Praise for
THE BURNING

"Another superb crime thriller from the prolific and talented father-and-son Kellermans. Set in the San Francisco Bay Area during one of the state's terrible wildfires, the story is . . . a riveting page-turner of a mystery with pulse-pounding action, and a compelling look at family dynamics and loyalty. The shock ending doesn't hurt, either."

—*Booklist* (starred review)

"Intriguing . . . The troubled familial relationships play an integral part in the unraveling of the whodunit and the why, adding pathos to the riveting finale. Once again, the bestselling Kellermans provide food for thought along with a tidy mystery."

—*Publishers Weekly*

"As always, the Kellermans guarantee that readers will turn pages rapidly to enjoy the complex characters and intricate plot turns. It's another winner for mystery readers."

—*Library Journal*

Praise for the
Clay Edison series

"Brilliant, page-turning fiction."
—STEPHEN KING

"Clay [Edison's] thoughtful narration is procedural gold."
—*Booklist*

"As for the keen sense of drama, it must be a genetic trait. . . . Unlike most crime writers (not to mention most of their readers), who revel in the bloody aftermath of a violent encounter, the Kellermans show compassion for the survivors, including conscientious officials like Edison."
—*The New York Times Book Review*

THE
BURNING

JONATHAN KELLERMAN
AND JESSE KELLERMAN

—

THE
BURNING

A NOVEL

BALLANTINE BOOKS
NEW YORK

The Burning is a work of fiction. Names, characters,
places, and incidents are the products of the author's imagination
or are used fictitiously. Any resemblance to actual events,
locales, or persons, living or dead, is entirely coincidental.

2022 Ballantine Books Mass Market Edition

Copyright © 2021 by Jonathan Kellerman and Jesse Kellerman
Excerpt from *The Lost Coast* by Jonathan Kellerman and
Jesse Kellerman copyright © 2022 by Jonathan Kellerman
and Jesse Kellerman

Published in the United States by Ballantine Books,
an imprint of Random House, a division of
Penguin Random House LLC, New York.

BALLANTINE is a registered trademark and the colophon is a trademark
of Penguin Random House LLC.

Originally published in hardcover in the United States
by Ballantine Books, an imprint of Random House, a division of
Penguin Random House LLC, in 2021.

This book contains an excerpt from the forthcoming book
The Lost Coast by Jonathan Kellerman and Jesse Kellerman.
This excerpt has been set for this edition only and may not reflect
the final content of the forthcoming edition.

ISBN 978-0-525-62013-6
Ebook ISBN 978-0-525-62012-9

Cover design: Scott Biel
Cover image: © Tim Robinson/Trevillion Images

Printed in the United States of America

randomhousebooks.com

2 4 6 8 9 7 5 3 1

Ballantine Books mass market edition: September 2022

To Faye
—Jonathan Kellerman

To Gavri
—Jesse Kellerman

THE
BURNING

CHAPTER 1

———

Monday. Nineteen hours in the dark.

T HE DEAD MAN lived up the hill. We could have walked, if the world wasn't ending and we didn't have to bring him back.

But it was and we did, so Harkless and I suited up and went out to the parking lot. As we exited the building a stunning fist of heat descended on us. The nearest wildfire was thirty miles away. Gritty sky and roaring air gave the illusion it was right over the ridge, climbing fast.

The apocalypse smells like a campfire and glimmers gold.

Through fierce raking wind we hurried to the body van, got in, and slammed the doors.

Above his respirator mask Harkless kept blinking. "God."

He pulled the mask down over his chin and wiped at the sweat ringing his lips. "You know where we're going?"

I nodded and started the van.

———

WE CLIMBED A steep, peaceful residential neighborhood crammed with split-level wood-frame ranch homes built in the late fifties. Long before anybody could imagine that million-acre fires, killing winds, and weeklong blackouts would become a season unto themselves. The houses weren't under direct threat, but tight spacing and a uniform color scheme made them look like rows of matchbooks ready to ignite.

No cars on the road. No children playing.

Wind pummeled the van, rocking it from side to side.

Scottish theme for street names: Aberdeen, Ayr, Dumfries, Inverness. Kilmarnock Court tapered south to a single potholed lane. Then large white painted letters issued a warning: BEGIN PRIVATE ROAD. The paving beyond was fresher, darker, glassy.

In lieu of a guardhouse, a stern sign limited access to members of the Chabot Park Summit Homeowners' Association and their guests, forbidding parking, loitering, or hiking, and promising to tow.

I eased the van over a speed bump. The gurneys jounced and gave a cough.

ENTERING THE DEVELOPMENT we passed through an invisible portal. The aesthetics changed as did the financial calculus. The guiding principle was no longer efficient rectangles but relaxed curves, the goal no longer maximizing units per acre but dollars per unit. Stately newbuilds shied back behind stone walls and high hedges. Slate roofs replaced asphalt tile. The architectural styles were varied. You had the money; you got what you wanted.

Less a community than a series of fortresses.

"I had no idea this was here," Harkless said.

This: rich people. *Here:* less than two miles from the county morgue.

We banked through stands of eucalyptus and California live oak to reach a long driveway that sloped up and out of view. An ultramodern fence of black metal slats set between concrete pillars stretched at street level. Double gates lay open. Flanking them were two larger pillars, one of which sported a security camera.

An Oakland PD cruiser with nobody at the wheel blocked the path. We waited for someone to appear.

"Rise and shine, sweetheart," Harkless said.

He leaned over and thumped the horn.

A uniform waddled out from behind a sycamore, tugging up his fly. "Sorry."

He signed us in and spoke into his shoulder. "Coroner's here."

THE DRIVEWAY WAS longer than I'd realized, switchbacking up through buckthorn, sagebrush, coffeeberry, manzanita—native species curated to simulate wildness. The effect was undone by drip tubes bulging through the ground cover like junkie veins. By the time we leveled out, we'd gained seventy feet of elevation.

The hilltop had been decapitated, smoothed, plumbed, and wired, then meticulously reassembled, stone by stone, shrub by shrub, like a monument to the vanquished. For all that, the house made no attempt to blend in: a towering stack of cantilevered glass boxes sandwiched between layers of whitewash.

The driveway broadened to a sprawling concrete motor court clogged with black-and-whites, an ambulance, the crime lab van. A wide concrete tributary slipped between the redwoods toward a mini-me guesthouse. To the west, the downslope had been buzz-cut. A clear day would give breathtaking views of the Bay, the city, all the bridges.

Lost, today, beneath a blanket of toxic haze.

Breathtaking, in a different sense.

We put on our masks and got out. Harkless hustled up the front steps. I followed with the Nikon slung over my shoulder.

Inside, a massive foyer opened out to a massive living room with double-height ceilings and vast glass walls. The décor was spaceship-chic: whites, blacks, Lucite, chrome. Furniture sectioned off zones serving various functions, all of them leisurely.

Mirrored wet bar with zebra-skin stools. White concert grand. Two white low-pile rugs, each large enough to swaddle a shipping container.

Only a scatter of yellow plastic evidence markers disrupted the color palette.

The power had been off for nearly twenty-four hours, and the interior had devolved to a greenhouse. I exhaled and my mask seemed to fill with warm syrup. I wondered how much it must cost to cool the place.

Anyone who could afford to live here wouldn't worry about utility bills.

Few people thought about their electricity, until it stopped flowing.

A sitting area near the bar was in disarray, end table overturned and puddles of broken glass. Criminalists in coveralls dusted, swabbed, tweezed.

No body.

I could smell it, though.

At the foot of the staircase Harkless greeted the detective, a trim middle-aged guy with a gaucho mustache and a slab of chocolate-brown hair. Despite the stifling conditions, he'd kept his suit jacket on, the ensemble medium tan with sharp creases sewn into the pant legs. The knot of his tie looked hard as a walnut.

"Cesar Rigo," he said.

The victim was a white male fifty-five to seventy-five years of age, dead of apparent gunshot wounds to the back and neck. The woman who'd called 911 confirmed him as the homeowner, Rory Vandervelde.

"Who's she?" Harkless asked.

"Davina Santos. The victim's housekeeper. She arrived for work at nine a.m. and discovered the body."

"Is she still around?"

"I have an officer attending her in the pool house," Rigo said. "I feel compelled to warn you, she is rather distraught."

He sprinkled his words like a chef does salt.

"We'll be gentle," Harkless said. "She mention anything about family?"

"According to her he's widowed. There's a girlfriend who stays over on occasion and a son in Southern California. She professes not to know the son's name. The girlfriend's name is Nancy."

"Last name?"

Rigo shook his head. "She referred to her only as Miss Nancy."

Either the smell was getting stronger or I was homing in on its source. I lowered my mask, craning.

Rigo gave a slight, curious smile. "Shall we?"

TWO DROPS OF BLOOD had dried on the marble near the hallway threshold. They continued as Rigo led us into a separate wing: coin-sized spots, widely spaced.

Harkless started to gag. An N95 might help with dust and smoke, but it's no match for decomp. A uniquely repellent odor, Mother Nature's way of alerting human beings to the presence of death, designed to send us running in the other direction. You never really get used to it, though most coroners manage to quiet the convulsive physiological response.

No such luck for Jed Harkless. Around the office he's known as Yak-Yak for the noise he makes, swallowing back waves of nausea. Why he's never transferred out is a mystery.

Cesar Rigo appeared unfazed, stepping nimbly through the evidence markers.

Around a bend the bloody ellipsis reached its end: a burst of spatter, a concentrated port-wine pool, drag marks curving through an open doorway.

A second clog, people instead of vehicles. Blood pattern analyst. PD photographer. LiDAR. Ballistics, meditating over a hole marring the baseboard. Everyone sweating and shifting on haunches.

The crowd parted for us, and we followed the drag marks into a capacious office. Piled against the near wall was a collection of lived-in furniture. There was a suede armchair with nailhead accents. A reading lamp hovered behind like a backseat driver. The windows over the desk looked west toward gray oblivion. Atop the blotter sat a lifeless computer and an old-school Rolodex.

Two snapshots in silver frames.

The first showed an Asian woman in her mid- to late forties. She was pretty, with caramel skin and liquid black eyes. She wore a lei and hoisted a cocktail. Tiki torches. Turquoise sea.

In the second photo, a young white male posed in cap and gown.

Both subjects were smiling. Both stood beside the same man. He was smiling, too, a mouthful of shiny veneers set in a prominent, pointed jaw. His hair was blond in the graduation photo. By Hawaii it had silvered and thinned, though he kept the same swept-back style. He had the brick complexion of one who burns easily but

nevertheless spends his time outdoors, unwilling to ca-
pitulate to the elements or bother with sunscreen.

He was gazing at the woman in the lei fondly.

He was gripping the young man around the shoulders,
fingers digging into the gown. The two of them didn't re-
semble each other.

The desk and its kin occupied maybe fifteen percent of
the floor space. The remainder was given over to sports
memorabilia: framed jerseys, pennants, helmets, ticket
stubs, trading cards, programs, game balls encased on
pedestals, a riot of team colors. Green and yellow for the
A's; yellow and blue for the Warriors; the Niners' red and
gold. Rory Vandervelde was a Bay Area native or he'd ad-
opted local allegiances.

I was impressed.

Rigo said, "You don't know the half of it."

Harkless didn't say anything, hiccuping and lurching
after the drag marks that snaked between display cases
and into a modest half bath.

Rory Vandervelde lay on his stomach, face cocked to
the left, wilting hair grazing the tiles. He wore black
terry-cloth pants with a grosgrain stripe down the side
and a gray silk shirt whose collar had partially torn off.
There was a crescent-shaped gash over his left eye, a hole
in his back, and another near the base of his neck. A third
shot had bitten off a chunk of his left trapezius.

Blowflies swarmed, emitting a bowel-tickling drone.
They'd colonized the wounds as well as the decedent's
mouth, nostrils, ears, and eyes. Eggs glistened like clumps
of rice. A few had broken out into maggots. Competition
was fierce. Most of the prime real estate was spoken for.

Heat accelerates postmortem processes. Tissue break-
down, rigor, livor, insect activity—they'd all been ripping
along, the off-gases collecting to create a fetid pressure
cooker. Condensation streaked the windowpane. My educated guess was that Vandervelde had been dead no

fewer than twelve hours, no more than a day. But that's what autopsy's for.

Rigo said, "Do you gentlemen require anything further at this time?"

Yak-yak went Harkless.

I said, "All set, thanks."

Rigo left.

I thumbed on the camera. "I'll get you when I'm done."

Harkless nodded gratefully and went to stand in the hall.

Capturing the correct angles required some acrobatics. I leaned over the toilet and against the wall, blinking and snorting and batting away flies that had seized on my orifices as the solution to their housing shortage. Dilute pink traces streaked the sink; a pink corona ringed the drain hole; watery pink spots on the wall implied wet hands shaken dry. Other than that, I saw no effort to clean up, and I wondered why the killer had moved the body in here.

Likely he'd been doing what most people did after they'd killed someone: freaking out and scrambling and committing one dumb messy error after another.

I finished up and stepped from the bathroom and called to Harkless. "All yours."

He soldiered past, gagging beneath the ineffectual mask. Pity him. He'd picked up the call. Examination of the body fell to him as the primary.

While he got to it, I returned to the foyer. By the front door stood a lacquered table topped with a silver dish for off-loading sundries. Sunglasses. Driveway clicker. Five keys on a sterling-silver fob engraved with the initials RWV, one of which fit the door.

No wallet. No phone.

I advanced toward the site of the altercation, taking photographs as I went. Mixed in with the broken glass was more dried blood—the origin of the trail. I traced it down the hall and around the bend. The scrum of investigators dutifully parted to give me a clear shot. Their reports would take days or weeks to prepare. Still, I'd seen enough homicides that I could speculate about the sequence of events.

It had begun in the living room. Maybe the assailant had broken in and stumbled upon the victim relaxing with a drink in hand. Although the front door, at least, didn't show forced entry.

Maybe the assailant and the victim had been sharing a beverage and had gotten into an argument.

Whatever the cause of the fight, it was violent enough to draw blood. The victim fled into the hall, flinging droplets as he went. The assailant caught up and shot him in the back and neck. Fueled by momentum, the victim kept going for a few more steps before reality kicked in and he collapsed, bleeding out, while the assailant panicked and freaked out and tried to decide what to do with him.

I photographed the kill zone. Exteriors and the rest of the house would have to wait until I'd helped Harkless turn the body.

I found him in the office-*cum*-museum, gazing at a 1989 World Series commemorative baseball autographed by Dennis Eckersley.

"Wallet?" I asked.

Harkless shook his head. "No phone, either."

"Okay. Ready?"

He exhaled noisily. "No."

We went into the bathroom.

A CORONER'S DUTIES include care of the decedent's body, determining manner of death, notifying next of kin, and securing property.

Rory Vandervelde owned a great deal of property.

Thirsty for air, I started upstairs.

The second floor held the living quarters, a horseshoe of bedrooms at one end and the master suite at the other, joined by a balcony that spanned the width of the living room. From that height the disorder below looked a carrion feast, scavengers in white coveralls swarming.

Each of the smaller bedrooms was pristine and impersonal, outfitted with a queen bed, hotel linens, a seventy-inch flat-screen, and an attached three-piece bath. Crash pads, maybe, for anyone too tipsy to get home safely. A spread like this cried out for parties, big and frequent. What determined who slept here and who got banished to the guesthouse?

The master, on the Bay-facing side, was predictably huge. Less predictably, it was unadorned, the walls white and free of art. But that was the idea. Anything that drew the eye would distract from the main event: an explosion of color every evening at sunset.

Tonight's would be more spectacular than usual.

The bed was a California king, half slept in. Atop the nightstand were the remote control for the AV system, a white noise machine, and a stack of magazines. *Cigar Aficionado*. *Vintage Guitar*. *Hemmings Motor News*. I opened the drawer. Foam earplugs. Eye mask. Reading glasses in an octopus tangle. No cellphone, but I did find a money clip with a California driver's license.

Rory Vandervelde's DOB was 02/05/1951. He stood five foot eight, weighed two hundred ten pounds, and was an organ donor.

I clicked on my flashlight and went to inspect the closets and bathrooms.

Two of each, his and hers.

Vandervelde favored luxe, neutral casual wear purchased in quantity. One shelf contained nothing but gray cashmere sweaters, all Versace, a few with tags attached. Its neighbor contained more sweaters, same brand, in black. I ran the beam over shoes and boots and loafers and slippers in every color from black to brown.

In the center of the closet stood a marble-topped island that merited its own census tract.

I combed through socks and underwear.

Burled maple boxes stacked on the floor. Wristwatch storage. Vandervelde owned at least a hundred. Three times as many pairs of cuff links.

You don't know the half of it.

The overabundance gave a whiff of anxiety. Stock up while you can; might be gone tomorrow. I wouldn't be surprised if he'd grown up poor.

Now it was all gone, forever.

I went into his bathroom.

Like basically every American over forty, Vandervelde took statins. Viagra, antacids, ibuprofen. That just about covered it. A man his age had aches and pains, but most days two fingers of single malt did the trick, thank you very much.

What sounds like voyeurism had a purpose. The physical environment we create for ourselves often speaks truths we prefer not to acknowledge.

Recreational drugs pose as prescriptions. A lack of hygiene can reflect mental decline. Regardless of how self-evident a cause of death seems, you never know what autopsy will reveal or what might acquire relevance.

So we open every drawer, every cabinet. Inevitably a picture of the person takes shape.

Rory Vandervelde's private quarters drew the portrait of a robust, vain, compulsive, fun-loving, clean-living individual.

I crossed over to Miss Nancy's territory.

A few couture sweat suits. Sneakers. Embroidered bathrobe. Built-ins meant for showing off handbags and shoes sat empty. Her island was close to bare, save half a dozen pieces of jewelry, each of which was dazzling. The warmth brought out remnants of perfume.

Her claim on the medicine cabinet felt equally tenuous: contact lens solution and a handful of cosmetics. The perfume was Chanel No. 19. Large bottle, mostly full.

Bringing luggage during stayovers? Valuing her independence? Or he didn't like having her clutter around.

Or a relationship teetering, commitment ambiguous.

A spiral staircase in the corner of the bedroom led up to a roof deck. Vandervelde had reserved the best views for himself, restricting the deck's footprint to a relatively compact twenty-by-twenty square. Enough for a hot tub, another wet bar, lounge chairs, and a vintage coin-op telescope aimed at what would have been San Francisco if the gods weren't angry.

The blurred sun hovered at its apex, unsure of whether to press on or retreat.

I stood by the railing to take in the property's full scope. Generous lawn, L-shaped swimming pool, pool house with its façade of French doors. The guesthouse, while smaller than its older brother, was enormous in absolute terms—what most people would consider a dream home. There was a putting green, a sunken garden with a pond, and steps descending to a lower-terrace tennis court.

Harkless came trudging over the grass toward the pool house to interview Davina Santos.

My eyes had begun to itch.

Back on the first floor I went room-to-room. Gym. Twelve-seat high-def home theater. Multiple eating areas, stocked kitchen with butler's pantry and regular pantry and a windowless wine gallery. I started running out of terms for "a place to sit and relax." Library. Conservatory. Parlor. Den. You could exhaust yourself, trying to sit and relax in all of them.

Every surface was dust-free. Credit Davina Santos.

Vandervelde's other collections included electric guitars, Americana, and antique pocketknives. Nothing looked to be missing, no busted locks or glaring blank spots.

If robbery was the motive, the killer hadn't done a very good job.

Or he'd done an incredible job, locating a single item of interest and leaving without succumbing to the urge to grab handfuls of plunder on the way out.

I still hadn't found a cellphone.

My final stop was the office. I'd bypassed it, saving the sports memorabilia for last. Amid the pens and paper clips in the desk I found an iPhone charger cord. But no phone.

Maybe that was the killer's object.

In the bottom left desk drawer was an estate planning portfolio, green pleather binder, four inches thick, gold embossing.

I set it aside, drew out the keyboard tray, tapped the space bar to revive the computer screen.

It stayed dark. No power.

I'd forgotten, just as I'd stopped feeling the heat or hearing the buzzing of the flies.

The Rolodex's plastic frame was riddled with hairline fissures and discolored by sun. I spun the dial to the V section. The absence of Vanderveldes puzzled me till I realized the cards were alphabetized by first name.

I dialed to N.

One Nancy listed.

Nancy Yap

Phone number with a 415 area code.

No sense wasting time hunting for the decedent's son: I didn't know his name. He'd be in the estate documents or we could locate him through Accurint.

An average scene, with an average amount of stuff to

sort through, takes an hour or less. In my decade-plus as a coroner I'd never worked a private residence this large or this lavish. Two hours in I still wasn't done.

I wandered the display cases, taking photos of the signed jerseys, the signed shoes, the stubs; quietly thrilled by the icons of my childhood, *where* and *when* rendered in sweat and leather.

Montana and Rice. McGwire and Canseco. Run TMC.

Memories, resurrected.

The heat of my brother's body against mine. On the floor, in front of the TV; elbow-jousting, *stop, idiot,* jumping up to embrace and scream victory.

On the court, in front of a crowd.

We watched anytime, played anywhere, loved everything, but basketball best of all.

Whatever else came between Luke and me, we always had The Game.

Yellow and blue are Warriors colors. They're also the colors of my alma mater, the University of California, Berkeley. Cal's reputation rests on academics, not athletics. The Golden Bears last won the NCAA tournament in 1960 and have since undergone something of a dry spell. There have been a few exceptions: the mid-eighties under Kevin Johnson, the mid-nineties under Jason Kidd, and then again a few years later, when I was the point guard and we clawed our way into the Final Four before I tore my knee ligaments into fettuccine.

Rory Vandervelde had my face on his wall.

It was a roster photo from the top of my sophomore season. A magical moment, pregnant with possibility. I knelt in the front row, balancing a ball on my thigh. I looked giddy. So did my teammates. We knew what we were capable of.

Our team made countless public appearances. For the boosters; for sick kids. I could never remember signing one particular photo. Yet the proof was in the margins, in black Sharpie.

CLAY EDISON #7

Neater than it would be today.

In time, everything breaks down.

"Pardon me, Deputy."

Rigo leaned in the doorway. I had no idea how long I'd been standing there or how long he'd been watching me.

"Your partner is looking for you," he said.

I nodded thanks. "I see what you meant."

"What's that?"

"This not being the half of it."

He smiled his small, odd smile. "There's more."

I WAS STILL reeling from confronting my younger self when Harkless met me on the motor court to relay the substance of his conversation with Davina Santos.

"She's worked for him eight years. Ever since she started he's been with Nancy. She's not sure when his wife died but she thinks about ten years ago."

"What about the son?"

"She's never met him."

"Ever?"

"I asked her twice. That long, I'm thinking they must be estranged."

Davina Santos came Monday, Wednesday, and Friday. She had a clicker for the driveway gates. Upon arrival that morning she discovered them open. Usually they shut after thirty seconds.

"Power's out," I said. "Maybe he opened them manually and didn't get a chance to close them."

Harkless mulled it over. "That's what happened, he was alive as of yesterday afternoon. There's cameras. Did you check the computer?"

I smiled. It hit him. No power. No footage.

"Shit," he said. "Is there a battery backup someplace?"

"Not that I've seen so far."

"Whatever. PD's problem. You get what you need?"

"Almost. I still have to shoot the outside."

"Hurry it up? I feel like I'm gonna suffocate."

"Tell you what," I said. "Let's get him loaded. You bring him in and intake. I'll text when I'm done, you come pick me up."

He jogged to the van for the gurney. I went to confer with Detective Rigo.

He was on the second-floor balcony, elbows on the balustrade, the suit coat taut against his narrow, muscular back.

"We're ready to remove," I said.

He straightened up. Only then did I register how short he was—about five-five, almost a foot shorter than me. The hair gave him several extra inches, as did his carriage: chest puffed, shoulder blades pinched. "Very good."

I shared our findings, giving him Nancy Yap's full name and phone number from the Rolodex. Rigo raised his eyebrows. Not expecting that much initiative from a coroner.

"Thank you, Deputy."

"No problem. I haven't seen a cell anywhere," I said. "Did you guys take it?"

"We did not. Is it possible you overlooked it?"

"Anything's possible," I said. "You'll keep an eye out and let me know if you find it."

"Our policy is open communication."

"Right. Considering how many valuables are lying around, I want to confirm that you're going to leave a uniform onsite till you're done and you can call us to seal up."

"Of course."

In my experience that was not *of course;* it was very far from *of course.* But it's wise to play nice, so I thanked him and we traded phone numbers and spent a few minutes divvying up who got what. He wanted the computer. I wanted the estate planning portfolio. He wanted any other financial documents. I wanted the money clip, house keys, and medications. The conversation was measured and polite, like an amicable divorce mediation.

"Anything else?" Rigo asked.

"Open communication. You tell me."

He chuckled and went to clear the hall.

WITH THE BODY van dipping out of sight, I followed the concrete path that led from the motor court down to the guesthouse, crunching over twigs and redwood cones knocked loose by the wind. Eucalyptuses creaked. Past a mountain of honeysuckle, the entrance came into view.

Entrances, plural.

A regular pedestrian door.

A hangar door, twenty feet wide and seventy-five percent raised.

Not a guesthouse. A garage.

It made sense. Rory Vandervelde had suites for his guests. The motor court was for their parking convenience. He had to put his own cars somewhere. Logic— and the size of the building—dictated that he had a whole bunch of them.

Rigo's smirk. *There's more.*

The hangar door gave onto a startling darkness. The garage's windows, I realized, were false.

I clicked on the flashlight.

Surfaces and shapes receded to infinity.

Not a garage. A museum.

I inched forward, playing the beam over polished glass and polished hardware and vivid high-gloss paint. Each time I took a picture the flash went off around me like fireworks. The floor was shiny, too, black-and-white checkerboard mimicking a final-lap flag. Vehicles clustered in twos and threes like the patrons of a cocktail party. Impotent track lights ran overhead.

Normally the space would gleam, bright and jaunty. Now I walked a crypt.

I'm not a car guy. Most of what I know I've learned in the course of being a cop. Meaning most of what I know has to do with extremely shitty cars. Give me a beat-to-hell '93 Corolla or dirty white panel van and I'm good. Anything over thirty-five-thousand dollars MSRP starts to get fuzzy.

Rory Vandervelde owned around thirty vehicles, none of them shitty.

The collection went for breadth over depth. Sports cars and luxury sedans, a three-wheeled oddity, a Harley and a Humvee. I recognized the better-known brands. Bentley, Lamborghini, Ferrari. The exotics I'd never heard of. What was a Koenigsegg? My brother would know. It looked supersonic and, for a person with long legs, super-uncomfortable.

Off the main display floor were nooks, man caves within the man cavern, side chapels in this cathedral of testosterone: billiards table, humidor, jukebox, yet another wet bar. Aerodynamic furniture and art picked up the same visual notes, but subtly. There were no images of cars per se, but rather art deco prints in black and silver and gold; photographs of the Rat Pack, Muhammad Ali exulting over a downed Sonny Liston. A wall safe with a thick glass front showed off the thirty-odd car keys. Several qualified as works of art unto themselves: tiny fantasies in precious metal and crystal, shaped like shields or rockets or the vehicles they started.

The air, already stodgy, grew hotter and denser the deeper I went. At the rear I came to a boutique repair shop set up with a hydraulic lift, chrome tools, and a broad worktable. Sharp stack of chamois. Clean white rags, suitable for an operating theater.

I took one last picture and started for the exit.

My phone buzzed.

Harkless had texted images from the bottom of the driveway. The gate mechanism was hidden behind a shrub. Someone had removed the housing to expose the motor and gears. A crank jutted, labeled with a double-headed arrow: OPEN and CLOSE.

I slowed, glanced up. The cars had to be the single most valuable collection. Yet I'd strolled right in without a second thought.

Not through the pedestrian door. Through the hangar door.

Which was stuck, partway open.

Adjacent to it, a portrait of Frank Sinatra hung askew, as though pulling away from the wall. I went over and touched the frame, which hinged out to reveal a recess containing the guts of the hangar door mechanism and a crank handle.

RAISE ← → LOWER

The hangar door looked heavy. Moving it would take elbow grease. Arm burning. Back cramping. You'd do it no more than necessary. Get the door only as high as you needed and stop.

As it stood, the opening permitted the passage of a low-slung car. Margin for error, eighteen inches. Don't scratch the roof.

I panned the flashlight. Just like in the main house, I could see no evidence of theft—no vacant hooks in the key safe, no gap in the display floor left by a missing vehicle.

I thought about the driveway gates, cranked open in anticipation.

The hangar door, ready to receive.

A vehicle coming in, then.

Who's the new guy?

You couldn't call me totally ignorant about cars. My

brother was a lifelong motorhead. Every November he made our father take him to the San Francisco Auto Show. Often I got dragged along. We're less than two years apart and grew up sleeping four feet away from each other. Inevitably some of his knowledge filtered over to me.

Luke's particular passion was muscle cars. Chargers and Firebirds and Thunderbolts, machines and names that conveyed raw power. In our bedroom he kept a *Bullitt* movie poster over his headboard. Not for the film or for Steve McQueen—both well before our time—but for its image of a Ford Mustang GT, tearing across the white background like an artillery shell exiting the muzzle. Other posters went up around it as we got older. Michael Jordan. Tupac Shakur. But the Mustang retained its place of prominence.

Rory Vandervelde owned a single classic American muscle car. It lurked in the shadows, off to the right of the hangar door, as though it had shown up to the party stag and had yet to join a clique. Like a wallflower. Which was funny, because the car itself was the antithesis of shy: a late-sixties Camaro, restored to perfection, painted a searing shade of green, and kitted out with aftermarket embellishments. Towering rims and a spoiler and a gnashing grille.

Short of acquiring the *Bullitt* car itself—maybe Vandervelde had tried—you'd be hard-pressed to find a more extreme example of the species.

I'd missed the Camaro on my way in. So much to gawk at. Eyes not yet adjusted.

I saw it now. It was, to be specific, a 1969 SS/Z28. V-8 engine, concealed headlights, black racing stripes, custom leather upholstery.

A hell of a car. One that I recognized, specifically. I had seen it before, not once but many times.

It was my brother's.

CHAPTER 2

———

WANTING TO DOUBT MYSELF, I moved the beam to the Camaro's license plate.

Do you know your own plate number by heart, let alone your brother's?

A brother you aren't especially close with?

It didn't have to be his car.

I swayed. My clammy shirt sucked against my back, sweat slimed the insides of my gloves. I was dehydrated and tired, eyes taxed from hours of straining.

How many 1969 Camaros existed? How many in that distinctive shade of green?

Had to be dozens. Hundreds, worldwide.

How many in California? Fewer. Still, we lead the nation in automobile registrations. Almost twice as many as number two Texas.

How many neon-green 1969 Camaros make their way to the East Bay? Our car culture isn't as strong as Southern California's. Still. No shortage of money. Enough interest to support the San Francisco Auto Show and a show in Silicon Valley. Danville has a smallish but well-regarded automotive museum.

It didn't have to be Luke's car.

We aren't close but we do see each other occasionally. He lives forty minutes from me and I live six blocks from our parents. Holidays. Birthdays. My mother can't or won't accept that her boys aren't best friends. Last year she'd instituted a monthly brunch. For the inaugural gathering she squeezed fresh orange juice and baked two kinds of mini-muffin. Chocolate chip and banana nut. This from a woman stumped by any kitchen tool more complicated than a microwave. Every successive menu got more aggressively elaborate, as if she could cook her way to family unity.

That was the last time I'd seen my brother: at brunch, at my parents' house, nine days ago.

Lemon sour cream waffles and virgin Bellinis.

Amy, Charlotte, and I walked.

Luke and Andrea pulled up in his bright, snarling, neon-green '69 Camaro.

He hadn't mentioned selling or trading the car. I couldn't imagine he'd ever consider it. And if he did, I couldn't imagine he wouldn't say so.

Maybe the opportunity had presented itself suddenly.

Or he'd loaned it out. Maybe he and Rory Vandervelde were friends. Car enthusiasts knew one another. They haunted the same events.

Why would a rich guy with thirty-plus hot-wheels need to borrow anything?

I ducked beneath the hangar door, pulled out my phone, and tapped a preset.

You've reached Luke Edison at Bay Area Therapeutics. Sorry I'm unavailable at the moment. Please leave your name, number, and a brief message, and I'll get back to you as soon as I can. Thanks and have a blessed day.

"Hey, it's me. Quick question when you have a sec. Thanks."

I stepped back into the darkness.

The Camaro was slick and menacing, like some venomous creature that had escaped the reptile house at the zoo. I circled it, my reflection swelling in the tinted windows. Luke had fixed up his Camaro by hand, over months, including applying a tint kit. I remembered him telling me about it. Along with Delaware and Iowa, California had the most liberal tinting laws in the country. You could go up to seventy percent in front and a hundred percent in back. The windshield had to be clear, though you could apply a four-inch visor at the top.

Rory Vandervelde's Camaro had a four-inch visor on the windshield.

I shined the light in at spotless seats.

Tried the door handles.

Locked.

The key safe, too, was locked, secured by a combination dial and fingerprint scanner. I didn't know what a '69 Camaro key looked like but none of the ones hanging behind the glass seemed to fit the bill. No logo for Chevrolet or GM.

It might not be Luke's car.

Even if it was his, that meant nothing.

If he had any tie to the crime, why would he abandon his car at the scene? How had he gotten home? You don't Uber away from a murder.

Near the scene. Not at it.

One of thirty-plus vehicles.

If it was even his car.

Which it didn't have to be.

Statistically.

I understood all of this.

I also understood how investigations work. Detectives look for the obvious suspect because the obvious suspect is often the right one. I understood tunnel vision. I understood the apparatus of the law, its unstoppable momentum.

My brother was a convicted felon.

I took a photo of the Camaro's license plate.

After a moment's contemplation, I deleted the image.

I copied down the tag and the VIN. I tore the page out of my notebook, folded it several times, and stuffed it in my back pocket.

Walked out of the garage, into the burnt and blinding air.

I STILL HAD to document the rest of the property. I had to act normal while I did it.

The pool house was roomy and sweltering. There were stalls for changing and a sauna; another wet bar, which made me irrationally angry. How many fucking wet bars did one man need?

Davina Santos perched at the end of a white chaise longue, taking up an inch of cushion, avoiding eye contact with the officer by her side. His name tag read B. SHUFFLEBOTTOM. He shot me an *SOS* look. The two of them had covered all topics of mutual interest.

I had questions of my own for Ms. Santos. Maybe she'd witnessed a recent visit from a man who stood six foot four and looked an awful lot like me, with the addition of a few pounds and a sandy-colored beard. Was this man wearing short sleeves? Did she notice a tattoo of a crown on the inside of his right biceps? When had he come? What was he driving? What did he and her employer talk about? Was the conversation friendly? Were voices raised? Maybe they'd been negotiating a sale; that could get testy.

This man—who looked like me, except he was a bit older and had endured hardship, mostly of his own making, the effects of which he packed beneath a goofy exterior but which broke through in occasional flashes of rage and depression—did Davina Santos know his name?

Had she mentioned him to anyone? Deputy Coroner Harkless? Detective Rigo? Officer Shufflebottom? What did they know?

Our eyes met. She smiled sadly. No recognition. So far, so good.

I left the pool house and cut through the landscaping, kicking up mulch. I photographed the pond and the putting green. A while later I found myself down on the tennis court with no recollection of having gotten there.

I tried Luke again.

You've reached Luke Edison at Bay Area Therapeutics. Sorry I'm unavailable at the moment . . .

I opened my messages, intending to text Harkless and let him know that he should come fetch me, ASAP. Instead I keyed *L*.

The screen autopopulated Luke Edison.

I touched his name, bringing up our chat history.

We had last communicated eight days ago, the morning after brunch.

R u around he'd written. Can we talk

The message had come in at ten thirty-three a.m. I would have been at work.

In any event, I'd never replied.

Now I typed Yo sorry what's up

I watched the screen.

It remained static.

Call me please I wrote.

Detective Rigo was standing at the far end of the motor court, immersed in his phone, one foot propped on an artfully placed boulder.

I had questions for him, too.

What did he make of the open driveway gates, the partially raised hangar door?

Did he intend to check for security camera footage? Or had he written off that possibility due to the outage, the way Harkless had?

With no cars missing, there was no reason for Rigo to zero in on the collection. Not before he'd done the basics. Talk to the victim's girlfriend, family, friends, business associates.

He noticed me coming and waved. "Were you able to find the phone?"

"Nope. I'm going to head back."

He nodded. Cocked a thumb toward the garage. "Remarkable."

"I'm not much of a car guy," I said.

"Nor am I. But one must admire the conviction."

"Oh sure. We can't leave it open like that."

"The driveway is the only way in or out," he said.

"You'll have someone here around the clock."

"That was what you requested, is it not?"

"Have they had a chance to dust out there?"

"Not yet."

"Once you're all set, ping us please, so we can seal up. My partner will email about the autopsy."

Rigo smiled. "Open communication."

"Good luck," I said.

"To you as well." He paused. "But."

I looked at him. His tie was tightly knotted and his suit jacket free of sweat stains.

"I saw your picture," he said. "In the office? Basketball. Also my sport."

I nodded, not catching the joke. Then he began waving his hand over his head to emphasize his short stature, saying "Eh? Eh?" and laughing.

I joined him. *Ha ha ha.*

"Actually, I was a gymnast," he said.

"Is that right," I said, because apparently we were having a conversation.

"Back in Brazil."

"Right. That's awesome. Okay, well, I'll have my guy pick me up. Be in touch."

Rigo turned and began climbing the front steps. I composed a text to Harkless. Held my thumb over the send arrow.

The detective disappeared inside.

I hit the arrow and sprinted down the concrete path to the garage.

Ducking beneath the hangar door, I drew from my vest a small packet of tissues.

I've been a law enforcement officer for twelve years. I've been a coroner for ten. I have never accepted a bribe, bowed to the influence of another, exploited my power, knowingly arrested an innocent person, or distorted evidence to suit my preferences. I'm a human being, I'm fallible, but I strive to be honest and to stay within the limits of the law and morality.

Without that, what am I?

All my life I have been the brother to a person I did not want to understand. Even as a child I considered him lazy and sloppy. Then he became reckless and volatile.

Then he became a criminal.

He is the action, I the equal and opposite reaction.

I wiped down the Camaro's doors and handles.

I wiped down the windows, the hood, the trunk latch, and the side mirrors.

I exited the garage and walked toward the motor court at a steady pace.

I stopped.

Rigo was back on the motor court, his foot on the same boulder. Maybe he'd sensed the awkwardness between us and gone inside to wait for me to leave.

He looked up from his screen. Gave his slight, inquisitive smile. "Deputy?"

I trotted forward with the tissue balled in my palm. "Had to take one more peek."

"And you claim to have no interest."

"You said it. Respect the conviction."

"Mm." He resumed scrolling.

I slipped the tissue in my pocket. Luke hadn't replied to my texts. He still hadn't, six minutes later, when Harkless pulled up to retrieve me.

CHAPTER 3

———

LIKE HOSPITALS, FIRE DEPARTMENTS, and other essential services, the Coroner's Bureau was running on generators. To conserve fuel, the thermostat had been set to seventy-six. Entering the intake bay I felt the mild air crush around me and started shivering violently.

"You okay?" Harkless said.

I said I'd meet him upstairs.

I pushed into the men's locker room, threw the tissue in the trash, and peeled off my sodden shirt, rubbing a towel over damp hair and gooseflesh, watching for a call or text from Luke.

Nothing.

I put on a clean shirt, composed myself, and went up to the squad room. Jed Harkless was in his cubicle next to mine, mired in the initial paperwork on Vandervelde. Deputy Nikki Kennedy had a pen between her teeth and was scooping her Kool-Aid-red hair. Deputy Lindsey Bagoyo murmured consolingly into the phone.

The techs: Carmen Woolsey in her big witchy skirt. Dani Botero and Lydia Januchak, gossiping by the printer.

Down the hall, Sergeant Clarkson laughed behind her office door. "I know it."

Everyone doing their jobs.

To them, it was a regular afternoon.

Ten years is a long time to remain a deputy coroner. I should be a sergeant by now, at the least. Higher-ranking friends have implied that I would be, if not for a couple of incidents that have earned me a reputation for insubordination.

Over the spring I'd applied for permission to take the exam. It was granted and I passed. The catch was that there were no openings in the Coroner's Bureau. Moving up meant moving out to another duty station. Amy and I agreed that we needed the extra money. But she wasn't going to push me to leave the post I've kept for so long and that I love.

Then fate brought a reprieve: Juanita Clarkson gave notice. Her husband's employer was relocating its HQ to Austin, effective January first.

Less than three months remained till I took her place.

My new shirt was already wicking. I put Rory Vandervelde's house keys in a desk drawer. The nub of paper with the Camaro's tag and VIN was in my back pocket. I felt it as if I were sitting on a nail. The urge to check my phone was a rag in my throat.

I reopened the drawer and buried the phone at the back behind the keys.

Focus.

I clicked on Rory Vandervelde's case file, opened the photo folder, and plugged in the Nikon to upload. Thumbnails sprouted in tidy rows, reproducing my run of the house in miniature. They dragged me, herky-jerky, across the foyer to the living room, around the fallen end table and bloody glass, over the marble tiles and along the bloodstained hallway and into each of the myriad rooms and through the trees toward the garage. What if I'd forgotten to delete the picture of the license plate? I had to stop myself from yanking out the cord. The hangar door appeared, followed by the flash-saturated garage interiors, opulent forms and lustrous colors; the key safe and the hydraulic lift; Frank Sinatra and the hidden crank mechanism, and then the camera skipped over to the pool house and the putting green and the tennis court, dusty and benign.

I minimized the window and moved on to Accurint.

Several addresses for Rory Vandervelde came up, the most recent being the mansion I'd just left. Built in 2013. No previous owners and all the personalization said Vandervelde had commissioned the house. He also owned property in Sonoma and Lake Tahoe.

Associates included Martha F. Vandervelde, born in 1952, and Sean C. Vandervelde, born in 1980.

I stood up and hung over the cubicle wall. Harkless was typing. The pleather estate planning portfolio sat on his desk.

"I can get started on that."

Without taking his eyes off the screen, he handed me the binder.

Fastened to its inside cover was the business card of a Palo Alto law firm.

TURLOCK AND BAIN, LLC
STERLING TURLOCK, PRINCIPAL AND FOUNDER

A cover letter, dated May 13, 2020, detailed the portfolio's contents: Rory Vandervelde's living trust, his last will and power of attorney and healthcare directive, plus numerous codicils and revisions thereto. The list of documents ran to three pages, allowing me to chart his emotional ups and downs with bleak precision.

The original will had gone into effect on April 17, 1983. In it Rory William Vandervelde declared himself a resident of Santa Clara County. He had married Martha Frances Vandervelde (née Roberts) on July 12, 1975. She was his sole beneficiary and personal representative, and vice versa. They had one child, Sean Charles Vandervelde, born on December 4, 1980.

By the early nineties the Vanderveldes had amassed enough wealth to establish a charitable foundation, to which they apportioned ten percent of their estate.

For a while that was all. Starting in 2013, however, the pace of change picked up.

First, a codicil transferred the Vanderveldes' place of residence to Alameda County. A house of that size didn't get built in a day. You had to get approvals, attend hearings, submit revisions. You proceeded on faith, dreaming of the future, like the architect of a medieval church that took centuries to complete.

Martha Vandervelde had never seen her dream realized: In November of that year, she died. A new will was accordingly drafted.

Eleven months later Rory amended his healthcare proxy, empowering Dr. Nancy Yap to make decisions on his behalf should he become incapacitated.

Two years after that, he cut Nancy in on the estate. Her ten percent came out of Sean Vandervelde's share. Soon that was upped to fifteen. By 2019 Rory had made Nancy Yap his executor and granted her burial rights. He declared for the record that he wished to spend eternity lying between the two women who had brought him joy in life. To that end, he had purchased an additional plot, next to his and Martha's, earmarked for Nancy.

The coup de grâce was a radical change to the estate distribution. Now Sean got a third, Nancy got a third, and one-third went to the foundation.

Even Sean's reduced portion would be more than most people earned in their lifetimes.

That wasn't the point. He'd been knocked down several rungs.

I found a Sean Charles Vandervelde living down in Pacific Palisades.

I dialed the law offices of Turlock and Bain, LLC. The receptionist patched me through.

"Deputy." Sterling Turlock's booming voice commanded attention with a single word. I could imagine the effect on a courtroom. "What brings you my way?"

"Good afternoon, sir. I'm calling about a client of yours, Rory Vandervelde. I'm afraid I have some bad news. Mr. Vandervelde's passed away."

Silence.

"Sir?"

"Oh no. Rory?"

"I'm afraid so."

"God. Another heart attack?"

"I'm sorry, but I can't discuss that before we've had a chance to speak to his next of kin."

"Right. Right. That'd be Nancy. You need her number? I can give it to you."

"It's Sean Vandervelde I'm trying to reach, actually."

Turlock cleared his throat. "He's not the one in charge."

I explained that I had been to the house and read the estate documents. "I'm not seeing anything about Mr. Vandervelde and Dr. Yap being married."

"No."

"In that case, we'll speak to Sean first. I was hoping you could confirm that I've got the right person." I read Turlock the phone number and address in Pacific Palisades.

"That's him."

"Thank you. We will speak to Dr. Yap, too, but for the time being I'd appreciate it if you'd hold off on informing her."

A beat. "Of course."

I had no more confidence in his *of course* than in Detective Cesar Rigo's. "I was also hoping to ask you a couple of questions. How long have you worked with Mr. Vandervelde?"

"Good grief. Forty years? Forty-five?"

"You must have known him well."

"Quite. We were good friends, all four of us, Rory and Martha, Diane and I. We belonged to the same club. That came later, though. When I first met them, they were living on peanut butter sandwiches."

"I'm not sure what he did professionally."

"How he made his money, you mean."

"Yes, sir."

"Well," Turlock said, "it's something of a Horatio Alger story. Rory and Martha had this little mom-and-pop shipping store over in Sunnyvale. One day a fellow walks in carrying a circuit board. It so happens the store's down the block from one of the big microchip companies. This fellow's an engineer. He needs to send a prototype to Washington, DC. Lightweight, very fragile. Their mailroom already broke two of them in transit. He's so fed up he decides to go out-of-pocket.

"He asks Rory, 'What do you have that I can pack this up in?' Rory shows him newspaper and Styrofoam peanuts. The engineer says, 'No, that's no good, we tried that.' Rory's about to tell him sorry, no dice. Then he remembers he's got a packet of balloons, extras from some promotion they ran. He blows some up, and they wrap the thing in tissue paper and snuggle it in there. Rory sends it off and forgets about it. I don't think he charged him for the balloons.

"Next week the engineer comes back. Rory's afraid the thing arrived in pieces and the guy is going to ream him out. Turns out the balloons worked like a charm, he's ecstatic, like Rory's some kind of genius. Rory thought that was hilarious, because the guy's an engineer, after all, and here he is, going wild about balloons. Now he's got another prototype he needs to send. So Rory does it the same way. This time he charges him for the balloons. Day after that, two more engineers come in. 'Can you pack this up for us?' You get the picture. Pretty soon Rory's buying balloons in bulk, and he realizes there's a business there. As an added benefit, there's less waste, and it keeps shipping costs down, cause it's mostly air. You ever order from Amazon? Those air pockets they use? You know the ones I'm talking about."

I did. I rarely took the trouble to deflate them, so they constituted half the volume of our weekly household trash output. "Yup."

"Rory's idea."

"Good idea to have."

"You bet your boots," Turlock said. "He wasn't what you'd call educated, but he had a head for things you can touch and feel. He got into manufacturing. That's about the time he brought me in. From there he branched out, cargo, trucking, storage, import-export, you name it. Did a lot of business overseas. Next thing you know he's joining the golf club, and the same computer fellows who used to ask him to pack their boxes are begging him for seed money."

He let out a gale of cathartic laughter.

"Dammit," he said. "I don't believe it. He was healthy as a horse."

I'd never understood that phrase. Horses get sick. They die. The slightest defect, people shoot them.

Maybe that was the idea. For a horse, anything short of perfection spelled the end.

"You mentioned a heart attack," I said.

"Well, sure, but it was minor. Anyway it was a long time ago."

"How long?"

"Eight, nine years ago. After Martha died."

Right around the time Vandervelde made Nancy Yap his healthcare proxy. "Do you remember the circumstances?"

"He and Sean had a fight."

"Fight?"

"An argument," Turlock said. "Words."

"Bad blood between them?"

"That kid's an asshole. He made life rough for Rory and Martha when he was growing up. Now he's grown up and he's *still* an asshole. I've told Rory a thousand times not to take it so hard. But it's his son. I'd feel the same in his shoes."

"What were they arguing about?"

"Who knows? Money, probably. Or Nancy. Sean didn't like his mother being replaced. What's he expect Rory to do, don sackcloth till the day he dies? He nursed Martha for years. He sat through every chemo session. God's sake, let him have a little happiness."

"I'm seeing a lot of changes to the terms of the estate."

"I discouraged that. I didn't think it would help matters. But Rory could be stubborn. The kid gets it from somewhere."

I mentioned the timeline on the mansion, how its completion coincided with Martha Vandervelde's death.

"Sad, her never seeing it. They tried to build here but got held up on permits and started looking elsewhere. They poured everything into that damn house. Emotionally, I mean. It kept Martha's mind off being sick, too. Boy, you should've seen their old place. Tiny run-down thing."

Which might explain the shopworn furniture crowded into Vandervelde's office: a reminder of his roots. "Before they moved, where'd he keep his cars?"

"The cars," Turlock said. "Wonder of the world, eh? Yeah, he bought those first. Used one of his warehouses over in San Jose. Bear in mind, he didn't have as many back then. Ten or twelve." He laughed. "Come to think, that is a lot."

"How did he acquire them?"

"I'm not sure what you mean."

"Did he buy them at auction? Through dealers, or private sales?"

"That I couldn't tell you. All of the above, I presume. Me, I couldn't care less about cars. I've driven the same Mercedes for twenty years. Rory ribbed me about it. 'You need to look the part, clients will think you're poor.' By the way, that was another thing Sean didn't like. After Martha passed, Rory got a lot freer with his money. He moved into the new place and had Nancy do the decorating."

"She doesn't live there full-time, though."

"No, no. Here. Palo Alto," he said. "Lily—that's her daughter from her first marriage, she's still in high school. Nancy stays at home with her most of the time. Rory would've loved for them to move in. You understand, she could say the word and never have to work again. But she's her own woman."

"What does she do?"

"She's a doctor, works at Stanford. Listen, Deputy, I've been doing this my whole life. Something's going on here or you wouldn't have called me. Is there going to be an autopsy?"

"Yes, sir, there is."

"You can't tell me why."

"I'm sorry, sir."

"Okay. Should I be there? Or Nancy?"

"I appreciate the offer, but that won't be necessary."

"Fine," he said reluctantly. "Good grief, what a lousy way to end the day."

We hung up, and I called the Los Angeles County

Medical Examiner-Coroner to request they make notification to Sean Charles Vandervelde.

THE SUN MELTED into the Bay. The sky glowed radioactive peach. It was an unnatural color, unsettling, beautiful. Impossible to get used to and sadly normal.

October in Northern California. And September. August and July and June.

Lindsey Bagoyo rose from her cubicle. "Night, everybody."

A chorus of farewells.

She started for the exit, pausing by my desk. "How's Amy holding up?"

My wife was fourteen weeks pregnant with our second child. Yesterday morning, with the outage looming and the air quality index climbing into the purple, she and Charlotte had gotten on a plane to the preferred destination for anyone yearning to breathe free: Los Angeles.

"My dude," Nikki Kennedy said. "Living that sweet, sweet bachelor life."

Carmen Woolsey said, "They're calling the wind a once-in-twenty-years event."

Dani Botero said, "Nice, just like last year."

Bagoyo patted me on the shoulder. "Stay cool."

I wished her a good night, too.

Harkless left soon after, followed by Kennedy and the techs.

Two and a half hours had elapsed since I'd tried to reach Luke.

I unearthed my phone from the back of the drawer.

No missed calls. Six unread notifications.

A photo of Charlotte, her face smeared with what I hoped was chocolate ice cream. They were having fun, Amy wrote, but they missed me. I wrote that I'd call them soon.

The next message was from a reporter I'd once made the mistake of talking to. She had since anointed me her go-to source. A Hayward man with COPD had died after his power cut out and his BiPAP machine failed. Did I care to comment? I did not.

A Berkeley detective named Billy Watts asked me to get in touch when I had a second.

A former Cal teammate who'd moved out of state had been following the news about the fires and wanted to make sure I was okay.

Texts five and six were automated alerts. Red flag warning for Alameda County. High wind advisory. Elevated fire risk. AQI hazardous. Sensitive groups such as the elderly and those with underlying respiratory conditions were urged to remain indoors. For more information visit their website.

The utility company announced that the public safety power shutoff had been expanded to cover additional areas and extended for twenty-four hours, subject to further expansion and further extension. For more information visit their website.

Nothing from my brother.

I was the only one left from my team. Night shift was settling in, getting coffee.

I reached into my back pocket for the nub of paper. I unfolded it in my lap and ran the tag for the green Camaro in Rory Vandervelde's garage.

It came back registered to Luke A. Edison, 1259 Jupiter Creek Road, Moraga, CA 94556.

The VINs matched.

Amorphous dread crawled through me.

"Closing time."

Brad Moffett, the night shift sergeant, was ambling over.

I closed the search window and stuffed the paper in my pocket.

Moffett pressed his chest like an opera singer. "You don't have to go home," he crooned. "But you can't. Stay. *Here*."

"DADDY, I GOT ICE CREAM."

"Hi, lovey. That's fantastic. What flavor?"

"Daddy, I can't see you."

"It's the connection, sweetie," Amy said. "You can talk, he can hear you."

"He looks silly."

"I often do," I said. "Hi, hon. How are you?"

"We're fine. How are *you*? Can you breathe?"

"More or less."

"Did they say when the power's coming back on?"

"They keep changing it. It was tomorrow morning. Now it's Wednesday."

"Uch. I'm so sorry."

"Tell him we went to the museum," Charlotte said.

"Why don't you tell him yourself?" Amy said.

"*You* tell him."

"Charlotte would like you to know that we went to the museum."

"Cool," I said. "Which museum?"

"Tell him there were dinosaurs."

"And there were dinosaurs."

"Wow. Were they scary?" I asked.

"*No*."

"Did you get ice cream before or after the museum?"

"We got it *at* the museum."

"Was it dinosaur-flavored ice cream?"

"Daddy, I can't *see* you."

"I know. I'm sorry. I love you so much. Are you having fun with cousin Sarah and cousin Jake and baby Liam?"

"He's a baby. He doesn't go on the potty."

"Not like you. You're a big girl."

"Their place is *bananas*," Amy whispered. "I feel like a Kardashian."

I thought about the crazy house I'd been in that day.

"Tell me," I said. "I want to hear all about it."

While she talked I stretched out on the living room floor and let her voice wash over me. I could smell the overdone air infiltrating our leaky windows and the dust in the area rug and the baked scent of the cardboard boxes stacked against the wall. We'd moved in months ago. Same week I passed my sergeant's exam, in fact. I'd thought that leaving the boxes out in the open rather than putting them in the garage would spur us to deal with them sooner. Instead we'd learned to ignore them. Now we had a cardboard accent wall.

Amy said, "Do you have enough to eat?"

"Beef jerky for days."

"Honey. That's not dinner."

"Many cultures would disagree."

"What about the leftover lasagna?"

"I ate it last night."

"Can't you order in?"

"Nobody's open. Drake's is pouring, but no food and cash only. Don't worry about me. How was your morning sickness today?"

"Better, thanks. On the whole it's definitely been easier than last time. Sarah says that means it's a boy."

"Sounds scientific."

"What should we name him?"

"I don't know," I said. "Hey, Charlotte, what should we name the baby?"

"Charlotte," Charlotte said.

"You want to name the baby your name?" Amy asked.

"It is a good name," I said. "But don't you think it might get confusing?"

"*No.*"

"Like if Mommy calls you for dinner, and she says,

'Charlotte,' how will you know which Charlotte she means?"

"They both need to eat dinner," Amy said.

"That's true. Let me think of a better example."

"Daddy, when are you coming here?"

I sighed. "I'm not sure, lovey. Will you eat some more ice cream for me?"

"Okay."

Amy said, "We're heading out with Sarah and the baby in a few minutes. P-I-Z-Z-A."

"Excellent. Have fun."

"I'll call you tonight after she's down."

"I might go to bed early. There's nothing to do. TV's out, Wi-Fi's out."

"Read by flashlight."

"It's too hot under the covers." I paused. "Maybe I'll tackle the Great Wall of Cardboard."

"Mm-hm."

"You sound skeptical."

"Mm-hm."

"Should I be insulted that you sound so skeptical."

"You should be happy that we understand each other so well. Try you around eight?"

"Sounds good. I love you."

"I love you, too."

"Bye, lovey."

"Bye, Daddy."

I opened the text thread with my brother. My last two attempts, hours old, unanswered.

Yo sorry what's up

Call me please

I'd balked at calling Luke's wife. I didn't want to worry her and frankly I wasn't sure she'd pick up. We're not close, either.

I tried her. She didn't pick up. I texted her.

Hey Andrea. Can you please ask Luke to give me a quick ring or call me yourself. Thanks

I considered calling my mom. Then I came to my senses.

I showered, hanging my work clothes over the towel rod to air out.

The house was fully dark. I fetched out LED lanterns and a box of candles, holdovers from the previous two blackouts, and placed them at intervals to create stepping-stones of light. It felt like I was stranded between the twenty-first and seventeenth centuries. The piercing glare of the lanterns hurt my head. I turned them off.

In the kitchen I fanned four packs of jerky and two slices of bread on a plate. I filled a glass with tap water. I surrounded the meal with candles and texted a picture to Amy.

#BachelorLife

She sent me a photo of their pizza, oozy cheese, golden crust.

I sent her a scowling emoji.

She sent me a kissy emoji.

I tore open my beef jerky. One and a half packs in I had lockjaw. Neither Luke nor Andrea had responded to any of my calls or texts. I put my plate in the sink and got dressed.

CHAPTER 4

———

MY BROTHER AND his wife lived off the grid, in the foothills of Las Trampas Wilderness.

The nearest town was Moraga, sleepier than usual tonight beneath the darkness and heat. Windborne snack wrappers waltzed the strip-mall parking lot. Past St. Mary's College I hooked sharply onto Jupiter Creek Road and wound through a tight, leafy canyon.

As I drove, my phone dropped bars, three to two to one, like a firing squad mowing down a row of the condemned. The gaps between mailboxes lengthened. Then several boxes formed a consolidated delivery point. After that, no boxes. The United States Postal Service had made its stand. *Not one inch more.*

Cruising with the window down, I could hear the creek that ran parallel to the road and gave it its name. The turn was easy to miss: a bike reflector, affixed to the trunk of a big-leaf maple, marking the spot where a crumbling culvert bridge jumped the water. On the other side concrete gave way to rutted dirt.

I bounced along at a crawl through alders and oaks, shrubs and creepers.

The genuine version of what Rory Vandervelde's landscaper designer had sought to evoke.

Six and a half acres had cost Luke and Andrea about the same as what Amy and I paid for sixteen hundred square feet. The trade-off was scant creature comfort and human contact.

I switched on my brights. The underbrush rippled with panic.

The parcel had come with a simple wooden longhouse, plonked in a clearing besieged by regrowth. There was an outdoor shower stall and an outhouse with a composting toilet. To these Luke and Andrea had added a chicken coop, raised vegetable beds, a potting shed. Late-season wildflowers flourished around an aboveground cistern. Solar panels made a modernist Stonehenge.

Charlotte loved it here. The setting brought out her latent savage. She harassed the chickens, ran through the grass in delirious circles, war-whooping and ripping up handfuls of vegetation. Every visit ended with me hauling her wailing to the car, her fingernails black, her diaper heavy as a sack of mud.

We didn't visit often.

On the far side of the clearing Luke had erected a shelter for working on his cars: a poured-concrete pad, four pressure-treated posts, and a corrugated tin roof. Tarp walls kept out the rain. While Charlotte gorged on freedom and our wives scrounged for conversation, he would take me out to show me the latest active project.

Tonight the pad was empty.

I parked next to Andrea's Nissan Leaf. Amber light filled the longhouse windows. Thin gray smoke twined from the stovepipe. I could not smell it because the air stank so deeply of char. Wind chimes rang unseen.

I started for the door.

The forest stirred.

I turned, took a few steps into the trees. "Luke?"

A deer exploded from the bushes. I stumbled and fell and it ran straight at me, rearing up to show the scraped undersides of its hooves and its belly taut with veins before it sprang laterally and punched through a dry shrub with a shattering of branches.

Hinges whined, light whipped the trees.

A woman's voice called, "I can defend myself."

"Andrea." I rose, coughing dust. "It's—"

She jabbed at me with her flashlight. "Who is that?"

"It's Clay." I'd dropped my own flashlight. I rummaged for it in the leaves, brushed myself off. "Do you mind . . ."

She lowered the beam from my face. She wore leggings and a T-shirt with the Bay Area Therapeutics logo: a green snippet of DNA sprouting marijuana leaves. Bare toes gripped the dirt. Her right hand trained a snub-nosed revolver on my groin.

I motioned for her to lower the gun, as well. "I'm trying to reach Luke."

"He's not here."

"I tried calling. Him and you." She didn't answer. "Can we talk?"

She went inside.

IN ADDITION TO a love of cars and "natural" landscaping, my brother and Rory Vandervelde had in common a preference for open-plan living, albeit not at the same scale. The longhouse lacked interior walls and was furnished with castoffs—a crooked armoire, unraveling wicker. The mattress lay on pallets. Over a meditation corner of rag rugs and zafu pillows, Buddha kept a serene watch. A folding table covered in food containers, vitamin bottles, essential oils, canisters of herbs, and utensils served as kitchen and pantry. Beneath it was a mini-fridge, beside it a wood-burning stove. Everywhere were lit candles. A close, oppressive atmosphere had built up.

Andrea set the gun on the kitchen table. Prying open a tin, she loaded powder into a tea infuser and reached for a kettle piping on the stovetop. Halfheartedly she offered me a cup.

"What is it?"

"Chamomile and valerian root." She filled a mug, dropped the infuser, and flipped over a small sand timer. "It helps to relieve stress."

I didn't ask why she felt stressed or why she thought I might, too. "No, thanks."

My brother and I had turned out different. The women we'd chosen to marry had amplified those differences by an order of magnitude.

Amy was five-ten, angular, pretty, and coltish, a middle blocker for her college volleyball team; an accomplished scholar and elegant thinker, confident yet humble, capable of assuming anyone's perspective without forfeiting her own.

Andrea stood five-two in Birkenstocks. Hippy, hippie, plate-faced, she had a habit of smiling up at you while you talked—smiling, but not nodding, for there was no assent implied, but rather martyrly forbearance. When you finished, she'd speak her piece. Even agreement tended to take the form of a rebuttal.

Nice day, isn't it, Andrea?

No, but it's so much better than yesterday.

It was Amy who'd first observed that Andrea's Zen-groovy-earthy persona was a coping strategy for profound anxiety. I hadn't cared to see that, too put off by her condescension. She boasted a cereal-box certificate in trauma counseling, others in yoga, mindfulness, and holistic aromatherapy. Despite all that, she rarely worked. The main advantage of having so many degrees was that they entitled her to refer to herself as a "therapist," which in turn entitled her to regard Amy, who held a PhD in clinical psychology from Yale, as her peer.

Amy didn't care. It pissed me off, though.

But I wasn't the one married to Andrea. Luke was, and they seemed to make each other happy. They'd met while he was at Pleasant Valley, when she came to the prison to teach meditation. She knew Luke's sins, accepted him; cleaved to him, after the world had turned its back. So he loved her, and doted on her, endorsed her wackiness and cherished it.

How curative that must have felt for him—to love and be loved. In his self-deprecating way he joked about being damaged goods. Which he was. But he wasn't a serial killer or a rapist. Plenty of women marry men far worse.

Andrea bobbed the tea infuser. Most of the time she piled her unmanageable brown hair beneath a kerchief or snood. Loose now, it swayed like seaweed. "What do you want with Luke?"

"He was on my mind. Both of you. With the . . . you know, everything. The fires."

"We're fine."

"I'm glad to hear it."

My attention had migrated to the revolver.

Andrea stiffened. "It's in my name. They can take away his rights but they can't take mine."

Were the police to show up with a warrant, I didn't think that argument would carry water. "Do you know where he is?"

"Out."

"Out where?"

She shrugged.

"When do you expect him back?"

"He'll be back when he's back."

"Have you spoken to him recently?"

"Define recently."

"Today."

"Not today, no."

"When was the last time you spoke?"

"Yesterday."

"Do you remember what time it was?"

"Not really."

Her calmness was maddening.

I said, "Did you see him?"

"When."

"Yesterday."

"No. I mean, yes. But not since then."

"He didn't stay here last night?"

"I don't keep track of his every movement."

"Sure. But"—*but he's your husband*—"did he mention where he was going?"

"We're two independent entities," she said. "You and Amy can choose to relate to each other however you want but that's not how we choose to relate. Sometimes he travels for work. Sometimes I'm on a silent retreat and we don't talk for a week. He's busy. We're busy people. You might not understand it, but you can't judge us for it."

"No one's judging anyone."

She bobbed at her tea.

"Is that where he is?" I asked. "On a work trip?"

"He definitely could be."

What the hell did that mean? "Did he say he was going somewhere?"

"Scott's always calling up last-minute and sending him some crazy place cause he knows Luke will agree to do it. He snaps his fingers and Luke jumps."

My brother's friendship with Scott Silber stretched back to high school. Even then Scott had shown an entrepreneurial streak: scalping concert tickets, sourcing rare sneakers, procuring kegs for a fee. His latest venture, Bay Area Therapeutics, launched right as California legalized recreational cannabis. Six months post-prison, Luke joined as employee number nineteen.

Both gambles had paid off. The company had twice upgraded their offices to accommodate rapid growth. It was the first decent job Luke had ever held. I understood his sense of obligation.

"But you're not aware that he's on a trip for Scott," I said.

"No, Clay, I'm not *aware*."

"Has Luke mentioned anything to you about planning to sell his car?"

"Sell—the Camaro? No. Why?"

"He took it with him when he left."

"I mean. It's his car."

"And this was yesterday."

"That's what I said."

I'd been holding out hope, telling myself that Luke could have sold the Camaro to Rory Vandervelde at any point in the last nine days. Andrea had shortened that window. Dramatically.

"You don't remember what time he left, though."

"Ask me all you want, it won't change the answer."

"How about morning, afternoon, night?"

She blew a raspberry. "Day. Okay? Happy?"

"Has he called you since then?"

"I haven't checked my phone."

"Can you check it now, please?"

"I don't have it with me," she said. "I'm not sure where it is."

"I'll call it."

"It's off."

The sand timer ran down. She reset it and faced me with crossed arms.

"Why are you so concerned about him all of a sudden?"

The premise of her question—that I'd failed to show concern for Luke until now—grated on me, not least because of the truth it contained.

How could I answer her?

Guess where I was earlier today.

Guess what I found.

Andrea stared at me defiantly.

She knew who my brother was.

She'd married him anyway.

Whatever's happened, I wanted to say, *you can tell me. I can help.*

But I didn't know if I could. And she'd never believe me. Why should she? I'd never gone out of my way to hurt Luke. But neither had I gone out of my way to help him.

Wind whistled through the wallboards in hot blades.

"Please," I said. "I just want to talk to him."

She made a put-upon face. "The phone's in my car."

"Do you want to give me your keys?"

"It's unlocked."

"Thank you."

She lifted out the infuser, watched it drip.

THE LEAF'S GLOVE BOX contained a heavy nylon pouch whose label read RF BLOQ. I unzipped it and found a cracked Samsung Galaxy. It refused to turn on, and I only had an iPhone cable with me.

In the longhouse Andrea was sitting cross-legged on a pillow, eyes closed, cradling her mug.

I held up the Galaxy. "You have a charger for this somewhere?"

She looked over at me. Recoiled. "Get that out of here."

She straggled to her feet. Tea sloshed from the mug and ran down her arms. *"Out."*

Mystified, I retreated outside. I could see her through the open doorway, moving around in a frenzy, as though she were on fire. "Andrea?"

". . . one second."

"Are you okay?"

"One *second* . . . Move back. *Farther*."

I stood among the trees.

A twisted black cable sailed out and pipped in the dirt.

I took the cable to my car, plugged in the Galaxy, and left the motor running.

I walked back to the longhouse, pausing on the threshold. Andrea huddled against the opposite wall with her knees drawn up protectively against her body.

"Can I come in?" I asked.

"Where's the phone?"

"In my car."

"Yours, too. Leave it outside. I don't want it in here. I should have told you before. Do you have anything else?"

"Like what?"

"A radio. A walkie-talkie. Anything that puts out a signal. A garage door opener."

"Not on me."

"Okay."

I set my phone atop a stack of firewood and stepped inside. "Are you all right?"

"No, actually. My head is throbbing."

"Is there something I can get you?"

She seemed unwilling to abandon the comfort of the wall. She pointed to her mug on the floor. I brought it to her. Pink blotched her wrists where the tea had run.

"I'm sorry I upset you," I said.

"Not your fault. You didn't know any better." She took a sip. "Don't look at me like that."

"Like what?"

"You know like what. I use it during the day, I have to. But I try to limit my twenty-four-hour total exposure, especially close to . . ." She trailed off. "You should, too, by the way, if you care about your health, or Charlotte's. Do you have any idea what those levels of radiation do to rats? Look up *cellphone tumors*. We're conducting this giant uncontrolled experiment on ourselves and we'll pay for it."

She turned vigilant, as if she'd heard a siren. "What time is it?"

"I—uh." I reached for my absent phone. "About eight thirty, I think."

"Shit."

She hurried to the makeshift kitchen, set the mug down with a thump, and knelt to open the mini-fridge. Light spilled out.

I shouldn't have been surprised. They had solar, and she'd plugged in the Leaf, so there had to be a power storage unit somewhere. But the candles and the woodstove—not to mention her patent terror of electronic devices—seemed to relegate functioning outlets to the realm of science fiction.

From the fridge she took four small glass vials and lined them up on the folding table.

From among the jars and canisters she picked out several vitamin bottles, a red plastic sharps container, a tattered piece of paper, a bottle of rubbing alcohol, a zip-top bag of gauze, a second of syringes. She removed four syringes and laid them in readiness next to the vials. Consulting the paper, she rearranged the vials to ensure they were in the right order.

I came closer. The paper was a calendar. Each day listed dosages for various medications.

She shook out capsules of vitamin C, vitamin E, folic acid, omega-3s, coenzyme Q10, bolting them down with gulps of tea.

I was also close enough to get a good look at the revolver. Roundish, .22 or .38 Special. A purse gun, meant to deter a mugger.

I wondered if it could inflict the kind of damage done to Rory Vandervelde's body.

I wondered if ballistics had recovered shells or slugs, and if so, what size.

Andrea stabbed a needle into the first vial and drew up a third of the chamber.

She held the syringe out to me.

I accepted it, reflexively.

She rolled up the hem of her T-shirt and pinned it in place with her elbow. The flesh near her waistband was mottled yellow and green and stippled with puncture marks.

She gathered a fold of skin, swabbed it with alcohol, and averted her eyes. "Don't tell me when it's going in."

"I don't know what I'm supposed to do."

"Put the needle in. Push down the plunger. *Slow.*"

"You can't do it yourself?"

"No. I can't."

"What do you normally do?"

"Luke does it for me."

"What did you do last night, if he wasn't here?"

"I did it myself."

"So—"

"And I threw up. Can you please stop talking."

I slid the needle into my sister-in-law's abdomen and injected her with Follistim. While the chamber drained she breathed out through her teeth.

I removed the needle. There was no blood.

"Put it in the sharps bin." Andrea laid her finger on day thirteen of the calendar, lips moving as she reviewed the next dosage.

Day twenty read *possible trigger*. Day twenty-two, circled in red, was *possible retrieval*. The top of the calendar read *Contra Costa Center for Reproductive Health*. Their logo was a stylized pair of hands holding a stylized baby whose face was also a daisy or maybe a shining sun.

She drew up the second syringe.

"Do I . . . Should I aim for a different spot, or—"

"Just do it."

I injected my sister-in-law with Menopur, with dexamethasone, and with Lupron.

I withdrew the last needle and she appeared to deflate, as if leaking from the holes in her body. She mumbled thanks, trudged toward the mattress, and flopped down.

"Do you need anything?"

She shook her head.

"Do you want the blanket on?"

"It's too hot." She squirmed, scratching at the dry skin on her calves, flexing and rotating her swollen ankles.

"Are you sure I can't get you anything? Water?"

"It'll just make me need to pee." Unable to get comfortable, she sat up and grabbed her left foot and ground at it with her knuckles. "They're like rocks," she muttered.

I thought better of sharing that Amy had suffered similarly. "I'm so sorry."

Andrea grunted.

I was about to excuse myself to check her phone when she spoke again:

". . . could you . . ."

She was holding her foot, staring up at me hopefully. I didn't understand what she was asking me to do. Then I did and I faltered. While the tone of her voice—of our entire relationship—had in it not one iota of sexuality, I had never touched her except to exchange wary hugs.

Like most anxious people she was highly attuned to any suggestion of wrongdoing. She lay down again and shrank into a ball. "Forget it."

"I—"

"I said never mind." She rolled over, hugging the pillow. I wanted to shake her, demand that she sit up and talk to me; could she please, for once, pause the Andrea Show. The shirt drooped against her ribs. She had lost weight, not a small amount.

Amy was thirty-three. We'd gotten pregnant with Charlotte by accident. The current pregnancy was planned but nearly as effortless. Say what you will about Luke's shortcomings—I've said plenty—he loved my daughter and was a good uncle to her, and I believed he would do the same for the new baby. When I called to share the news he congratulated me enthusiastically.

Andrea was forty-four, three years older than Luke. She'd never offered us congratulations. If the subject arose at Edison family brunch, she didn't leave the table or make snide comments or do anything so overt. She didn't participate, either, biding her time until a new subject arose, as though pregnancy and children were as arcane and unrelatable as Hammurabi's code.

I looked at her now, fetal on the mattress, and thought about her loud disavowals of Western medicine. I thought about the lab-made hormones coursing through her and the desperation that had driven her to resort to them.

Her eroded body, radiating tension. Her feet, small and distended and unwashed.

I sat on the bed, lifted her ankles onto my lap, and began massaging the soles of her feet. She made a brief show of resistance and went limp.

"Too hard?"

"No, it's okay."

"Let me know."

"He does this every night," she said miserably. "Every night, until I fall asleep."

I nodded.

"He'll come home," she said. "He has to."

I let a minute go by. "How do you guys coordinate your schedule? Do you share a calendar?"

"No."

"Where's his computer?"

"He keeps it at work."

"He doesn't bring home a laptop or anything?"

"I've asked him not to." She yawned and scratched her upper arms. "God, I'm so itchy."

"I'm thinking of anything that could tell us what he's up to. What about his email account?"

"What about it?"

"He has two, right? Work and personal? Do you know either of the passwords?"

"I'm not going to tell you that."

"You check. Or put the password into my phone."

"I said *no*, Clay."

The wind keened.

"Do you have a key to the Camaro?" I asked.

"Why do you care about his car so much?"

"I have a friend in the market. I thought maybe Luke'd be interested."

She didn't react to the obvious lie. "I don't have a key. I never drive it."

"Does he keep a spare around? In the car shelter?"

"I have no idea." She yawned again. "You can look if you want."

The candle at her bedside guttered and went out.

I said, "Is he keeping up with going to meetings?"

No reply.

I thought she might've nodded off. I leaned over. Her eyes were open.

"He's clean," she said.

"You're sure of that."

"I'm his wife."

"All right. I'm going to take a quick peek at the phone. What's the PIN?"

"Our anniversary."

"Remind me, please."

She did.

"I'll put it back in your car," I said. "Are you going to be all right?"

She tugged up the blanket.

The Galaxy's lock screen showed Andrea and Luke in hiking gear, holding hands on a rocky outcropping. I keyed in the PIN, unleashing an avalanche of notifications, an indication that the phone had been off for some time.

I called him. It struggled to connect, and his voice came through chipped into digital packets.

You've reached Luke Edison at Bay Area—

The log showed several missed calls from him, all made the day before between two thirty and five thirty p.m.

No voicemails. No recently deleted voicemails.

I opened the text messages. The thread with Luke was at the top of the list.

One unread.

Sun, Oct 1, 5:54 PM

Baby I'm sorry

CHAPTER 5

———

SPAM OVERFLOWED the phone's inbox. The most recent email from Luke was weeks old, a forwarded invitation to the Bay Area Therapeutics Labor Day cookout. Vegan and gluten-free options available.

When he and Andrea communicated electronically, texting was their medium of choice.

I scrolled up the thread. They sounded like any happily married couple, covering practical matters (pick up chicken feed; home by seven), sharing photos and jokes, proffering affection.

Also a few squabbles. Luke had canceled a doctor's appointment, arousing Andrea's ire.

Call them and reschedule TODAY

Nothing suggested real trouble.

Nothing explained his final message.

Baby I'm sorry

The timing gnawed at me.

Sunday, five fifty-four p.m. Soon after the power went out.

Right around the time of Rory Vandervelde's death.

What did Luke have to be sorry about?

I texted him from Andrea's phone.

Can you call me please

The wind chimes clanked and banged.

Are you there I wrote.

Please call when you get this

Call your brother too

If Luke and Andrea shared a plan, his phone ought to show up in her device-finding app.

It didn't.

I debated whether to take the Galaxy with me. Andrea clearly didn't want it around; in that sense I'd be doing her a favor.

But I'd told her I would put it back. She might wake up to the fact that her husband wasn't home, panic, and rush to her car to check. I zipped the phone in the pouch, tucked the pouch in the Leaf's glove box, and crossed the grass toward the car shelter.

IT WAS SORELY out of place, a ludicrous contradiction to their carbon-neutral lifestyle. Oil cans littered the concrete pad. The surrounding soil was stained with coolant and paint overspray. Luke had stockpiled enough gasoline to supply a Parisian riot.

That was my brother. Meek and macho. Thoughtful and careless. Generous without warning and staggeringly self-involved.

The shelter's tarp walls had been drawn back and secured to the posts with bungee cords, like a crude canopy bed. A chain saw with bark-crusted teeth hung from a hook. Grubby rags; a mechanic's creeper; extension cords and buckets and jacks. Everything looked well used. By comparison, the repair station in Vandervelde's garage was the Sistine Chapel.

No spare key on a nail.

A mug sat atop the tool chest. I sniffed coffee, stale and cold.

I went through drawers. No keys there, either.

Bins held paint cans, mementos of cars come and gone.

Cherry red: '73 Dodge Challenger, the first car he bought after his release. He wasn't allowed to drive yet. The DMV had deemed him a negligent operator and suspended his license indefinitely. He was working at Walmart and living with my parents rent-free. They'd hired a lawyer to help him get his license back. Presumably they gave him money for the Challenger, too. He picked it up in wretched shape, on the cheap. Whenever I stopped by I'd hear him hammering away in their garage.

Mustard yellow: '71 AMC Javelin. On a Wednesday morning he rang my doorbell and invited me to take a spin. Amy was at work and I had Charlotte. I tried to fend him off. Another time. But Charlotte lit up when she saw him, and I caved. I remembered wrestling her car seat into position.

A few other colors I couldn't place. Glittery metallic blue, basic black, gray, silver. Bought and sold without fanfare? Or samples he'd tried out.

The last can: neon green. For his baby; his favorite. He'd stop at a light and the guy in the next lane would roll down the window. *Cash money. How much?*

Declining, always, with a smile. *She's so sweet, think I might hold on to her a little while.*

One edge of the green can lid stuck up.

I touched it. It wobbled, imperfectly closed.

Recently used?

Touch-ups, for a big sale?

Rory Vandervelde had the bankroll to make an offer no one could refuse.

I tamped the lid and shut the bin, took the coffee mug and crossed back to the longhouse.

Inside the revolver lay like an anchor on the kitchen table.

Andrea was snoring.

I put the mug next to the gun and tiptoed around, blowing out candles.

I PHONED AMY from the freeway.

"Hey," she said. "I thought you'd gone to bed early. I didn't want to wake you up."

"Thanks. I—" A smoky gust knocked me halfway into the adjacent lane. "Gah."

"Are you driving?"

"It's super-hot in the house, and this is the only way to charge my phone. How was pizza?"

"It was pizza. Can I tell you something funny Charlotte said?"

Grateful for small talk, I said, "Please."

"She ordered anchovies and the waiter was like, 'Whoa, anchovies. Are you sure?' And she goes, 'I have a sophisticated palate.'"

"She said that?"

"I swear to God. Did you teach her that?"

"Not me. It must've been your dad," I said. "He loves setting these verbal land mines that go off under us."

"She did use it correctly."

"Do you think we're doing enough for her?" I asked.

"What else should we be doing?"

"I don't know. Sending her to enrichment? Getting her a violin?"

Amy laughed. "She's three."

"If I'd started the violin at three I could be a professional musician today."

"My love. You're tone-deaf."

"I'm just saying."

"Are you volunteering to drive her to and from lessons?"

"I changed my mind," I said. "No violin."

"That was easy."

"Our children will be forever stunted because we're too lazy to get in the car."

"I'm a hundred percent fine with that," she said.

I said, "I miss you so much."

"I miss you, too. I hate that you're alone."

"When do you want to come back?"

"I rescheduled my clients through Wednesday, and Maria said I can have the whole week. Hopefully it doesn't come to that. The Cal Fire map says nothing's more than ten percent contained. You're sure you can't get away and come here?"

I'd thought about asking my sergeant for a few days off.

That was before a green car in a murdered man's garage.

Amy said, "Honey? Did I lose you?"

"Sorry," I said. "I'm here."

"No pressure. I know you've got your hands full."

"Thanks." I should tell her everything. No doubt she'd reassure me, gently point out that I was catastrophizing.

No need to drag her into my paranoia.

"What's on tap for tomorrow?" I asked.

"Sarah and I talked about the beach."

"Have a great time. Check in when you can."

"Good night, honey."

"Good night."

OUR HOUSE WAS MURKY, as lonesome as if no one had ever lived there. Wind rattled the windows like a mouthful of loose teeth. We'd only been able to afford a fixer-upper. Wobbly front porch railing. Seismic cracking in the bedrooms. Dingy nylon curtains throughout, scarlet tartan faded to pink in patches. Not our forever house. A foothold in the market. I had a promotion in the pipeline. Three to five years, some sweat equity, and we could ratchet up. DIY could be fun. We'd watched online spackling tutorials, followed rosy chronologies on HGTV.

We had yet to take on any project more technical than changing lightbulbs.

We lived with a wall of cardboard.

My damp work clothes hung over the bathroom towel rod. They'd absorbed the smoke and smelled like a musty pipe bowl. I took the paper with the Camaro's tag and VIN from my pant pocket and went to the kitchen.

I rinsed and dried my dinner plate by candlelight. Through the window my neighbor's cypress trees writhed in chaotic worship.

I put the candle in the sink and touched the paper to the flame. The paper was damp, too; it steamed and didn't want to catch. I held it there till it did, till the surface curled and the characters blackened into ash.

CHAPTER 6

Tuesday. Thirty-five hours in the dark.

SLEPT POORLY and woke up coughing.

I groped on the nightstand for my phone. The battery had dwindled to seven percent.

No missed calls. No texts.

The air quality index had worsened overnight. Maroon splotched the map, as if the northern third of the state had suffered a vicious beating.

I settled against the rank pillow, breathing stale, pungent smoke.

Luke hadn't told me about their fertility problems. I had no idea if this round of treatment was their first or tenth. I did know that even a single round was expensive and that insurance rarely covered it. Selling the Camaro might lessen their financial strain.

If Rory Vandervelde wanted the car, the deal could've closed easy and quick. Andrea had narrowed the delivery window, yes, but it was possible that Luke had brought the car to Vandervelde's house on Sunday, shaken hands with the new owner, and left him healthy as a horse.

Left and gone where, though?

Where was the Camaro's key?

Andrea claimed not to know about any sale. That, too, had an explanation: My brother was constantly wheeling and dealing. The paint cans attested to that. Cars were his thing, not hers. She was too preoccupied—or too apathetic—to keep up. Or maybe he was worried she'd try to talk him out of it. She loved him and he loved that car.

The very fact that he loved it so much made it all the more likely he'd sold under duress. Had he wrestled with the decision? Was that why'd he'd texted me the day after brunch?

R u around

Can we talk

Maybe I was reading too much into Andrea's evasiveness. I'd shown up unannounced, at night. She was highstrung by nature. Add in supersized doses of hormones and she had to be jumping out of her skin.

The embarrassment of having her secrets revealed.

The indignity of having to ask for help. From me, of all people.

She'd never liked me and the feeling was mutual.

She said it herself: She was Luke's wife. She knew him better than I did, better than I ever had. A twenty-four-hour radio silence would have been inconceivable for Amy and me. But who was I to judge?

Look at where Luke and Andrea lived. How they lived. They thrived on solitude.

You could live that way without kids. BC—Before Charlotte—Amy and I had spent much of our free time together. But not all of it. We'd talked and texted, but not like we did now, the never-ending flow of questions, re-

minders, photos, videos; the banal urgency of parent-
hood.

Maybe Luke was traveling for work. A last-minute
thing, for Scott.

Maybe he'd taken off on a vision quest, selling his car
first, hours before the murder.

Ugly coincidence. It happened.

I wielded these thoughts, trying to beat back the uglier
alternatives.

Failed.

I told a cold shower. I breakfasted on protein bars and
tap water and Advil.

Flakes of burnt paper stuck to the sides of the kitchen
sink. I rinsed them down the drain with the vegetable
sprayer.

A fine layer of ash covered my car. I ran the wiper fluid,
sluicing runnels of gray sludge.

AT MY DESK twenty minutes early, I plugged in my cellphone to finish charging and stashed it at the back of the
desk drawer, behind Rory Vandervelde's house keys. The
cord poked out, creating a quarter-inch gap, and my mind
overlaid a nauseating image of the garage hangar door,
stuck open.

I stapled my attention to paperwork.

Day shift trickled in. Night shift clocked out.

The sun came up, just.

By nine a.m. I couldn't stand it any longer and reached
into the drawer for the phone.

One text from Amy. The beach it was. She'd try me
later. She loved me.

Another text from the reporter. Did I want to comment yet? I did not.

My former teammate hadn't followed up and neither
had Billy Watts, the Berkeley detective. I texted my team-

mate that I was hanging in there and called Watts. His line went to voicemail. I told him to give me a ring whenever.

Nothing from Luke.

Dread resurfacing, stronger, sharper.

I texted Andrea.

Hey hope you're feeling well. Please lmk if you hear from Luke

My desk phone rang. I put the cell away and pressed SPEAKERPHONE. "Coroner's Bureau."

A curt male voice said, "Sean Vandervelde for Clay Edison."

"This is Deputy Edison. Thanks for getting back to me, Mr. Vandervelde."

"Yeah, so, I'm at work and I have two people standing outside my office, saying my dad's dead, except that they won't tell me a thing about it because they're saying I have to speak to you. So maybe you can tell me what the fuck is going on."

"I can, yes. I'm sorry to tell you that your father has passed away. My condolences."

"I *know* that part. They *told* me that part. What I *don't* know is anything else, so I'd appreciate it if you'd stick to that: the parts I *don't* fucking know."

"Right now we're not able to say exactly what happened, but—"

"Why not?"

"It appears your father was the victim of a crime."

Silence.

I said, "I realize that hearing that can be—"

"Fucking bitch. Hang on." He spoke to someone else: "You can leave, please. And tell them to leave. Goodbye. Thank you. *Goodbye.*"

He came back on. "Do you have a suspect?"

"That's a question for the detective. I'm with the county coro—"

"Who's the detective?"

I gave him Cesar Rigo's contact information.

"I don't fucking believe this. Oakland? It has to be them?"

"That's where the crime took place."

"Yeah, I *understand* that, I'm saying the *reason* you have murders in Oakland is because your police department is a grade-A shitshow run by a dickless prancing clown crew with a single-digit solve rate, so you'll forgive me if I don't sound psyched at the prospect of them *sleuthing*. How do you know he was murdered?"

"It appears he was shot. We—"

"The fuck is that, 'appears'? Was he shot or not?"

"The autopsy is scheduled for tomorrow. Once that's complete, we'll have a better sense—"

"No autopsy, I do not consent."

"Respectfully, sir, the law requires us—"

"I want him out of there. I want it done in a private facility."

"If you'd like him reexamined—"

"No. You do nothing. Do you hear me? Nothing. I will get a court order."

"Mr. Vandervelde, I appreciate that you're upset—"

"What time tomorrow?"

I started to check the calendar. Instinct kicked in. "Just so you know, sir, the procedure is closed to the—"

"Get fucked," he said and hung up.

Dani Botero leaned out. "No chill."

I got up to refill my coffee and came back to find my drawer buzzing.

Pictures from Amy. They were at the Santa Monica Pier. Charlotte, ear-deep in a cloud of cotton candy. I texted them to have fun and put the phone away.

I looked up OPD's homicide clearance rate.

It wasn't great, but it wasn't in the single digits. Getting better every year.

I looked up Sean Vandervelde's LinkedIn profile.

He was the young man from the graduation photo on Rory Vandervelde's desk. Since his college days he'd lost hair and gained weight. He was an attorney at a multinational firm. Their L.A. office was on Wilshire Boulevard, not far from where Amy and Charlotte were having a delightful beach day. He specialized in entertainment law.

MIDMORNING NIKKI KENNEDY and I responded to a call from Oakland Fire at the Ace Hardware on MacArthur Boulevard. Earlier that day the store's assistant manager, whose name was Russell Andrews, had arrived for work. The store wouldn't open for ten minutes but people were lining up along the sidewalk.

Andrews entered the store through the rear and went to his locker to put on his red vest. He and a co-worker discussed the crowd out front. Same as yesterday. Andrews shook his head. Somehow, these folks had managed to disregard dozens of emails and text alerts from the utility urging them to stock up on batteries and flashlights. Now they needed batteries and flashlights.

He fought his way into the vest. It didn't fit right, they never did. Russell Andrews was a big guy. He sweated a lot and kept extra vests in his locker so he could change during lunch.

Laughing, he told the co-worker he didn't know if he was going to make it that long. The forecast called for a scorcher.

Might be a three-vest day.

The first few hours kept him busy. Without power, the registers were inoperable. They had to write up receipts by hand, count out change. By eight thirty a.m. they'd run out of lanterns. By nine the paper towels were gone. Signs limited customers to one pack of batteries apiece. Nobody obeyed. They'd stuff four under each arm, waddle up to the customer service desk, and plead their case. Likewise all the other rationed items: masks, TP, generators, portable light sources. Everyone had a reason for why they, more than anyone else, needed multiples. Life-and-death-type excuses that got them nowhere.

By ten thirty supplies were dangerously low, tempers brittle. Russell Andrews phoned the distribution center to see if he could get an ETA for restock. The distribution center put him on hold. Andrews flagged down a woman from the paint department who was passing by. He asked her to listen on the line while he ran and swapped out his vest real quick.

He hadn't donned the new one when a cashier burst through the swinging doors: fight on register three.

The cashier would explain to me that he'd come looking for Andrews because he was the supervisor. Plus, when you needed someone to break up a fight, Russell Andrews—six foot two, two hundred ninety pounds, erstwhile offensive lineman for De Anza High School—seemed like the right dude for the job.

Andrews lumbered out to the floor.

Two women were rolling around on the linoleum, scrapping over the last unsold twenty-four-pack of Energizer D-cells. They had toppled an endcap display of ChapStick. A crowd of shoppers and employees had gathered. Several people, including the store security guard, were filming.

Like King Solomon in Timberlands, Russell Andrews waded into the fray, patient, confident in his size. He instructed the women to simmer down. That didn't have the desired effect, so he lunged for the batteries. Now all three of them were grabbing and shoving and cussing. Not since senior-year two-a-days had he had performed such strenuous physical activity.

With a heave from Andrews the batteries flew free, arc-ing over his head and tumbling along aisle five, Small Kitchen Appliances. He flopped back.

The women flopped back. They recovered and went scrambling after the batteries.

The crowd shifted to watch them.

Russell Andrews stayed down, flattened by sudden cardiac arrest.

A customer noticed him, ran over, felt his neck, and shouted for help. A cashier ran for a defibrillator. The customer began chest compressions. She was a graphic designer, untrained in CPR. She only knew what she'd seen on TV. Afraid of hurting Andrews, she didn't push nearly hard enough to goad the circulatory system of a man more than twice her weight.

Starved of oxygen, Russell Andrews's brain began to die.

Nobody had called an ambulance. The graphic designer told me she thought the cashier had done it. The cashier had the opposite impression. The security guard had moved up with his phone to get a better view of the brawl. The woman from the paint department was still on hold.

Russell Andrews died at register three.

In advance of our arrival, EMTs had sent the rubberneckers packing and herded the employees, teary-eyed, into the break room. We took pictures, took statements, examined the body. Turning him was a bit of an adventure, Kennedy and me squatting and grunting, her ruddy cheeks gone raspberry red to match her hair.

She began the dorsal exam. I went to the van for the gurney. The sidewalk was deserted, customers having dispersed in search of batteries and flashlights.

My phone buzzed. Jed Harkless.

"Am I right in thinking you got the keys for Vandervelde?" he asked.

"In my desk. What's up?"

"Oakland called. They're finished. Me and Bagoyo are gonna head up there to seal."

I pulled out the gurney. The legs unfolded and it clattered upright in the gutter. "I can come with you. I'll be back in an hour."

"Not sure we can wait that long."

The gurney had started to roll down the street. I grabbed a rail. "What's the rush? There's a uniform on site."

"Not anymore, there isn't. The detective said they can't spare the bodies. They already left this morning. All that stuff, I want to get up there soon as I can to safeguard."

The very rationale I'd given Cesar Rigo: big house, full of expensive things to steal.

An old FBI agent once told me he'd never met a cop who asked for more work. I couldn't demand to accompany Harkless without coming off like a major try-hard, and the desire not to call attention to myself outweighed the desire to revisit the scene and have a look around.

"Whatever you want," I said. "Just trying to spare you the smell."

I thought Yak-Yak might jump at the chance to bow out. Instead I triggered a defensive reaction. "Naw, bro. I'm good. Keys?"

"Top left."

"Thanks."

I pushed the gurney to the hardware store entrance. A man on Rollerblades was tugging on the locked door. The EMTs hadn't turned over the hours-of-operation sign. It still read OPEN—PLEASE COME IN!

"They're closed," I said.

"But I need batteries," the man said, his feet sliding.

I braked the gurney and knocked. "Pretty sure they're sold out."

"Are you going inside?" the man asked. "Can you ask?"

An EMT unbolted the door for me.

"Godspeed," I said, flipping the sign to CLOSED—SEE YOU SOON!

Nikki Kennedy knelt by the wrapped body. She took the feet. I took the shoulders.

"You want a hand?" the EMT said. He smiled gallantly at Kennedy. "Don't want you to hurt your back."

She shot him a look that would burn toast.

I counted down from three, and we lifted what used to be Russell Andrews, two hundred ninety pounds of *never again,* onto the gurney.

The pads squeaked. The frame shuddered and settled without further complaint.

Kennedy did not injure her back.

Near the freeway, I saw the man on Rollerblades testing the door of an unlit 7-Eleven.

AT FOUR THIRTY Harkless returned from sealing the house.

"Holy Moses," he said. "Why didn't you tell me about the garage?"

The Camaro flashed through my mind, its bright colors dulled down to something sickly.

I saw my hand, racing across the paint, removing marks, destroying evidence.

Of what? Luke was on a work trip.

I said, "I wanted it to be a surprise."

"Oh, it was."

Lindsey Bagoyo entered, unstrapping her vest. "We didn't know where to start. We ran out of bags."

Triumph in their voices, as though they'd returned from a successful hunt.

I opened my desk drawer. Rory Vandervelde's house

keys were no longer there but were in a storage locker with his watches and cuff links and jewelry and everything else Harkless and Bagoyo had managed to gather. The key for the locker, in turn, was upstairs with Edmond, the property clerk.

I reached to the back of the drawer for my phone.

Twenty-seven hours since I'd written to Luke.

CHAPTER 7

——

BAY AREA THERAPEUTICS occupied a converted warehouse on Washington Street, a block and a half in either direction from the old morgue building and from Jack London Square. Before leaving work I called and secured permission from Scott Silber's chief of staff to come by.

I took side streets. Traffic lights vibrated in the wind and signs ricked spasmodically. In the residential neighborhoods everyone had hunkered down for the evening, but the markets along 8th and 9th in Chinatown did a brisk trade. Masked shoppers shouldered twenty-five-pound sacks of rice up the sidewalk, the stream parting and rejoining around an elderly man glacially advancing a wire cart bricked solid with toilet paper.

I parked beneath a snapping banner that invited me to DINE PLAY SHOP STAY. The area had long served the adjacent Port of Oakland. Growing up, Luke and I referred to it as POO, because of the acronym and because you could smell it from the freeway.

Gentrification had sanded down some of the rough

edges. Not all. A few edges you kept for character. The eye relished the reclaimed waterfront with its gastropubs and bowling alley and purveyor of artisanal beef; the nose wrinkled at stagnant brine and bunker fuel.

That evening's special was Added Smoke.

The grid functioned this far west. I could hear the thud of bass as I passed the CrossFit box Luke frequented after work. Along with reforming his character, he'd devoted serious effort to reshaping his body. No longer did people confuse us from behind.

In a fit of brotherly insanity I'd once agreed to join him. For twenty interminable minutes I climbed a rope and stepped up onto a high wooden box and flung kettle-bells. The wall timer hit zero and I puddled on the rubber mats, knee screaming.

Luke lay beside me.

Pain is weakness leaving the body he said.

Pain is pain paining the pain I said.

Feels good when it's over.

You could also try not making yourself feel horrible to begin with.

He laughed and bumped me with his elbow. *How I do.*

In retrospect the remark felt telling. We'd seldom discussed his years in prison and never the crime that put him there. His outwardly easygoing manner could lead you to conclude that he had shed any lingering sense of remorse.

Amy, again, had seen deeper, identifying a masochistic streak in Luke's character—the need to test, limit, and punish himself. He'd become, successively, a vegetarian, a vegan, and a paleo vegan. Pretty much he ate cashews. As a recovering addict, he'd placed himself in an awkward position by working where he did. He didn't exercise so much as scourge his body and, by extension, his soul.

I came to the warehouse. No signage out front. I rang a buzzer set into the brick and a voice instructed me to show my ID to the camera eye. I started to reach for my badge, swapped it for my driver's license.

The woman who opened the door was in her mid-twenties, with pixieish features and a persecuted, watchful expression.

"Evelyn Girgis," she said.

She handed me a timestamped visitor sticker and escorted me over the main floor, a warren of communal desks and freestanding glass conference rooms beneath exposed ductwork. At quarter to six the pace of activity was strong. I said as much to Evelyn, who shrugged.

"Scott's almost always the last to leave," she said.

"I appreciate his seeing me on short notice."

Her smile implied that she'd made an effort to prevent this meeting from taking place.

Among the employees, a few blatant stoner types stood out. The majority were Silicon Valley technocrats, extruded by the same die that made worker bees for every Bay Area start-up. Mostly white, mostly young, full of energy and FOMO. Dreamers for whom *hope* was spelled with an *I* and a *P* and an *O*.

The place was set up for their gratification, with bike racks, videogame cabinets, and branded swag from the annual retreat. The kitchen offered electrolyte water and healthy snacking choices. Dogs wandered or snoozed underfoot.

The most significant difference between this and most workplaces within a thirty-mile radius was literally in the air—a resinous funk emanating from dozens upon dozens of marijuana plants. They replaced standard office greenery, livening up dead spots and nodding beside the recycling bins in decorative planters, thrusting forth lush masses of leaves and glistening alien cones of orange and purple. Staked placards identified the strains.

I'm no stoner, but I live where I live. OG Kush and Cheesequake I recognized. The unfamiliar ones had me stifling a smile. Purple Monkey Balls. Bob Saget. Alaskan Thunderfuck. Dank Ewe. They exuded melon and pepper, skunk and tangerine. And just plain weed.

High along a brick wall ran a series of eight-foot-tall signs bearing the slogan I AM CANNABIS. Soft-focus portraits accompanied testimonials to the plant's manifold benefits: medicinal, social, economic. The subjects represented a wide slice of humanity. A firefighter with a herniated disk. A female veteran with colon cancer. A man with debilitating OCD. A man who had served a lengthy prison sentence under the old drug laws. A fieldworker. A minister.

I'd slowed to read. The content was engaging, the execution stylish and empathic.

Evelyn Girgis said, "Part of a campaign we created for our expo booth last year."

"Nice work."

"Luke's idea, actually."

"Really?"

Another thin smile. She checked her phone. "Scott's ready for you."

I followed her up a floating staircase toward a glassed-in pod elevated on I-beams and overlooking the main floor like an aerie. There was no desk. The computer and keyboard mounted to a rolling stand, similar to those found on hospital wards but made of bleached wood and designed by Scandinavians. An altar table displayed twenty-odd bonsai marijuana trees under bell jars. Cucumber slices floated in a jug of ice water beside a stack of compostable cups.

Scott Silber lolled in a bamboo papasan, boat shoes kicked off, talking to the ceiling.

He held up a finger. Evelyn froze on the top step.

He finished his call, plucked out his earbuds, and gestured permission.

Evelyn unfroze and held the pod door for me.

Scott bounded forward to give me a pound hug. "Bro . . . Thanks, Evvie."

She withdrew and shut the door, zeroing out the ambient noise.

"Please please please," Scott said, reseating himself. "Shit, man. What's it been?"

I took a slingback chair. "Not since Luke's wedding, I think."

"Right. Right. You look *good*."

"You too." I meant it. Scott had hardly changed since high school. Same curly black hair, three-day beard, Mick Jagger lips. Gone were the FUBU denim and Wu-Tang hoodies; navy slacks and a pink button-down open at the neck probably made it easier to raise capital.

"Yeah, well, I gotta keep up with all these fucking kids I work with. On that note: You got a family."

"A daughter."

"Pssh."

"We're expecting again."

"*Psssh*. Respect. Luke told me about your little girl. He said she's a genius. I expect nothing less, you guys come from brains."

By "you guys" I didn't know if he meant me and Amy, or me and Luke. "And? What's your deal, Mr. Silber?"

Sheepishly he held up his left hand, wiggling the bare ring finger. "Did my mom send you? For real, though, that's dope. You guys must be busy as shit."

"Coming from you, I'll take it as a compliment."

"I know, right? Wild. I knew we had something special but I never imagined it'd blow up like this. You have a dream, and for a long time that's all it is, a picture in your mind. Then you wake up and there's all these people, it's this giant organism taking on a life of its own. Five years ago you told me I'd be in this position . . ." He shook his head. "Dreams have a life of their own, too."

His speech had the practiced quality of an investor

pitch. He dropped the starry-eyed act and grinned. "I'd be lying if I said it wasn't fun as fuck."

"I saw Luke's posters. Very compelling."

"Oh my God, we are so lucky to have him. He's such a huge value-add." Scott clapped and sanded his palms. "So what's up? If you're going to ask about throwing in, I'm straight up gonna have to disappoint you. At present we're fully subscribed."

In the company's early days my brother had approached me, asking me to act as his proxy investor. When I refused, he enlisted our mom.

I glanced at the hive of commerce beyond the pod walls and wondered how much their shares were worth today. It made me question why he'd need to sell his car. "No worries. But it's not that."

"Okay. So what's up, man?"

"I'm having trouble getting in touch with Luke. Has he come into the office today?"

"I don't think I've seen him."

"Is there a way to find out?"

"I can ask downstairs to check if he's used his keycard."

"You mind?"

"Not at all." Scott took his earbuds from his breast pocket and inserted them. " 'Call Evelyn Girgis . . . ' Yo, Evvie. Real quick do me a solid: See if Luke's scanned in today. Thanks."

He took out the earbuds. "Everything cool? You look kinda stressed."

"I'd feel better if I could talk to him."

"Did you ask Andrea?"

"She said he took off sometime on Sunday but hasn't heard from him since. She thought he might be on a work trip. She mentioned you ask him to travel on occasion."

"Time to time. He's amazing in a room. Get him in front of buyers, it's practically a lock."

"But not in the last few days."

"*Yeesh* . . . Honestly, bro? I don't remember. We have two hundred seventy-seven employees. Even if I wanted to micromanage them, I couldn't." He wiggled his fingers. "You have to let the baby birds fly."

"If he did leave, he'd put it on his work calendar."

"Yeah, I assume."

"I'd like to have a look at it. The rest of his accounts, too."

Scott arched his eyebrows. "For real?"

"Unless you can reach him."

Holding his gaze on me, he reinserted the earbuds. "'Call Luke Edison.'"

I counted the length of five rings, watched him listen to the silent words.

You've reached Luke Edison at Bay Area Therapeutics. Sorry I'm unavailable at the moment. . . .

Have a blessed day.

"Yo yo, Dookie," Scott said. "Checking in. Hit me up when you got a sec. Love you tons."

He disconnected. "Look. It's no big deal. How often do you pick up your phone?"

"When was the last time he called you?"

He worked his cell out of his pocket. The slacks were tailored and it took a while.

". . . Thursday. Around two p.m."

"Did you talk to him?"

"I don't remember. Maybe."

"Did he leave a voicemail?"

"Nobody who knows me does. They know I'm not going to listen to it."

"When's the most recent text?"

He thumbed. "Saturday. Ten in the morning."

"What does he say?"

"It's work stuff. It's not going to mean anything to you."

"Humor me."

He read: "'KPL passed on piece about sales dip in Oregon cause they think it's old news. Will circle back.'" A mocking smile. "Did you get any of that?"

"Try texting him now. Ask him to call you."

He sighed. He thumbed, tapped, and set the phone on the floor. "Listen, Clay—"

"When was his last email?"

"We really need to do this?"

"Not if you let me look at his account."

"You understand I can't just do that. He's entitled to privacy."

"I agree. Can we also agree not to put that ahead of his welfare?"

"His welf—what's that even mean?"

I'd run and rerun so many disaster scenarios that I had a hard time picking just one. And I could see why Scott found my persistence confusing. I knew about the Camaro. He didn't.

I said, "If you had reason to believe that he was in trouble, you'd agree that takes priority."

"Sure. But I don't have reason to believe that." He laced his fingers behind his head. "Go ahead. Persuade me."

"Nobody's heard from him in more than a day."

"Okay."

"You don't think that's a problem?"

"Andrea's not worried, I don't know why we should be."

"She doesn't know the old Luke. She never met him."

"Yeah. Cause it's the *old Luke*."

"Something weird is going on, Scott. Whether you believe me or not is up to you."

"I get that you're wound up. But can we be, like, parsimonious? Worst case he took off for a few days to clear his head."

"Of what?"

"*I* don't know." His shoulders bunched. "Dude. Why are you coming at me like this?"

"I'm worried about him."

"Let's just breathe, please, okay? Here," he said, standing, "let me get you some water. Or you want a gummy?"

"Who at the company would know where he is? He must report to someone."

"Technically, I guess, yeah."

"Who?"

"The CMO."

"Can you ask him?"

"Her," he said pointedly. He sat and touched his headset. " 'Call Tanisha Dubuque.' Hey, T. Yeah. Sorry to bug you. Real quick: Have you spoken to Luke lately? Yeah. No. Do you know if he's on the road . . . ? Okay. No no no. No need. Thanks, T."

"What did she say?"

"Look, he reports to her. But that's not . . . I mean, we have—it's more of a flat hierarchy."

Said the CEO in the glass watchtower.

"What's he doing, day-to-day?" I asked.

"That's what I mean. We're fluid. It changes, day to day. I don't believe in fitting the person to the task. You fit the task to the person. Luke . . . He's a Swiss Army knife, you know? A free safety."

"Who does he interact with?"

"How do you mean."

"Does he deal with people on the black market?"

His lips tightened but his voice remained soft. "Look. Clay. When you called, I dropped everything and carved out time. But this is not cool."

"I'm asking a question."

"It's not a *cool* question, the way you're asking it. So I suggest you check yourself and whatever preconceived notions you have about what we do here. This is a legal enterprise."

"Not saying otherwise. But don't you sometimes have to expand your sources?"

"That's the way the supply chain operates. We couldn't meet demand otherwise."

"What if Luke got involved with one of those people?"

"'*Involved*'?" He sputtered a laugh. "Bro. Please. 'Those peop . . . ' You know who 'those people' are? OG hippies who haven't stepped foot out of Mendocino in fifty fucking years. They got kids older than us. Their *kids* have kids. It ain't MS-13. You're using an obsolete framework. It's not twenty fifteen, we're not schlepping around Hefty bags of cash. Luke doesn't handle that shit anyway."

"What does he handle?"

"*Other* shit. This"—Scott waved at the office floor— "is not one business. It's business*es*. We have extracts. We have edibles, infusions, flower. That's the plant-touching side. We also have lifestyle consulting, corporate consulting, brand consulting, event planning. Everything's siloed, legally. Luke's strictly non-touching. And FYI, that was *his* choice. He didn't want his record causing issues. I told him don't trip but he insisted."

"You've got weed growing everywhere."

"For *decoration*. That's not *product*. You know how often we have to replace those motherfuckers? They're not happy in here. They need sunlight. They need *warmth*. They die like it's a horror movie. Fuck, bro. Luke doesn't even like weed, it makes him puke."

"What about other drugs?"

"I'm not going to answer that."

"You know his history as well as I do."

"Yeah, well, if he relapsed, I guess he decided not to share that with his boss."

"You're his friend," I said.

He said nothing.

"Have you noticed any changes in his behavior?"

"No."

"Has he asked to borrow money?"

"*No.*"

"Has he sold his shares?"

"He can't. We're not at that stage."

"How much does he make?"

"For fuck's sake, Clay. You want a job, fill out an application." He paused, sliding his jaw. "Maybe he just doesn't want to talk to you. Did you ever think about that?"

"That's why I went to Andrea, and it's why I'm talking to you."

"Okay, then, maybe you want to take a moment to follow up and ask yourself why *not*. Here's my theory: You're kind of a dick to him. For real, what do you have against him?"

"Nothing. If I did I wouldn't be looking for him."

"All I hear is you making one assumption after another."

"About what."

"About me. About my business. Him, what he does, who he *is*. He doesn't want to talk to you? I don't blame him. Know what," Scott said, "I don't blame you, either. You're a cop. You think like a cop. It's *good* or it's *bad*. News flash: Life ain't like that. *Human beings* aren't like that."

"I'm talking about one specific human being," I said.

"Your brother fucked up, big-time. And he knows that. Believe me. He paid his debt to society. Now he's out here trying to make it right and improve the world and all you can think is *oh, he's getting high* or *oh, he's involved with 'bad people.'*"

My temper was starting to slip. " 'Improve the world.' "

"You don't get it, do you?"

"Enlighten me."

"You saw the posters. Did you read them?"

"I did."

"Then you should know. This isn't about getting idiots high. It's about helping individuals who are sick. Who are in pain. It's about using a natural product, a beautiful gift from Mother Nature, to help wean people off truly *toxic* shit pushed by Big Pharma. It's about supporting independent farmers, and independent business, and starting to undo some of the damage done to communities of color who've been fucking *decimated* by the War on Drugs and the prison industrial complex. That's what I believe in: restorative justice. It's what your brother believes in. So you ask me if he's improving the world? I say yes. At least, he's trying, which is more than most people can say. Shit," he said, clawing at his stubble, "I don't know what I'm expecting *you* to say. You're part of the system that created this whole fucked-up situation in the first place."

"None of that has anything to do with Luke."

"Of course it does. It informs your entire mindset. You're going on about the 'old Luke' cause that's all *you* can see. You don't get an answer to a text and instead of taking a good hard look in the mirror you start jumping to all these batshit conclusions. I mean, listen to yourself."

His phone twitched on the floor. He stuck in his earbuds. "Yeah what's up. Okay . . . He last scanned in on Friday afternoon."

"What time?"

"Evvie, did you . . . Three twenty-five. Shit. I know. I know. Tell them two minutes. And can you come up, please? My friend needs to be shown out. Thanks."

He disconnected and took several cleansing breaths. "All right. I don't want to cut this short, because I hear you, and I totally empathize with how you're feeling. I have to jump on a call now. Let's not leave our shit in a state of tension. That's not good for anyone. As soon I hear from him, I'll ask him to reach out to you. Okay?" He stood and put out a hand. "Can we . . . ?"

"I need to see his accounts."

"Dude. Come on. We just did this."

"Maybe you're right. I'm overreacting. But ask yourself what happens if I'm right, and he needs our help and I came to you and you screwed around. What's that going to feel like for you?"

Evelyn came up the steps. Scott gestured for her to wait. The vitality had gone out of him. I noticed now the furrows in his forehead, the slack beneath his chin.

"Who's asking?" he said. "Clay his brother or Clay the cop?"

"Who's asking me? Scott the CEO or Scott his friend?"

He laughed and shook his head. "Man, fuck you."

I said nothing.

He beckoned Evelyn in. "Evvie, please ask the powers-that-be to grant my friend here temporary permissions for Luke's data."

She blinked. "Which permiss—"

"His calendar."

"Email, too," I said.

Scott pursed his lips and nodded.

I stood up. "Thank you. One more thing. Did he ever talk to you about his car?"

"His—which car."

"The Camaro. Did he ever talk about selling it?"

"Not that I can recall. Now, if you don't mind . . ." He started working in his earbuds.

Evelyn said, "Um, Scott. Should I—"

"Just—handle it, please," he said. He turned away and activated his call.

"*Lo siento*, peeps," he said. "You have my undivided attention."

CHAPTER 8

DOWN ON THE OFFICE FLOOR, the tide had begun to ebb as employees departed for the night. A substantial number stayed put, eating delivery at their desks. Start late; end late. Or they had power here but not at home. So many young faces. How many of them had families or partners waiting for them? Why sit alone in a stuffy apartment without Netflix, watching your phone run down?

Better to expense your açaí bowl and establish bona fides as a hard worker.

Evelyn said, "We'll need a few minutes to get you set up." As if she were prepping for a colonoscopy.

"Thanks. While you do that I'd like to have a look at Luke's desk, please."

She stopped walking. She glanced up at Scott's pod, back to me. "What for?"

"Is that going to be a problem?"

"It depends. What's going on here?"

"I'm concerned about him," I said.

"Why?"

"Nobody knows where he is."

Another quick peek at the god in the sky. "This way."

THE FLAT HIERARCHY applied to everyone but Scott Silber. Luke's workstation was identical to every other workstation: a black mesh ergonomic chair and a narrow allotment of gray desktop. Writing implements filled a mug tiled with images of him and Andrea. There was a monitor with a dangling cable hookup for a laptop and a printer-paper photo of Charlotte taped to one corner.

The laptop itself was absent.

The workstation to the left was unoccupied. The twenty-something white guy to the right swiveled to greet me: "Yo, what's—whoops." He laughed and returned to his screen. "Sorry."

"Back in a bit," Evelyn said.

She went.

"Excuse me," I said to the guy.

". . . yyyyessir." He swiveled.

"Sorry to interrupt. I'm Luke's brother. You thought I was him."

"Yeah, I thought he shaved and I was like *Noooo* . . . Sorry, you guys must get that a lot."

"Can I ask your name?"

"Matt."

"Are you friendly with him, Matt?"

"Me and Luke? Yeah, of course."

An Asian American woman across the desk spoke up: "Everybody likes Luke. He's Mr. Positive."

A few people seated within earshot smiled to themselves.

I asked the woman her name.

"Annie."

"He was here on Friday afternoon," I said. "Did either of you see him?"

"Friday I was out," Matt said.

"I was here," Annie said.

"Did you talk to him?"

"I think a little?" she said.

"Did everything seem normal?"

"Normal?"

"Did he seem preoccupied or upset?"

She and Matt exchanged a look.

"Is everything okay?" Annie asked.

"I'm wondering if you noticed anything out of the ordinary."

"Not really."

"Did he mention any weekend plans?"

"I don't think so. I mean, he's Luke, he's the best. But he doesn't socialize, per se."

I looked around at young, guileless faces.

Why would they hang out with a guy in his forties?

Evelyn turned up the aisle.

I took a pen from the mug, unstuck the printout of Charlotte, and wrote my contact information on the back. "If you do think of anything, this is me. Any of you. If you remember something, please get in touch."

I placed the paper in the middle of the desktop. Nobody moved to take it. They all looked obscurely traumatized.

Evelyn approached. She eyed the paper. "This way."

SHE PUT ME in a conference room and gave me water in a compostable cup.

"We'll be ready in a second."

Thirty minutes later she returned with reinforcements. Olivia from HR fanned out a sheaf of waivers and NDAs. Rita from Legal stood by as I signed them. Harold from IT opened up a laptop.

"This is Luke's?" I said.

"You don't need the physical device to access his data," Harold said. "Everything's in the cloud."

Apart from a trip to Portland at the end of the month, my brother had no travel scheduled.

"What about his meetings yesterday and today?" I asked.

"He's been out of office," Evelyn said.

"Did he call in? Or cancel?"

"You'd have to ask the people he was supposed to meet with."

"Great. Can we do that?"

A beat. Evelyn glanced at Olivia, who glanced at Rita. Harold picked at his chapped lips.

Rita said, "May I ask what the purpose of this is?"

"I told Evelyn. We don't know where he is. It'd help to know who's seen or spoken to him."

"You're a police officer?"

"I'm his brother and I'm here as a private citizen."

"Be that as it may, I'm not comfortable with you interrogating our employees."

"It's not an interrogation. Nobody's under arrest. It's a yes–no: Did Luke make his meetings or not? It doesn't have to be me who asks them. You do it. Or ask Scott. He'll be happy to help."

Three heads rotated toward the glass pod, where Scott could be seen at a distance, pacing and fluttering his pink broadcloth arms like a tropical fish in a tank.

Harold tore off a piece of skin. His lip bled and he dabbed at it with the hem of his hoodie.

Rita said, "Let's hurry it up, please."

Evelyn took out her phone. She checked the laptop screen and thumbed a message. A moment later the phone emitted a cutesy bubble-popping noise.

She checked the laptop, thumbed again. *Pop.*

Olivia smiled at no one. Rita stared at the floor, wishing she billed by the hour.

Harold was rolling the piece of skin between his fingertips like a tiny joint.

Pop, pop, pop.

"No," Evelyn said at last.

"He didn't call in."

She shook her head.

"Didn't cancel."

"Everyone's telling me he never showed up."

"All right," I said. "Let's check his inbox."

Harold flicked away the skin, opened the mail client, and slid the laptop to me.

Evelyn, Olivia, and Rita drifted forward to read over my shoulder.

I turned in my chair. "If you don't mind, I'd like to respect Luke's privacy."

Evelyn stepped back. Olivia stepped back.

Rita threw me a look of loathing and stepped back.

Luke's mailboxes were untouched since Saturday. Ditto the documents and chat feeds.

No mention of the Camaro anywhere. Nothing to or from Rory Vandervelde. For that Luke more likely would have used his personal email.

Thinking he might have used one account as a backup for the other, I opened the login page in a new window and keyed in lukeedison29. I clicked FORGOT PASSWORD? and followed the steps.

A few seconds later a recovery link showed up in his work inbox.

I clicked it.

The screen prompted me for a code sent to his phone.

Accounts and usernames and passwords and PINs, a giant knot of electronic yarn.

"Say I did want to find the physical device," I said to Harold. "The computer he uses belongs to you? Do you have a way to track it?"

"As long as it's actively connected to the internet." He drew the laptop over, typed, shook his head. "Off-line."

"Are we almost done?" Rita asked.

Harold said, "What about his phone?"

"I don't know where it is," I said.

"Do you want to know?" He angled the screen out to show an employee profile, tabs for payroll and benefits and so forth. Under the PROPERTY tab, two entries appeared.

MacBook Air   LOCK—ERASE—LOCATE
iPhone 11   LOCK—ERASE—LOCATE

"We don't issue employee phones," Olivia said.

"You did to Luke," Harold said.

I believed Olivia from HR that Bay Area Therapeutics did not issue phones, and I believed Harold from IT that they'd made an exception in my brother's case. He'd been hard up when Scott made him employee number nineteen. Probably Scott had said something to soften the impression of charity. *Just till you get back on your feet.*

They'd since forgotten about it. Or maybe they justified the perk on the grounds that Luke made a lot of work calls. Andrea would have her own phone plan, predating their relationship.

I pulled the laptop over and clicked LOCATE.

A new window opened, a map marked with a red pin: Castro Valley, south of the freeway.

"That's where it is?" I said.

"It's where it was, last time it pinged," Harold said. "It might not be there anymore."

I clicked the pin, bringing up coordinates and a timestamp.

Monday, October 2, 12:04 a.m.

CHAPTER 9

SITUATED DUE EAST of San Leandro, Castro Valley is the first of several bedroom communities strung along the 580 Tri-Valley Corridor. Our high schools had a rivalry. In Luke's final game before he dropped out, he got tossed for clotheslining their point guard.

To everyone else in attendance it must have seemed like he'd picked a strange moment to lash out. We were up by double digits with two minutes left on the clock. To me—sitting on the bench, watching it happen—the gesture made a perverse kind of sense. I wouldn't have done it. But it resonated at the center of my id. He and I had learned to play against each other, battering like bighorn sheep, our blood staining the driveway concrete. There were no fouls called. Fouls were for pussies. Get hit? Hit back. Hit *first*. Don't wait. Suckers waited.

Then came middle school, Saturdays at the park, developing a fluent two-man game, running rings around the competition; misdirecting, talking trash, calling out schemes in a shorthand akin to the language of twins. *Becky* or *bubble* referred to Sir Mix-A-Lot's "Baby Got

Back" and meant: Set a back screen. We had lyrics for a
pick-and-roll, a pick-and-pop, a give-and-go, V-cut,
switch. The code was elaborate and protean. You had to
be inside our heads. And then, older and taller, riding the
bus to Mosswood, the most storied game in Northern
California. For two kids playing against grown men, the
atmosphere was Darwinian.

Hit first. Hit hard.

So while I considered it dumb of Luke to swing his
arm, and felt smug in the belief that I had greater self-
control, I also appreciated the act's internal logic. It was
an act of self-preservation, programmed by years of battling for dominance and status; the act of a competitor.

It's not enough to defeat an opponent. You have to de-
grade him. Tear out his heart.

The competitor in me also understood that Luke's loss
was my gain. The conference board suspended him for
three games. Coach gave me the next start. I never gave it
back.

PAST THE MAIN Castro Valley shopping district, suburban
tracts dissolved and died out. The earth rose up in welts.
Then began five depopulated, mountainous miles.

Take the exit for Eden Canyon Road.

Off-ramp signs pointed left for food and lodging, right
for gas.

Turn right.

I came to a deserted intersection.

You have arrived at your destination.

Across the road, chain-link hemmed in a decrepit
ranch house. Opposite was an off-brand service station.
Everything else was dirt and rocks and weeds.

Why would my brother drive to a remote location in
the middle of the night?

To clear his head.

Stopping for gas, bound for someplace yet more remote.

Or he'd done something bad and needed to get rid of a phone.

I rolled into the service station. The lights were off. The pumps were off. There was a shuttered garage and an office with the shades drawn.

I opened the center console. Half its contents reflected the father in me. Diapers, wipes, expired applesauce pouch. The other half belonged to the cop. Gloves, flashlight, Ka-Bar knife. I dug out an old N95, soft from overuse, that had been living in there for probably two or more years. No point tossing it. There would always be another fire.

My phone lit up. *Amy Sandek would like FaceTime . . .*

The screen pixelated, grayed, and set tentatively.

"Hey," Amy said. She squinted. "Are you in your car? Do you want to try me back?"

I switched on the dome light. "It's okay, I'm not driving."

"I've been calling."

"Sorry. I lost track of time. Is she asleep yet?"

"I kept her up so you could say good night."

"Thanks."

The screen flipped. Charlotte lay on her stomach, scribbling in a *Frozen* coloring book.

"Hi, lovey," I said.

"Say hi to Daddy."

". . . hi, Daddy."

"Hi, lovey. How was your day?"

". . . it was fun."

"What did you do?"

". . . lots of things."

"Honey, please put down the crayon for a second and talk to Daddy."

Charlotte scooted onto her knees. She was wearing

Frozen pjs. A hank of dark hair draped her shoulder. It was my hair, until you got close enough to see the fine golden filaments woven throughout. A gift from her mother. In sunlight they imparted a sheen, less color than light itself, so that my daughter seemed to glow from within.

I said, "What was the most fun part?"

"We went to the beach and there was a man who was naked."

"No way. Really?"

"Really," Amy said.

"Like, full frontal?"

"He was playing the bongos," Amy said.

"I saw his penis," Charlotte said. "What's 'frontal'?"

"It means his penis," Amy said.

"What the heck kind of beach did you go to?" I asked.

"Tennis Beach," Charlotte said.

"Never heard of it."

"Really it's *Venice* Beach but cousin Sarah called it *Tennis* Beach."

"You should have called it Pennis Beach."

"What's that?"

Amy said, "We had pizza for dinner again."

"Lucky girls," I said. "Hey, lovey, I heard you like anchovies."

"No I don't. Daddy, baby Liam had a poop-mergency."

"He did, huh? Did you call the poop police?"

"It got on cousin Sarah's hands."

"Yuck."

"Her shirt and pants, too," Amy said. "It was epic."

"Daddy, I went potty at the beach."

"That sounds like fun."

"I went in the green porkapotty."

"You did? That's awesome. Great job. How was that experience for Mommy?"

Amy didn't answer.

"I'm proud of you, lovey. Did you get cotton candy?"

"No, I got ice cream."

"That was for dessert," Amy said. "You got cotton candy at the beach, remember?"

"Lovey, please make sure Mommy brushes your teeth really well."

"I will."

"Do you know how much I love you?"

"Yes."

"How much?"

"So much."

"More."

"So so much."

"Even more."

"So so so so so so so *so* much."

"Close enough. Good night, lovey."

"Good night, Daddy."

The screen flipped again. Amy said, "I'm sure you are, but: Are you fixed for food?"

I pressed on my stomach, as though to gauge its contents. I hadn't eaten since breakfast and I was still wearing my VISITOR sticker. "All set."

"Jerky again?"

"Dinner of champions."

She smiled. "Call me before you go to bed."

"Will do. Love you."

"You, too."

The screen went black.

I put on the mask.

My knock at the gas station's office door went unanswered. The garage had a rolling steel shutter. I pounded on it a few times. Sharp reports echoed down the road.

The station backed up to a scrubby rise screaming with katydids. Along one side were a dumpster and the restroom door, locked with a mechanical keypad. A headless broomstick leaned against the wall. I took it and walked around the station, poking through trash receptacles. Candy wrappers, Mountain Dew bottles, losing lottery tickets.

No phone.

I heaved open the dumpster with a boom. Flies billowed out. I ran the flashlight beam over bags and rags and cans. A phone might work its way down through the cracks. One by one I began removing items from the dumpster and setting them on the ground.

Soon my arms and shirt were smeared in ripe black grime, and I was feeling stupid. The fact that Luke's phone had last pinged in the area didn't mean it was still here. He just as well could have chucked it out the window from the road or shut it off while pumping gas. I couldn't get much dirtier, though, and I was almost finished. I bent to grab another bag.

"Can I help you?"

Twenty yards away a man stood pointing a rifle at me. He was in his late fifties, medium height, with thin wrists and thin calves and a long pleated neck. All middle, his mass concentrated powerfully from shoulders to hips. A shaggy gray comb-over levitated in the wind. The skin of his forearms shone dark with grease. He wore a brown bathrobe, greasy smashed moccasins, and flannel pajama pants. Reading glasses hung on a chain around his neck.

I showed my hands. "Alameda County Sheriff."

"The hell you say."

"My badge is in my pocket."

He said nothing.

"Do you want to see it?"

"I want to know why you're in my trash."

I wondered how he could have gotten here so fast. I hadn't heard him coming, hadn't heard a car. The station didn't have security cameras and moreover there was no electricity. Then I spied the ranch house across the road, and I remembered pounding on the office door and the garage, and the crash of the dumpster lid, sounds that carried on a quiet, untrafficked night.

"I'm looking for someone," I said.

"In my trash?"

"Not my intention to disturb you. I knocked."

"We're closed. Take your mask off . . . Now get out your badge and throw it over here."

I did.

"You aren't dressed like a cop."

"I'm off duty."

"Who're you looking for in my trash?"

"My brother. This is the last known location of his phone."

"Here?"

"Near here. Yesterday, about midnight. You remember if anyone came by?"

"We were closed then, too." He tossed me the badge. "No power, we can't dispense."

"I was hoping the phone might still be around somewhere. Do you mind if I look?"

"I mind you making a mess."

"I'll put everything back. Promise."

He said nothing.

"He hasn't come home," I said. "He has a history of drug use and we're worried sick."

He sniffed. "I'm going to stand right here."

"Okay."

"I was in the Marine Corps. You get it in your head to try anything funny I'm not going to miss."

"I believe you."

Removing the deepest items from the dumpster required that I lean over so far my feet left the ground. The floor and interior walls were unspeakably foul.

No phone.

I came up for air. "Has there been a collection since Sunday?"

"No. You going to clean up or what?"

I refilled the dumpster and shut the lid. "The bathroom? Has it been cleaned out?"

"I told you, we've been closed ever since they shut the lights off."

Then he said, "First you said yesterday, then you said Sunday."

"Twelve oh four a.m. Monday. What most people call Sunday night."

He sniffed again. "One second."

From his bathrobe pocket he took a cellphone. He dialed and put it to his ear.

"I need you to cross the street. Yes, now. Get some clothes on, then."

He put the phone away. "First night I had my son wait up. In case anyone saw this blackout and got clever and decided to rip the place off. You can ask him."

"I appreciate it. I'm Clay, by the way."

"I know, I saw your badge. Tom."

"I appreciate it, Tom."

He nodded.

"What did you do in the Marine Corps?" I asked.

A one-sided smile. "Motor pool."

A young man shuffled up from the direction of the ranch house. Late teens to early twenties, medium height, robust through the torso like his maker. The clothes he'd gotten on were black mesh shorts, a San Jose Sharks jersey, and black Adidas slides. Meaty shoulders sagged with fatigue.

Tom said, "Tommy, this gentleman is looking for his brother."

Tommy regarded me as though I had asked him to recite the *Iliad* in the original.

I said, "He might've come through Sunday night, Monday morning, around midnight. You were here?"

"All freakin night," Tommy mumbled.

"People take advantage," Tom said.

"I don't see *you* doing it."

"Mind your tone."

"Did you see anyone, Tommy?" I asked.

"A few people stopped wanting gas."

"Did you talk to any of them?"

"I told them, sorry, no gas."

"Do you remember what they looked like?"

"Not really."

"Hang on, I can show you a picture."

I went through hundreds of photos of Charlotte to find one of my brother: a group shot, Edison family brunch. The very first, if memory served. Fresh-squeezed OJ and mini-muffins. Luke was corkscrewed, trying to fold himself into the frame. A tall-guy problem. It made for a poor likeness. His nostrils looked big as Oreos and his face was foreshortened.

I zoomed in on him and held the phone out to Tommy.

"Maybe. I don't know."

"Let me find a better one," I said, scrolling. "Try this: See if you can estimate how many people stopped that night. Are we talking two? Five? Ten?"

Tommy mugged helplessly.

"You heard the man," Tom said.

"I don't *know*," Tommy said.

"What about their cars?" I asked. "That might help you remember who was driving them."

He got a faraway look and his lips started quivering, as if he were about to channel the dead. "I think there was a, like a Civic, or something like that."

"Okay. Good. Now see if you can remember the driver."

". . . a guy. Not the guy from the picture."

"You're sure about that."

"Yeah, this guy was Asian."

"Good. See? You remember more than you think."

Tommy glanced happily at his father, who remained stoic.

"What's the next car you remember?" I asked.

". . . a sedan. A nice one. A BMW. It was a guy and a woman. The guy was like, 'Turn on the pump,' and I said I couldn't. He sorta lost his shit. 'What's wrong with you, you're supposed to be a gas station, how can a gas station have no gas.'"

"Can you describe his appearance? Was he white, Black, Asian?"

"White."

"Tall? Short?"

"Maybe more tall than short."

"How tall? Like me?"

"I don't know."

"How old was he? Compared with you, me, or your dad."

"You're closest, I guess."

"So around forty."

"I guess."

"Did he look like me?"

"I just wanted him to leave," Tommy said.

"I know it's hard. Concentrate and try to see him. Does anything about him stick out?"

"Like what?"

"Anything. Facial hair. Was he wearing something distinctive, or maybe he had a scar or tattoo. His clothes were messed up, or had blood on them, like he'd been in a fight."

"Nothing like that."

"What about the woman? Can you describe her?"

"She stayed in the car. I didn't see her too good. I mean, it was dark, all I had was the flashlight. I didn't want to, like, shine it in her face."

"Do you remember what time it was when they pulled up?"

"I mean, I was tired."

"Who was driving, him or her?"

"She was, I think."

Luke was forty-one. The right age for a midlife crisis.

How stressful had things gotten between him and Andrea?

Stressful enough that he couldn't handle it with a cup of chamomile and valerian root tea?

Enough to run off with another woman?

For most guys, a midlife crisis meant buying a car, not selling one.

Maybe he needed quick cash for his new adventure.

Dealing the Camaro to Vandervelde.

Texting his sidepiece. Pick me up bae

She was driving the BMW. Her car.

Baby I'm sorry

Did it make sense for him to apologize to his wife in advance?

Maybe the BMW had belonged to Rory Vandervelde. Straight trade for the Camaro.

"You said it was a nice BMW," I asked. "Do you remember the model?"

"Nuh. It was black, or—actually, gray, maybe. I mean, it's a nice car."

Tom made an impatient noise, at his son or at me or both of us.

As we talked I'd been hunting for a clearer photo of Luke. I stopped at one taken the night he and I went to CrossFit. A moment of fragile camaraderie, both of us bedraggled, me putting on an exaggerated frown and giving thumbs-down, Luke doing the opposite.

I showed it to Tommy. "Is that him?"

He stared for a ten-count. "There was a guy with a beard sort of like that."

"The guy in the BMW?"

"No, a different guy. He was driving a truck."

"The guy from this photo was driving a truck?"

"No, I don't . . . I don't think it's the same guy. I mean, maybe. But—like, the beard, it reminded me."

"You're sure it's not the same guy in the photo?"

"This guy was kinda younger."

"How much younger?"

Tommy thought. "More like me."

Luke had lived hard and it showed. I doubted anyone would cut twenty years off his age.

"Can you describe him? Aside from the beard."

"He was white."

"What about him, did he look anything like me?"

"You don't have a beard."

"The shape of his face," I said. "Take your time."

"I mean, he was pretty big."

"Big as in tall, or big as in big?"

"Both, I guess."

"Do you remember what he was wearing?"

"I don't know, man. He was just some guy."

"What about the truck? Did you get a make and model?"

"I think it was . . . white? Okay. Okay. It had one of those things on the bed . . ." Tommy chopped his hand to describe a horizontal plane. "Like a top."

"A tonneau cover," Tom said.

"That's great," I said. "What else?"

"I heard it pull up," Tommy said. "I went out to say, sorry, no gas. He said he needed to use the bathroom."

"Did you let him?"

"Yeah. I didn't want him to, like, piss on the ground. I gave him the code."

I looked to Tom, who went over to the restroom door and keyed in the code for me.

I stepped inside. Fluorescent tubes on a motion sensor snapped on, filling the confines with abrasive blue light. It was an off-brand gas station restroom. A little cleaner than average. Eight by eight, nubby beige plastic wainscoting; floor tiles with a drain inset and a toilet with a gouged seat. There was a cloudy stainless-steel mirror and a pedestal sink with a crack in the base and an unfilled paper towel dispenser and a stainless-steel trash bin screwed to the wall, liner knotted at one corner to prevent slippage.

I grasped the knot and lifted the bin liner free. In the bad blue light it turned like some deformed afterbirth, strata of garbage visible through the filmy plastic, a crumpled cigarette pack, toilet paper wads, a tampon. A heavier item would fall straight through and settle at the bottom in a bulge. That was what had happened. At the bottom of the bag was a gun.

CHAPTER 10

───────

Tommy couldn't tell me anything else about the guy with the beard. He couldn't remember any of the truck's identifying details beyond its color, maybe, and the tonneau cover. Not the tag, not its first letter, not if it was in- or out-of-state; not the time of the truck's arrival, the direction it had driven in from, or where it had gone when it left.

For twenty more minutes I kept at him, my forearm starting to burn from clutching the bin liner in a fist that grew tighter and tighter as I demanded information he could not provide.

I don't know he kept saying. *I don't remember.*

The harder I pressed, the more muddled he got, until his father laid a hand on his shoulder and said, looking at me, "That's all right. You did good."

Tommy bit his lip.

I said, "Thank you. Both of you."

Dolefully Tommy shuffled off toward the house.

I held up the bin liner. "I'm going to take this."

"Far as I'm concerned you can take them all."

I gave him my number in case Tommy remembered more. I stripped off my soiled shirt, tossed it in the footwell, and drove away, pulling over beneath the underpass.

Gloved up and drew the gun out of the bag.

Walther PPS semi-automatic 9mm. It had seen better days. The grip and slide were worn; the serial number had been filed off. The crime lab could recover the number with acid. But that would require turning the gun over to the crime lab.

At the base of the grip, around the bottom of the magazine, was a thin layer of dried blood.

Rory Vandervelde had a gash above his eye. Typical pistol-whip injury.

I ejected the magazine. Six-round capacity, half full.

Rory Vandervelde had been shot three times.

I replaced the magazine. I put the gun in the bag, tied it off, and lowered it into the footwell beside my shirt. Setting it down gingerly, as if it might explode on contact.

A BLUE NISSAN Leaf sat at the curb outside my house. Andrea was hunched on the porch steps, knees gathered to her chest. She sprang up as I turned into the driveway.

I gestured one second to her and texted Amy.

Can we talk tomorrow? Sorry super tired

Sure. Sleep well. LY

LY

I reached down for my dirty shirt, leaving the gun and bag behind.

Andrea met me at the driveway's edge. She didn't register that I was bare-chested. It can be that way with self-obsessed people. I half expected her to shove a syringe into my hand.

She said, "I need to talk to you."

———

IN THE KITCHEN I lit candles, filled her a glass of water, and told her to hang tight while I cleaned up. I soaped myself to the shoulders in the bathroom sink and got changed. When I came back to the kitchen she was pacing, the water untouched.

I sat at the breakfast table. She hesitated, then joined me.

"Have you heard from Luke?" I asked.

She shook her head. "I've been trying him all day." She looked down, gnawed a thumbnail. "I haven't been completely honest with you."

I waited.

"We had a fight. Saturday night. The next day he wanted to forget about it but I was still upset. We started arguing again and he got in his car and left."

"What time?"

"I told you, I don't remember. I think it was around lunchtime."

"Did he say where he was going?"

"For a drive."

"Where?"

"He didn't tell me."

"Is this something he's done before? Left the house?"

"Never for more than a night," she said. "And he always calls."

"That's what you thought was going on when I talked to you yesterday."

A beat.

"I'm scared," she said.

"Of?"

"He's not coming back."

"Did he say that? Do you have any reason to think it?"

Her eyes flashed. "It's what *you* think, isn't it?"

"Where does he go, when he leaves?"

"I don't know . . . a motel."

"Any particular one?"

"I don't think so. Sometimes he just sleeps in his car."

My brother had experience making do at night. "What about friends? Who would he go to? Who's he closest with?"

"Scott, probably."

"He hasn't heard from Luke, either."

"You spoke to Scott?"

"Earlier today."

"You went to his *work*?"

"Nobody's heard from Luke since Sunday," I said. "My parents? Does he ever crash there?"

"The last thing we need is them getting involved."

"Have you talked to them?"

"*She'll* just blame me." A strange look came over her. "Haven't you?"

Same barrier I'd hit with Scott.

I knew about the Camaro. The gun, too, now.

Andrea didn't. To her, Luke's absence was personal, not criminal.

So why hadn't I taken the next sensible step and called my parents?

I hadn't, because I knew my parents. For Luke's sake I needed to control the flow of information. My mother was the last person capable of that.

I said, "Let's hold on talking to them for the moment."

"Why? Just call them and ask."

"I will, when it's right."

"What are you talking about? Call them." She slapped the table. "Give me your phone."

"Andrea. Please listen."

"Forget it," she said, standing. "I'll go over there myself."

I reached for her. "Hang on."

"Let *go* of me. Let go of my *fucking arm*."

She wrenched free, grabbed her purse, and ran outside, headed for her car. Seeing me coming after her, she made a mewing sound and bolted up the sidewalk toward my parents' house.

"Andrea. Wait."

"Leave me *alone*."

I closed the gap between us in a few strides but hung back. Anyone peeking out a front window would see a six-foot-three man chasing a much smaller woman, fumbling with her purse and in evident distress.

Domestic dispute. Mugging in progress.

We continued up the block, me pleading with her as she hollered at me to go away.

At the corner she spun, waving a can of pepper spray. *"Stop following me."*

I said, "I found his car."

I saw it spread to her, the dread I'd been carrying, saw it envelop her like a poisonous cloud.

"What do you mean, you found it."

"We can't have this conversation here."

"Found it *where*."

"Someplace it shouldn't be."

"*Where*."

"Let's go inside and talk."

She said nothing. The can shook in her hand.

"Yesterday I was called to a homicide. Luke's Camaro is in the victim's garage. Can we go inside, please?"

"You're wrong."

"I—"

"It's not his. You're wrong."

"I ran the tag. It's his."

"No, no. No."

"I tried calling Luke to ask if he'd sold the car. If he left because of a fight, he should pick up when I call. He's not. Scott can't reach him, either. I traced his phone to a gas station. I went to look for it and found a gun, in the trash, with blood on it. So we *cannot* call the police and we *cannot* call my parents. Do you understand me?"

She began to cry.

A red SUV slowed at the curb. The window lowered and the driver leaned over. Middle-aged guy, bald, glasses. Bag of groceries belted into the passenger seat. "Everything okay here?"

"We're good," I said.

"Ma'am? You okay?"

Andrea stuck the pepper spray in her purse. She wiped her face. "Yes."

"You sure?"

"I'm fine. Thank you."

The guy frowned. "Do you need me to call someone?"

She brushed past me and walked toward my house.

I followed, allowing a ten-foot margin.

The SUV edged along behind until Andrea had turned up my front walk. Then it sped off.

CHAPTER 11

——

BACK AT THE KITCHEN table Andrea drained her water in one go. "You've been lying to me," she said.

"We'll call it even."

Silence.

"What do we do?" she said.

"The main thing is figuring out where he's gone. I need your help. You know him better than anyone."

She tilted her chin upward in grim satisfaction: Of course she did.

"I need to ask some questions without you getting upset. Can you do that?"

"I'm not a child, Clay."

"No, you're not. Besides the gun that I saw at your house, do you own any others?"

"No."

"Is there a chance Luke might've gotten ahold of one for himself?"

"No."

"Would he have told you if he did?"

"Why are you asking me if you don't believe me?"

"I do believe you. But we both know he's not allowed to own a firearm. He might've kept it a secret to avoid incriminating you."

"We trust each other."

I decided not to touch that one. "Fair enough. How's your financial situation?"

"Why does that matter?"

"The only other explanation I can come up with for the Camaro being at the victim's house is that Luke sold it to him. Why would he do that it unless he felt he had to? You know how much he loves that car."

"Not everything is about money, Clay. Not everyone thinks that way."

"What round of IVF are you on?"

Her mouth pinched.

"Eight," she said. "Plus four courses of IUI."

"That's expensive."

"I know what it costs." She tucked her feet under her. "We borrowed."

"How much?"

"Two hundred thousand."

"How much is left?"

A shake of the head: *Nothing*. "Luke wants to stop."

"Is that what you were fighting about?"

She barked a laugh. "He said we should get a horse, instead."

"Are you behind on your payments?"

"No."

"When does the loan come due?"

"It's . . . There's no deadline." A beat. "It's from your parents."

My mother is an office manager. My father teaches middle school math and science.

"How can they afford that?" I asked.

"They took a second mortgage. What's the first explanation?"

"What explanation?"

"You said money was 'the only *other* explanation' for the car being there. What's the first explanation?"

I didn't answer.

Andrea shrank back in revulsion. "You think he did it."

"I didn't say that."

"You don't have to. I can *read* you. You're *thinking* it."

"What I think is we need to find him before anyone else does, and to do that we need to line up all the facts, regardless of how unpleasant they might be. He might not be in any trouble."

"You just got through telling me he *is*."

"I said might. I could be wrong. I hope I am. Scott thought Luke could've taken off to clear his head. Maybe he talked to my parents. I'll find out. But I guarantee that if you tell them he's missing, they're going to panic. They're going to want to know why we haven't called the police. It doesn't matter what I say. They'll make an end run around me. Then it's out of our hands."

"So?" she said. "We *should* call the police."

"A missing adult, they won't do a thing. The only way to get them interested is if there's an indication of foul play, and the only way to do that is either to lie to them or to tell them about the car. And you don't want to do either of those things. Because whatever you believe *I* think about Luke, I guarantee it's better than what some random cop is going to think."

She wiped her face again, roughly.

I said, "I'm sorry to have to ask this, but is there a chance he could be seeing someone else?"

"That's what you come up with? One fight and he's having an affair? No. There's no one else. I know him and he knows me. If he wants to be free, I'd let him."

"Okay. Who else would he turn to in a pinch? Who's he close with?"

"Scott's who comes to mind."

"People from his gym? Couples you socialize with?"

"We keep to ourselves."

"You must have friends."

"Of course we have friends."

I took a pad and pen from the counter. "Make a list."

"They're not going to talk to you. You could be anyone. I'll do it."

"The whole point of this is to keep things quiet."

"No, Clay. The whole point is *Luke.*"

The thought of her ad-libbing made me uneasy. But I'd involved her. She was a variable I now had to account for. On top of that, it was in my interest to keep her occupied. "Fine. Call them and let me know what they say. Call your credit card companies and see if he's used his recently. The more dead ends you can eliminate, the better. What about people from NA?"

"I told you, he's clean."

"Okay, but he spends time with them, and he might tell them things he doesn't tell you. Where does he attend meetings?"

She rolled her empty water glass between her fingers. "We've moved on."

"Moved on from what?"

She did not answer.

"He's stopped going," I said. "Am I hearing you right? Is that what you're saying?"

"I'm saying we're beyond that."

"What happened to 'Once an addict, always an addict'?"

"A one-size-fits-all approach might help in the beginning, but an individual's needs change over time. You want to be rigid, be rigid. Are you the same person you were when you were twenty?"

"Why would you stop doing something that's working?"

"It wasn't working. Not for us. You're not listening."

"How do you know he hasn't relapsed?"

"We've been managing this way without a problem for two years."

"Managing with *what*."

"Diet. Exercise. Self-care. You need to read a little, Clay."

I gave myself a second. "How about this: Where did he used to go for his meetings?"

She named a church in Moraga. "You're wasting your time, though."

"I'm covering all the bases. What about people from prison? Does he associate with any of them?"

"He's been out for five years. That's in the past."

"Did he have a beef with anyone inside? Anything that could follow him out?"

"No . . . I don't know. Who is this person?"

"Which person?"

"The man who died."

News about the murder would go public soon enough. Withholding Vandervelde's name served little purpose. And she might know something about him.

"Rory Vandervelde," I said.

Her silence read as despair, not deception. Her face was moist and flushed. Candlelight scooped out her cheeks, the cavities beneath her eyes. I felt her sorrow touch mine.

"Who is he?" she asked.

"A car collector. That's the only connection I can see between them. If Luke was looking to sell the Camaro, this guy had the means to buy it."

"I've never heard of him."

"It's okay." I tapped the pad with the pen. "Please write down the password to Luke's Gmail account."

"Why?"

"So I can see who he was in contact with. Starting with the victim."

"Why do you have to keep calling him that?"

"That's what he is."

"You're acting like it's Luke who made him into a victim."

"I—"

"What happened to lining up facts?"

"That's what I'm doing."

"No, it's not. All you want to talk about are things that make him look guilty. What does he have to do to prove himself to you?"

"That's not the issue here."

"Oh please. *Please.*"

She rolled her eyes. My face got hot.

"You know what, Andrea? You want to know what I think? Okay. Here's what I think. I think it's one hundred percent possible he did something terrible."

"Great, well, at least you're admitting it."

"I think it's totally possible. But there are *other* possibilities, such as that he's overdosed. Or he's out somewhere, suicidal. Or he owes someone money, he pissed someone off, and they did something *to him*. What I'm trying to do is sort through all that, but unless you cut the self-righteous bullshit I'm never going to get anywhere."

She lurched from her chair and vomited into the sink.

I went over to help her. She swung her arm to keep me at bay. She retched, spat, wiped her face on a dish towel, and hobbled past me to the living room sofa.

I stood in the doorway. "I'm sorry."

Her eyes were shut, her fists clenched over her heart. "It's not you, it's the medication."

"Do you need anything?"

"An ice pack would be nice."

I opened the freezer and was greeted by the warm breath of over-thawed meat. Tepid pink water had pooled on the shelves. It dripped onto the kitchen floor. I'd forgotten.

I soaked a dish towel under the faucet, wrung it out, and brought it to her. "No ice. Best I can do."

She spread the compress on her forehead. A weary, resentful peace settled over the room, like a drowning man giving in to his fate.

"He loves you," she said.

"I know. I love him, too."

"Do you?"

"Of course I do."

"That's not what I meant. I meant do you *know* it."

"Yes."

"I don't think you do."

I kept silent.

"You should hear the way he talks about you." She shifted onto her side. "Like you're some kind of god he needs to beg forgiveness from."

"I never him asked for that."

"It doesn't matter whether you did or you didn't. It's there."

"Since when does he care about my opinion?"

"You really believe that."

"He never has."

"Then you've never paid attention."

I said nothing.

"He has a few different passwords he uses," she said.

I brought her pen and paper. She jotted down strings of letters and numbers.

"Thank you," I said.

She stretched out again and put the compress on. I sat on the floor against the Great Wall of Cardboard.

"It's not my forgiveness to grant," I said. "If that's what he wants, he should talk to the families of the women he killed."

"He wanted to."

Restorative justice.

It's what your brother believes in.

"Is that what he said?"

"He said he wished he could apologize to them."

"When?"

"I don't know. A while ago. I told him not to contact them. That he'd only be reviving their trauma."

For once I agreed with her. "Did he listen to you?"

She peeled off the towel and rose on her elbows. "Why?"

"If anybody has a good reason to want to hurt Luke, it's them."

Her throat was pulsing, her eyes bright with terror. "I told him it would be a bad idea. I—"

A knock cut her off.

A voice called, "San Leandro police."

I said, "Wait here."

Through the peephole I made out two blocky shapes at the foot of the porch steps.

I opened the door. A flashlight shone in my eyes.

"Evening, sir. We received a call about a disturbance at this location."

The bald man, driving the red SUV.

The uniforms introduced themselves as Officers Broder and Huang. They asked my name and who else was home. I called Andrea over. She came to the door holding the wet compress against her forehead. Just the kind of thing you'd put over a bruise, if the power was out and you didn't have any ice.

Broder said, "Is everything okay here, ma'am?"

Andrea looked at me. "What's going on?"

"Somebody decided to be a hero," I said.

"If you don't mind stepping outside," Huang said, "we'd like a word with each of you individually."

"I'm fine," Andrea said.

"Do what they say," I said.

———

EVEN AFTER WE had established that she and I were not partners; that it was my residence and not hers; that I was a peace officer; that there was no allegation of violence; that neither she nor I knew the man in the red SUV or had asked him for help; even after Andrea began to lose her patience and complain that this was harassment, and their focus shifted from me to her—*aha, she's the crazy one*—Broder and Huang were reluctant to leave the scene before Andrea did.

It was almost midnight. We'd been standing on the front lawn, two islets of two people each, for an hour. I had to force myself not to look toward my car, where a trash can liner containing a handgun sat in the footwell.

I said to Huang, "One minute to talk to her in private, please."

He conferred with Broder. They backed off to the sidewalk.

"Go home," I said to Andrea. "Get some sleep."

"How am I supposed to sleep?"

"Lower your voice, please."

"We can't sit around and do nothing."

"We're doing what we can. Keep your phone turned on and nearby."

She glanced at the cops.

"Andrea. Promise me you'll listen for your phone."

"Yes. Fine. Yes."

"Okay. I'll call you tomorrow."

She walked to her car. I started for the house, waving to the cops. "Have a good night."

Officer Huang nodded. They were still there when I went inside.

CHAPTER 12

I N THE FALL OF 2005 I was twenty-one, entering my se-
nior year at UC Berkeley. I arrived on campus with
guarded optimism. The team that I'd led to the Final
Four was largely intact. Three guys had graduated and
two more had transferred, leaving nine familiar faces.

At our first team meeting I thanked everyone for their
support throughout the long recovery process. Last season hadn't been fun for anyone. I'd ridden it out on the
sideline, in a brace, clapping as we dropped game after
game. Nobody liked to lose, especially after you'd tasted
success. What counted was what you learned from the experience. The time had come to start back up the mountain. We had our new guys to help us reach the top. We
had our core guys. We had Coach.

It was a pretty good speech. I'd had fifteen months to
refine it. I got a big round of applause. Everyone crowded
in to rub me on the head.

One of the new guys was a redshirt sophomore named
Patrick Starks, a transfer from San Diego State. Over the
spring Coach had shown me tape and asked for my ap-

praisal. I gave it to him: The kid's jump shot was a work in progress. He needed to log some hours in the weight room. What he did have was a quick first step, a devastating handle, and that ineffable quality known as court vision: the ability to slow down time and move people around in mental space like chess pieces.

Call me naïve, but I'd had no idea, not the faintest suspicion, that I was watching the future.

My own court vision didn't extend that far.

The Patrick Starks who greeted me that fall had logged the hours. All summer long he'd been running the same drills I had, except on two perfect knees. He bumped my fist, welcomed me back, and proceeded to dismantle me.

I'd never been the tallest or the strongest or the fastest. I'd gotten as far as I had by harnessing and taming a certain reckless instinct. I'd pull up from the hash mark. Run straight at guys half a foot bigger. Sometimes these impulses cost me. On good days they made me deadly. The key was using them judiciously, enough to sow uncertainty in a defender and chaos in his team. They never knew what I might do. I didn't know it myself till I did it.

You practice and plan and scheme and diagram, and then you go out there and it all falls away, because your opponent is fighting for his life, just like you.

Advancing in the backcourt, I saw Patrick Starks ready for me, his smile hungry, his feet light below hips that slid as if on ball bearings. Now I was the uncertain one, and he was brash and unpredictable. He wanted to tear my heart out. And he could, and he knew it. I pressed against stiffness and heard the echo of pain, and I allowed myself the one emotion no great athlete can afford to feel: fear.

At the end of practice I shook his hand, knowing I'd never start again.

For his part, Coach lobbied hard to keep me around. So what if I couldn't perform at my previous standard? The guys looked up to me. Without question Starks had talent, but he also had room to grow. I could mentor him. It didn't have to be martyrdom. I'd get minutes.

No, thanks, I said.

Pride prevented me from using the word *quit.* Coach was kind enough not to use it, either.

Leaving the athletics complex felt like jumping out of a plane without a parachute. I wandered, bewildered, through the hot smell of laundry blowing behind the PE building, through the eucalyptus grove, over lawns. Around me whirled a startling busyness. Students were talking, reading, running to class. In theory I was one of them. But not really. For three years I'd existed in a bubble of teammates and staff.

Who were all these strangers, lounging on their blankets and throwing their Frisbees and brandishing clipboards? There were so many of them, and their activity was indecipherable, these thirty thousand souls in pursuit of a goal alien to me: getting an education.

My academics were a train wreck. I didn't see how I could graduate, short of staying on another three years.

I made my way to Tolman Hall, the psychology building, and gazed up at its cratered façade. I had more psych units than any other. Two whole classes. One of those had been taught by a genial, enthusiastic man named Paul Sandek, himself a former college basketball player. We'd chatted a few times after games. I had never been to his office hours, let alone confided in him. I didn't know then that his playing career, like mine, had ended with an injury.

I could barely remember the names of my other professors.

I consulted the directory, climbed to the second floor, and walked a gloomy hall. Sandek's door was shut. Hearing his raspy laugh, I turned to go; changed my mind and scrawled a note on his whiteboard.

The door opened. Sandek leaned out, phone pressed to his shirt. *Clay. What a nice surprise.*

I told him I was thinking of dropping out.

He rubbed his beard. In those days it was more pepper than salt. He apologized to the person on the other end of the line. He'd have to call them back.

It took summer sessions, two course waivers, and an extra semester, but under his guidance I finished my degree. Throughout those months, as Luke caused our family to implode, Paul took me into his, inviting me home for dinner, where his wife, Theresa, a business school professor, put out heaping portions of moussaka or chicken cacciatore. Afterward I rinsed the dishes and handed them to their daughter, a leggy blond high schooler named Amy, to slot in the dishwasher. Cleaning up was as crucial as eating. It was what normal people did, and I needed normal like a blood transfusion.

One night, after Amy had gone upstairs to do her homework, I sat with Paul and Theresa in the living room and they grilled me about the rest of my life. It was one thing to earn a diploma, quite another to find purpose. What interested me? What did I care about?

Initially, I had no answer. Every choice I'd made since fourth grade reflected the single-minded goal of playing professional basketball. In its absence I confronted an existential void.

My parents had shared the same goal. I say that to their credit. My mother, in particular, was unflagging. She'd driven me to every practice; traveled to every game, home or road. Hers was the first face I saw in the recovery room when I woke up after my surgery, and she accompanied me to physical therapy multiple times a week. She had her own reasons for throwing herself into the role of sports mom. I had a bright future, and it was simpler and more directly rewarding to invest in that than in trying to halt Luke's deterioration. Given a choice, though, I doubt she would have opted to spend her forties driving to Fresno to scream her lungs out. Like every other narcissistic adolescent, I'd never asked her permission. I wanted what I wanted and she took on wanting it, too.

Then I stopped wanting it, leaving her staring into a void of her own. On some level she had to feel cheated: She'd backed a horse that came up lame. In doing so she'd also failed my brother. A new, unshakable conviction took hold of her. She could claw back time; she could and would save him.

But he had broken out of the stall to run wild.

In 2005 Luke was twenty-three. He worked at minimum wage, illegally, or not at all. He moved often, ditching one unthinkable living situation for another. He slept in his car, if he happened to have one. He slept rough.

He tells these stories now like they happened to someone else.

Looking back I feel guilt for how little thought I gave him and sadness at what my parents endured. It's not as though they forgot about him, and my mom periodically let her pain show. Sitting beside me at PT, she'd yawn, and when I asked if she was okay she'd confess that she'd been up all night, bailing Luke out of jail. Or that he'd cropped up after a month, asking to have our old room for a few nights.

Dull resignation colored her voice, as though he were a leaky faucet.

Always I urged her not to let him in. Always, she did, even though she knew he'd soon vanish along with the cash from her purse.

My father bricked himself up in work, books, hobbies, DIY. Only once, that December, did he lose his temper. Luke pawned a necklace passed down from our paternal great-grandmother. My father discovered the theft and confronted him about it. They ended up getting into a fistfight in the living room. My dad threw him out with a warning not to come back.

My mom called me, sobbing. She was afraid Luke might hurt himself. We needed to find him and get him checked into the hospital.

I thought it was pointless. This wasn't the first time Luke had gone off the radar. He'd run out of money and come home. He always did. No, she insisted, this was different, it felt different.

Not wanting her to suffer alone, I told her to pick me up. We trawled the streets, taking turns at the wheel. We checked the emergency rooms. We checked with his friends. They weren't his friends anymore. He had new friends whose names we didn't know. Nobody'd seen him in a while. Last time they did see him, he didn't look too good.

At daybreak she dropped me at campus. I napped for two hours and went to my nine a.m. class. My mother went to work. She didn't call the police. She knew what they'd say.

In 2005 Rosa Arias was twenty-eight years old, a full-time mother to three children: Max, six, Stephanie, four, and the baby, Christian.

She lived in Concord, a middle-working-class city in Contra Costa County, where she and her husband had both grown up. Ivan made good money as a statistician for Chevron. They owned a three-bedroom, two-bath house.

They'd met through Ivan's younger sister, Vanessa, with whom Rosa worked, at Macy's in the Sunvalley Mall, the summer Rosa turned seventeen. Ivan was five years older, bookish and mild-mannered. In addition to Vanessa he had four more sisters. Rosa liked that he came from a big family. Having so many women around meant he knew how to treat a lady. She'd always longed for a sister. The house she grew up in, with one brother, was always seething with angry male drama.

The Ariases' house was loud and full of laughter. People fought, but there was too much going on to stay mad or sad for long. Shy by nature, Rosa decided she would learn to be a part of that kind of family. She decided she wanted that kind of husband and that kind of home.

She was nineteen when they married. She would've liked to start having kids right away, but Ivan preferred to wait a little. So she concentrated on nieces and nephews; Ivan's three older sisters had kids ranging from infants to college-aged. Nobody would turn down free babysitting.

She loved getting together with everyone for backyard barbecues or birthday parties in the park. Once Max came along her sisters-in-law would pass him around, cooing over how delicious and fat he was. They gave her bags of baby clothes, and in the first eight weeks of his life, when he was colicky and Rosa thought she would lose her mind, they took turns coming over and holding him so she could have some temporary relief.

Although she'd met the Ariases through Vanessa, it was Janet—the second oldest, the quiet one—to whom Rosa felt closest. Those big get-togethers could stretch for hours. Ivan and the brothers-in-law happily pulling Budweisers from the cooler, Lisa and Paula and Rachael yakking it up. Hyperactive kids running everywhere with frosting on their faces.

Rosa loved them all, loved being part of it, but after a while her nerves just felt so fried. Sometimes she had to go stand behind a tree. She could hear Gladys asking Ivan *Donde se fué, tu delicada florecita?* And Janet saying *Leave her alone, Mama, can't you see she's tired.*

Janet was unique in another respect. Lisa had five children. Paula and Rachael had four apiece. Vanessa popped out three, boom-boom-boom, and wanted more. Janet married young and had Lucy right away but then couldn't get pregnant again. Nobody knew if she and Craig had stopped trying or if there was a problem. To compensate everyone heaped praise on Lucy and made sure her cousins included her in their games.

Lucy Vernon was nine when Rosa came into the circle. Over the next decade Rosa watched her niece evolve from a sunny pigtailed child to an intense, driven, creative young woman. Lucy loved clothes and from an early age talked about being a fashion designer when she grew up. It was Rosa, a skilled amateur, who taught her to sew.

After school, on weekends, Lucy would walk over to use Rosa's Singer. From the scraps Rosa gave her, Lucy fashioned small items to sell to her classmates, reversible headbands or a clever pouch that attached to a keychain and could be used to hold a tube of lip gloss or Chap-Stick. Soon she'd saved up enough to buy her own machine. When Rosa was pregnant for the second time, they collaborated for six months on Lucy's quinceañera dress, beading the bodice by hand.

In 2005 Lucy Vernon was nineteen. The same age Rosa had been when she married Ivan. Lucy's life looked different. She lived at home, worked part-time at Chipotle, took classes in fashion design and business. She still didn't have her learner's permit, let alone her license, relying on friends and family to chauffeur her where she couldn't walk, bike, or bus. She was an only child. She tended to get what she wanted.

On a December Sunday afternoon Lucy called Rosa to ask if her aunt would drive her to a fabric store in Fruitvale. She was copying a dress worn by Rihanna in *Us Weekly*. She described it: chartreuse leopard print against a white background, cut high, with a black lace neckline, decorative lace stripes up the front, lace edging the thigh slits.

Ivan—listening in on the conversation as he spooned cereal into Christian's mouth—saw his wife make a gagging face. He laughed.

Lucy had tried the local stores. None of them had the lace she wanted. A place on International Boulevard showed one on their website that looked close. She needed to see the fabric in person, touch it with her fingers, move it in the light, you couldn't tell from a screen, Rosa had taught her that. But Lucy's parents couldn't drive her. Her dad was on a fishing trip and her mom had taken Gladys to visit a friend in the hospital.

Rosa hesitated. Ivan could see she didn't want to strand him with three kids, though he often encouraged her to get out of the house. It'd been a while since Rosa and Lucy spent time together. Ivan thought he could detect the same wistful note in his niece's request. She could have called a friend.

Go, he said to Rosa.

Rosa kissed the kids and told them to behave. She kissed Ivan and got into her car, a 1997 Kia Sportage. It had served her well, but with two car seats and a booster, she'd been talking about getting something with a third row.

She stopped by the Vernons' to collect Lucy and they drove to Fruitvale, entering the fabric store at approximately four fifteen p.m. and shopping for thirty to forty minutes. Despite their closeness in age, the salesclerk mistook them for mother and daughter. In her recollection it had to do with the fondness on Rosa's face as she watched the younger woman run her hands over bolts of cloth and imagine, out loud and with excitement, what they might become.

MY BROTHER WOKE beneath the freeway. The sun was almost down, though he didn't realize that at first and in his disorientation took it to be dawn.

He sat up. He was in an abandoned parking lot surrounded by a chain-link fence. Train tracks ran nearby. There were tents, as well as other bodies lying inside sleeping bags, under tarps, and on the fissured, weedy asphalt. Someone had shaken out his backpack. His clothes were strewn everywhere.

He checked himself for his most precious possessions: a glass pipe, three glassine envelopes of crack cocaine, and a small sum of money left over from pawning our great-grandmother's ring. These he kept close by, sleeping with the pipe tucked in his armpit or cradled in his limp fingers, drugs in the folds of his crotch or between his butt cheeks. The cash he split between his socks.

Now his feet were bare and the money was gone.

The pipe lay within arm's reach, its tip broken off.

He reached into his underwear and found the drugs.

He gathered the rest of his things, including a mostly full fifth of vodka that he drank furtively and quickly. One shoe he found behind a concrete pillar. The other was nowhere to be seen. He went around, kicking up piles of garbage, till he found some other shoe that sort of fit.

He stole a pipe off a guy passed out cold and smoked one glassine envelope.

Rolling up his sleeping bag, he shouldered his backpack and left the encampment through a hole in the fence.

At the corner of 8th Street and 5th Avenue he passed a sign for Laney College. He couldn't remember when he'd last eaten. It must have been a long time; crack suppresses the appetite, yet he felt a gnawing hunger. He turned down 12th Street and entered a convenience store opposite Clinton Square. The owner caught him slipping a banana into his pocket and chased him out, waving a gun and yelling at him in Vietnamese.

Luke went around the block to get away from him. He sat down on the curb, ate his banana, and smoked a second glassine envelope.

Across the street, a bright-green Mustang was parked outside an apartment house.

Sweet wheels. It made him smile. He knew about cars. He hadn't had a vehicle in forever and never anything remotely as cool as the Mustang.

He finished his smoke and went over for a better look. Mid-seventies. It was really nice. It was fucking amazing. Stars shone in it. The owner had taken good care.

He tested the door handle. Locked.

A bag of Cheetos sat open on the passenger seat. There were crumbs on the leather. It changed Luke's opinion of the owner and pissed him off. That was no way to treat a beautiful machine, the most perfect car he had ever seen. He tried the passenger door but it, too, was locked. He still felt mad about the man at the convenience store who'd threatened him. He felt so furious he started pounding on the hood. He climbed atop the Mustang and stomped on the roof.

The hell are you doing. A man had materialized on the sidewalk. *Get down from there.*

Cheetos, motherfucker? Luke said.

The man's name was Orlando Flores. He lived in the apartment house and was the owner of the Mustang. He registered Luke's crazed mien and dishevelment and began backing away.

It's a beautiful machine Luke said. *It deserves respect.*

Orlando Flores took out his cellphone.

People often refer to a mustang as a wild horse, but that's incorrect. The mustangs that roam the American West descend from domesticated horses brought by the Spanish, cast back into nature.

A mustang is a feral horse.

That reckless instinct. Never harnessed. Never tamed.

Luke jumped down. He charged at Flores, dragged him to the sidewalk, beat him, and took his wallet and keys. One key fit the car door. Luke got in and fired it up. It roared.

ON THEIR WAY home from the fabric store, Rosa Arias and Lucy Vernon stopped to pick up dinner. Rosa called Ivan to let him know that Lucy would be joining them. Rosa was ordering garlic shrimp for herself and plain noodles and chicken for the kids. She read Ivan the menu so he could choose. Pineapple curry pork sounded good.

The last person who remembered hearing Rosa Arias speak was the hostess who handed Rosa her bags of Thai. Rosa double-checked that there was no spice in the noodles or chicken. Otherwise her kids wouldn't eat it. The hostess assured her that there was zero spice.

At approximately five forty-five p.m., Rosa and Lucy exited the restaurant. That late in the year, it was dark. They got into the Kia and Rosa drove north on International Boulevard to 29th Avenue, which led to the freeway. She signaled left and edged into the intersection. The light turned yellow. She started to make the turn and a green Mustang traveling in the rightmost oncoming lane at seventy-five to eighty miles per hour crushed into the Kia's passenger-side door.

Based on the point of impact, one would expect Lucy Vernon to be more grievously hurt. But it was Rosa who was killed outright when her head struck the window.

Lucy hung on for nine more days before dying.

Luke sustained a broken femur, broken ribs, a punctured lung, and a lacerated spleen. He spent four days in a coma and woke up cuffed to the bed rail.

CHAPTER 13

———

FROM MY FRONT WINDOW I watched the San Leandro cops finally drive away. Once the cruiser had turned the corner, I brought in the trash can liner from my car and crossed the living room to the Great Wall of Cardboard.

Amy's neat handwriting identified the contents of each box. BOTTLES/NURSING. WINTER COATS. GRAD SCHOOL BOOKS. BOOKS (CLAY). GIRLS CLOTHES 6–12 MO. BABY TOYS. An index to our lives. It made me think about my job: meeting dead people, trying to reconstruct their lives from the way they'd perished and paper trails they'd left. Property records and traffic fines. At that moment the work of ten years seemed as flimsy as inferring an ancient civilization from a few shards of pottery.

I took down a box marked BREAD MACHINE.

A wedding present. Not once had we made bread with it. In our previous home, a tiny mother-in-law cottage, I'd used the machine to store my personal firearm and ammo. Now we had a gun safe in the master bedroom closet.

I sliced open the packing tape. The lid of the bread

machine was also taped shut. I peeled it back and put the bin liner, its tampons and toilet paper wads and the bloody Walther PPS, inside the baking chamber. I shut the lid, shut the box, fitted it back in.

Everything looked just like before.

I lay on the sofa in the dark, creating columns in my mind.

Luke left of his own volition.

Luke committed a crime.

Luke is the victim of a crime.

The first column I subdivided into *Luke is okay* and *Luke is not okay.*

Okay included a business trip, taking off to clear his head, or an affair.

Not okay included an accident in some far-flung or inaccessible place. Suicide. Relapse, him strung out in some rat-infested shell, hallucinating, eyes dilated and dry as husks. In which case he could resurface tomorrow or in a month or never. I've collected the bodies of people like that. I've met their families. They're rarely surprised to get the news.

My brother's criminal history and the discarded handgun made the second column—*Luke committed a crime*—hard to ignore. He could have acted alone or with an accomplice: someone to drive him away from the scene, which was why his car was still there. A young man, maybe, with a beard and a white truck.

But it was the third set of realities, that Luke had come to harm by the hand of another, that I found myself dwelling on. In part because Andrea had accused me of bias. In part because of the Camaro; accomplice or no accomplice, a car was a conspicuous piece of evidence to leave behind. But mainly because of the many bad actors my brother had encountered in his time on earth.

Laying out my fears systematically was useful. And soothing. Working a case like any other.

It was also disheartening. I had none of the usual tools a cop takes for granted. Partners to share the burden and reflect ideas. Databases. Support teams.

Not to mention a complete lack of legal authority.

The two people I loved most were hundreds of miles away.

I had never been so alone in my life.

Too keyed up to sleep, I opened the browser on my phone and searched for Luke's victims. I knew next to nothing about them. Despite my mother's pleading I hadn't attended the trial, believing I could exempt myself from the nightmare.

An article from the archives of the *Contra Costa Times* discussed the crash and included photographs of both victims. Lucy Vernon's friends had put up a virtual memorial on Myspace. No one had ever taken it down so it persisted, ghost-like. She had dimple piercings and wore dark purple lip liner. She would never be forgotten. Rosa Arias's obituary called her a beloved wife and mother. She was survived by her husband Ivan and three young children, unnamed.

That was as much as I could find with the resources at hand, though I looked for a while longer. Rosa and Lucy had died right before social media erupted and made everyone's private lives a matter of public record.

I tried logging into Luke's Gmail account using the passwords Andrea had given me. None of them worked. Maybe she'd forgotten it. Maybe he'd forgotten it and been forced to change it.

I composed an email to my father. I had a question for him. House-related, I called it. I thought that was the best way to pique his interest while minimizing the chance he'd mention it to my mom. Otherwise she'd insist on getting on the phone.

At four a.m. I used the last two percent of my battery to google Patrick Starks. He'd declared for the NBA draft but was not selected and spent years bouncing around leagues in Italy, China, Australia, and Israel, winding up as head coach of the Division III Susquehanna River Hawks. These days he went by Pat.

Wednesday. Sixty-one hours in the dark.

A new fire had broken out in Napa County, on the western side of Lake Berryessa. Air quality was expected to worsen. Everyone, not just sensitive groups, was urged to remain indoors. To avoid exposure to unhealthy wildfire smoke, a "clean room" should be established. The public safety power outage remained in effect.

I pulled into the bureau beneath a sky peeling like old varnish.

Rory Vandervelde's autopsy was scheduled for eight a.m. At ten to, the booth officer called the squad room to notify Jed Harkless that Detective Rigo had arrived.

It was all I could do not to jump up. I was desperate for an update. I watched Harkless pour two cups of coffee and disappear down the hall. His keycard beeped.

Fifteen minutes later he returned.

"What's up?" I asked.

"Hm?"

"He have anything interesting to say?"

"Who?"

"Rigo."

Harkless shrugged. The criminal investigation was no business of his or mine. But he knew my reputation: I was a meddler. "We didn't really get into it."

I nodded and he sat behind the cubicle wall.

I decided to give it a few minutes, then saunter downstairs myself. Just to say hi.

I glanced over my shoulder.

Carmen Woolsey was staring at her screen.

Lydia Januchak, staring at hers.

Dani Botero's chair was unoccupied. She was in the morgue, assisting with the autopsy.

I opened Accurint and typed in Ivan Arias's name.

The system returned several individuals. The Ivan Arias I wanted was fifty-one years old, with a current address in Concord. He was the property's sole owner. He owned no watercraft and had no criminal record. Associates included Rosa Arias, deceased; Maxwell Arias, twenty-four; Stephanie Arias, twenty-two; Christian Michael Arias, nineteen.

Either of the sons would seem to qualify as a young man.

I wondered if either of them had a beard or owned a white truck.

My desk phone rang.

"There's a Sean Vandervelde here for you," the booth officer said. "Seems kinda mad."

"Don't let him in." I closed the search window. "I'm coming down."

Through the lobby glass I recognized Sean from his LinkedIn page. He wore a grape-colored polo shirt and jeans and was stalking the narrow landing that connected the building to the visitor lot. Dragging a Rollaboard, as if he'd come straight from the airport.

I came outside. "Mr. Vandervelde. Deputy Edison. We spoke on the phone yesterday."

"What time are we getting started?"

"Started with what?"

"The autopsy."

"I'm sorry to disappoint you, sir, but as I informed you, it isn't open to the public."

"I'm not the public."

The booth officer startled and reached for her radio.

I motioned for her to wait. "I understand that this is stressful, sir, and I want to help."

"Sure you do."

"But you need to calm down. Otherwise you're going to have to leave the premises. Okay?"

The vast majority of bereaved people are polite. If anything, they go out of their way to express their gratitude. Tiny kindnesses feel like saintly acts when we're at our lowest.

The angry minority—the bellowers, saber-rattlers, danglers of lawsuits—do their worst over the phone. Get them face-to-face and they almost always fold.

Almost always. We still wear bulletproof vests.

Sean Vandervelde glanced at the booth. The guard was waiting on a sign from me.

"Yeah," he said. "Okay."

"Thank you. How about we discuss this in private."

He nodded, and the guard buzzed us through.

I showed him to the small room reserved for next of kin. The walls are beige. There's a potted ficus and copies of *Real Simple* magazine; a bland sofa and matching chairs and a coffee table set with a box of Kleenex. The wastebasket is emptied out after each visit.

Vandervelde dropped his bag and dropped onto the sofa, one knee jogging. He grabbed a tissue and began twisting it into a rope.

I offered him water or coffee. He didn't answer. I took a chair. "When did you get in?"

"What . . . ? An hour ago."

"Are you alone?"

He stopped torturing the tissue and stared at me. "What are we doing? What is this?"

"It's part of my remit to ensure that next of kin are taken care of."

"You want to take care of something, take care of her."

"Who?"

"Who do you think? That fucking parasite bitch."

"I take it you mean Nancy Yap," I said. "Have you been in touch with her?"

"I don't want to talk to her."

"I understand she and your father were in a long-term relationship."

"She was my mom's oncologist. That tells you what you need to know."

He slumped, resting his head against the wall, atop a faint grease stain left by thousands of other weary heads. "You can't let her take his body."

"I assure you, sir, nothing's happening until we've completed our investigation."

"She's going to try. She had his lawyer call and threaten me."

"With what?"

"She's the executor. Allegedly."

"Are you in possession of a copy of his will?"

"There's no will."

"Then—"

"I don't care if she has a piece of paper with his signature on it," Sean said. "It doesn't mean a thing if he's not in his right mind."

He jackknifed, hurling the shredded tissue at the wastebasket. It missed. "You see what's happening here, don't you? It's *his lawyer*. Now he's representing her? *That's* not a conflict of interest? Senile old shitbag, I should have him disbarred. A buck gets ten she's sucking his dick, too."

He was working himself up again. I said to him the same thing I've said to countless others in his position, to refocus them on what matters: "Tell me about your father."

Sean frowned. "Tell you what?"

"What do you remember about him best?"

"I don't . . ." He faltered. "He was my father."

I nodded.

"He wasn't a bad father. Don't think that's what I'm saying."

"Not at all."

"He was involved, he could be a lot of fun. I have good memories. All right? Is that . . . Have I said whatever it is you want me to say?"

"You don't have to say anything."

Silence.

"I was at his house," I said. "It seems like he had a wide variety of interests."

Sean snorted. "No shit."

"Did you share any of that with him?" I paused. "Cars?"

"When I was six, maybe. But come on. Grow up."

He leaned back again. "People look at him, 'Oh, here's this guy, he's a master of the universe, he must be some sort of genius.' But the fact of the matter is he was incredibly gullible. He was like a child. He'd be the first to admit that. His own father walked out, his mother was an alcoholic. He was basically dyslexic. Nobody ever set boundaries, nobody told him you couldn't do certain things. You give a person like that too much money, it's like giving a gun to a toddler. I graduated law school and he bought me a Maserati. For the life of him, he couldn't get why that was inappropriate. 'Why don't you ever want to enjoy yourself?' I told him, 'I can't show up to work in a car nicer than the partners'.' The one person he listened to was my mother. She spoiled him, but at least she kept him grounded. She goes and next thing you know, that cunt's moving in and I'm getting lectured about it's his life, he gets to decide."

Easy narrative. Victim; villain. "Sounds tough."

"It's not tough, it's disgusting. They didn't even wait till my mom was dead. And now this bitch has the balls to sit there and tell me what I'm entitled to? Fuck you. Listen, I appreciate what you're trying to do, but I didn't fly up here in the middle of the workweek to explore my feelings. I need to speak to someone who can move the needle. When's the detective coming?"

I glanced at the clock. The autopsy was well under way. "Did you call him?"

"He wasn't interested in what I had to say."

"Detective Rigo is a thorough investigator," I said, though I didn't know that and on some level hoped it wasn't true.

"He's shitty at returning phone calls."

"You can share your concerns with me, and I can relay them to him."

"My concerns are that she murdered him. That's my concern. Relay that."

"You believe Dr. Yap—"

"Don't call her that. She should lose her license. Don't call her that."

"You believe she killed your father."

"Not on her own. Does she seem like the kind of person to get her hands dirty?"

"I haven't met her."

"Trust me. She hired someone to do it. With his money."

"Do you have cause to suspect that?"

"Are you deaf? She got him to put her in charge of his estate."

"I'm asking if she's made threats against him in the past, or if their relationship was violent."

"How the fuck do I know? I don't live with them."

"Besides Ms. Yap can you think of anyone else who might want to hurt your father?"

Sean Vandervelde smiled bitterly. "Besides me, you mean."

"I mean in general."

"No. Is the detective coming or not?"

"Hard to say. They don't always."

He crossed his arms. "I'll wait."

"What time's your flight home?"

"I don't have one. I'm not leaving till I've sorted this mess out."

"Do you have a place to stay tonight?"

"Are we friends?"

"I just want to make sure you're set up. A lot of hotels are closed because of the outage."

"I'm in the city. Okay?"

"Okay." I stood. "Anything else I can do for you, sir?"

He shut his eyes. "I'll take that coffee."

I BROUGHT IT to him in a paper cup and went to the morgue viewing station. Cesar Rigo was there observing the autopsy on the flat-screen.

At table four, on the far side of the morgue, Dani Botero was assisting the pathologist, Mahalia Millsap. Rory Vandervelde's abdominal cavity was butterflied, his organs removed and sampled. His stomach had been opened and its contents decanted into a basin for analysis.

Rigo had on a royal-blue suit, same slim cut, purple tie tightly knotted.

I felt my own throat constrict. "Morning."

"Good morning, Deputy. I didn't expect to see you."

Dani Botero saluted me through the window. I saluted back. Dr. Millsap kept her eyes on the body, narrating over the intercom as she traced the path of the bullets.

"Sean Vandervelde is here," I said to Rigo.

"Is he?"

"He has a theory he'd like to share with you. He flew in from LA."

"Is he aware that I am here?"

"No. I have him in a room. I told him you might not come but he seems intent on waiting."

"What is the theory?"

"Nancy Yap had his father killed."

"Fascinating. When I spoke to her, she advanced a similar claim about Sean."

"The will cuts him out and puts her in charge. Either side, there's motive. She stands to benefit and he's on the warpath."

"Thank you, Deputy. I will take it under advisement."

The shot to Rory Vandervelde's trapezius was a clean through-and-through. The shot to his neck had chipped the left transverse process of the C5 vertebra. The fatal shot, number three, was an unlucky fluke. The bullet had sneaked between the third and fourth ribs, missing the scapula but tearing open the descending thoracic aorta and causing rapid internal hemorrhage, Vandervelde's own heart pumping his trunk full of blood.

I spoke into the intercom. "TOD?"

"Late Sunday to early Monday morning," Dr. Millsap said.

"After the power went out."

"Probably, although don't hold me to that."

"Did you get into his computer?" I asked Rigo. "Anything from the security system?"

"The footage terminates with the outage. The neighbors cannot recall a vehicle entering or exiting the property. One assumes they were preoccupied with their own problems."

On the screen, Dr. Millsap tweezed out a warped, bloody slug. She held it up to the camera. "Small-to-medium caliber." She dropped it into a metal pan with a *clack*.

I asked Rigo if ballistics had recovered intact rounds.

"One. Nine millimeter."

Same as the Walther PPS.

"Any luck finding the murder weapon?" I asked.

Rigo shook his head. "I informed your colleague that

we were able to locate the victim's phone. A neighbor discovered it while walking her dog. It had been smashed and thrown to the side of the road. Forensics is attempting to recover the data."

If my brother had a legitimate reason to be at Rory Vandervelde's house, they had likely communicated prior to the appointment. The fact that the phone was damaged didn't change much. What was true of Luke's laptop was true of any connected device: You didn't need the physical object to access its activity. I assumed Rigo had submitted a subpoena for cellphone records. Landline, too. It's what I would have done. Depending on Vandervelde's carrier and the detective's pushiness, it could take anywhere from a couple of days to weeks for the request to trickle through the layers of compliance.

I had a more immediate concern. "Were you able to pull prints?"

"Unfortunately not. It appears to have been wiped clean."

"Too bad. What about from the rest of the scene?"

Rigo moved his eyes from the flat-screen to me. I had the disconcerting sensation he could see through my skull. "There is evidence of numerous individuals throughout the house."

"Right." Too many questions. I had to stop. But I also had to learn what I could; I had to know. "So what's the thinking."

"Pardon?"

"If not Sean or Nancy." Sweat tickled my breastbone. "Robbery? Business dispute?"

"It's early to say."

"You can't stop Clay," Dani said through the intercom. "He's got a thirst for knowledge."

"I'm just a fan of open communication," I said.

Rigo smiled and returned to watching the screen.

Dr. Millsap announced that she would commence dissection of the head.

"What do you want me to tell Sean?" I asked Rigo.

"Must we tell him anything?"

"I can't leave him sitting there all day."

"From your previous remarks I took that to be a viable option."

"One thing he said I thought was kind of strange. I asked if he could think of anyone else who might want to hurt his father. He goes, 'Besides me, you mean.'"

"I am making the intermastoid incision," Dr. Millsap dictated.

She drew a scalpel across the crown of Rory Vandervelde's head. Sunburnt scalp parted to reveal flat gray bone. Together with Dani she peeled the flesh to the hairline.

"Perhaps I will have a word with the younger Mr. Vandervelde," Rigo said.

I led him to the next-of-kin room and knocked softly.

The room was deserted, the paper coffee cup sitting on the table.

The booth officer told us that Sean had left a few minutes ago and gotten into an Uber.

"Did he say where he was headed?" I asked her.

"He didn't say anything."

"Do you have his number available?" Rigo asked me.

"My phone's upstairs but I can text it to you."

"Thank you, Deputy." With sudden uninvited intimacy he stepped in and squeezed my biceps. His small hand was like a snare. "You've been most helpful."

CHAPTER 14

AMY AND CHARLOTTE had gone with Sarah and the baby to Huntington Gardens in Pasadena. I thumbed through photos of Charlotte in a bamboo grove, looking contemplative beyond her years.

I had another missed call from Billy Watts, the Berkeley detective, one from Andrea, and one from a number I didn't recognize. I listened to the attached voicemail.

Mr. Edison, my name is James Okafor. I work with your brother. I understand you were here asking about him. Feel free to give me a ring . . .

I went out to the employee lot and called him from my car.

"Hello."

"Hi, Mr. Okafor. It's Clay Edison, Luke's brother."

"Oh, hey." His soft, gravelly baritone faded into the bustle of the office floor. "Hang on a sec, let me find a room." A brushy sound as he walked. The noise dampened. "Okay."

"Thanks for calling."

"No problem. Sorry I missed you yesterday, I had to

leave to pick up my kids. Annie Lin told me you were by. She said you can't reach Luke."

"He's been AWOL since Sunday. Have you spoken to him?"

"Not recently. You mind if I ask what's going on?"

"I don't really know. His wife hasn't heard from him, either."

"Uh-huh. Well, I don't want to alarm you, because I don't know if this means anything."

I'm alarmed. "Go ahead."

"Your brother thought he was being followed."

IT WAS A WEEKDAY. Four, five months back. Okafor arrived at the office early. He and Luke were among the few who did. They were the Old Guys. His was the workstation to the left of Luke's. They joked about it, like there was a designated zone for anyone over thirty.

He stopped to get coffee and ran into Luke, standing at the kitchen counter, unmoving.

"I'm like, 'What's up, king.' He told me he was driving in and almost got into an accident. One block from the building, he stops at a hard yellow and the guy behind him almost rear-ends him. I could see he was shaken up. I thought because, you know, he loves that car. I'm like, 'At least nothing happened, right?' Then he tells me he went out to get his lunch. He was distracted on account of the near miss and forgot to bring it in with him. He steps outside and there's the same truck that almost hit him, parked across the street."

My scalp prickled. "A truck."

"That's what he said. He said it was like it was waiting for him. The driver has the window down, and Luke expects the guy to start cussing him out. But he doesn't say anything. He just points his phone at Luke, like he's taking a picture of him, or filming him. Luke goes and gets his lunch from the car. The whole time the guy's following him with the camera."

"Was he able to describe the driver?"

"Not that he said. I told him, 'It's probably an insurance scam, the guy's gonna say you hit him so he can make a claim.' Luke's like, 'Maybe, I don't know.' But he looked nervous."

"What about the truck? Make and model, a plate number?"

"All he said was white. I remember, because I went out myself to see. He told me what to look for: white truck, across the street. But it was gone."

"What about if it had a cover over the bed? Or any detail, no matter how small or insignificant it might seem."

A chair creaked. "That's as much as I remember."

"Okay. First off, Mr. Okafor, thank you."

"It's James. My pleasure. I mean, not my pleasure. You know what I mean."

"Do you think Luke might've mentioned the incident to Annie or anyone else?"

"I'll ask her but I wouldn't count on it. Luke . . . He's not a sharer. Neither of us are."

"There's a security camera at the entrance. Is it possible it caught the truck?"

". . . could be."

"Could you find out? Scott knows what's going on, tell him it's for me. Or Evelyn Girgis. They'll need you to tell them what dates to look at."

"I'll try. Is there anything else I can do to help?"

"Not right now. Thanks, James. It's really helpful and I appreciate it. If you remember anything else please get in touch."

"I will. Hey, I'm sorry about this. Your brother's a good dude."

The temperature inside the car had climbed. Every

breath tasted like an ashtray tipped into my mouth. I put on the AC and unfastened the top three buttons of my shirt and slapped myself in the cheek a couple of times to wake myself up.

Andrea answered on the first ring. "What is it? What's going on?"

"Nothing bad. I'm checking in. Any word?"

"No. I did what you said and called our friends." Her voice was abraded, as if she had been crying nonstop since leaving my house. "No one's seen him. I still have a couple left to ask."

"Credit card activity?"

"There haven't been any charges since Saturday."

"What did he buy?"

"Fish oil. I was with him, we went together."

"All right." I paused. "How are you doing?"

"How do you think? I was up all night. I feel like I'm going crazy."

"I'm sorry you have to go through this. Do you need me to come over tonight and help with your shots?"

"I did them myself. I threw up. Whatever. Stick to finding Luke. What about you?"

"Me?"

"How are you feeling?"

Coming from her, the question invariably preceded a lecture.

Clay, you should be more mindful of . . .

As a therapist, *I feel it's unhealthy to . . .*

But she added nothing.

I said, "I'm fine. Thanks for asking."

"Have you talked to your parents yet?"

"I emailed my dad. I want to run the conversation through him."

"Your mother called me."

"Shit. When?"

"This morning."

"What did you tell her?"

"I didn't pick up."

"Thank you. Just keep putting her off and I'll get to them as soon as I can. Listen, I spoke to one of Luke's colleagues."

I recounted my conversation with James Okafor for her and got silence.

"You've never seen a truck like that," I said.

"No."

"Okay. And Luke didn't—"

"No."

"I'm sure he didn't want to upset you."

"*You're* upsetting me."

"We don't know what it means. It could be nothing. I just want to keep you in the loop."

A text appeared from Sergeant Clarkson. Where r u

"I'm going to have to get off in a minute," I said. "Keep trying your friends. Call the places he hangs out. The gym. Go to the motels, show them his picture. Can you handle calling the hospitals?"

Andrea began again to weep.

I said, "Don't worry, I'll do it."

"No. No. I can do it."

"Are you sure?"

"It should be me." She blew her nose. "What are you going to do?"

"I have a few things on my list. The NA meeting is tonight, I was going to start there."

"I'll go."

"You don't have to."

"It's right in town. I'd rather be doing something than nothing."

"Fine. Let me know. I tried the passwords you gave me. They don't work."

"I don't know what to tell you, that's everything I

could think of. Isn't there a way we can—get in? Can we contact Google and explain what's going on?"

"They're not going to listen to us."

"They have to, you're a cop."

"It's not that simple."

R u here Sergeant Clarkson wrote.

"What about the families?" Andrea said. "The ones . . . you were going to check them out."

"I will," I said, typing Sorry on my way 5 min

"When?"

"Soon as I can."

"You need to go now, Clay. They could be doing something to him *right now.*"

"Andrea. Listen—"

"*No, you listen.* You told me you were going to find him. I *trusted* you."

"I am on it. I promise. I have to go so I can follow up on all this stuff. We'll talk later. Okay?"

Silence.

"Yes," she said. "Let's talk later."

She sounded stupefied, as if a tranquilizer had just hit her bloodstream.

The line went dead.

BEFORE HEADING INSIDE I made one final call to the office of Terrence J. Milford, warden of Pleasant Valley State Prison, ending up talking to an assistant warden named Keith Gluck who spoke in a low, bored nasal drone. I gave my name and badge number and told him I was interested in reviewing the file of a former inmate.

"Date of release?"

"Mid-twenty-eighteen."

"That case," Gluck said, "we're not going to have it here. You can order it up from CDCR."

In four to six weeks.

"Maybe someone's around who remembers him," I said.

"What did you say the name was?"

I hadn't. "Luke Alan Edison."

"What was this concerning?"

"It's an ongoing investigation."

"And remind me your name?"

"Clay Edison."

Gluck said, "That's a coincidence."

"He's my brother. Do you remember him?"

"I'm not sure what I want to tell you over the phone."

"If I were to come down there, could we talk?"

"When did you want to come?"

"I could be there by eight."

"Tonight?" He laughed. "How's tomorrow at . . . two. That work for you?"

Another bottomless night of wondering. "Two it is."

I SWIPED INTO the squad room. Sergeant Clarkson leaned out from her office.

"Hey there. Where'd you go?"

"Had to take a personal call."

She nodded slowly. Prior to becoming a sheriff, Juanita Clarkson had served two tours in Iraq. Her reputation was tough, but fair. But tough. "Body in Fremont. You're up. Lindsey's prepping the van." She looked me over. "Everything okay?"

My shirt was untucked, the buttons undone to mid-chest. "Yes, ma'am. It's just . . . hot."

"Mm," she said. "Hydrate, hydrate, hydrate."

EARLIER IN THE DAY, Cindy Albright, thirty-seven years old, an employee of the utility company, had responded to a report of a downed power line near the campus of the

California School for the Blind. As a rule, any such report called for a bucket truck and repair crew. Deluged with complaints since the start of the shutoff, dispatch had begun sending a customer support unit van to verify the situation and, if justified, secure the area till a full crew became available.

Seeing nothing amiss, Cindy Albright circled the block a few times and phoned her supervisor. He checked the incident log.

Overacker Avenue he read. *South side of Walnut, by the train tracks.*

She told him she was right there, looking up at the lines running pole-to-pole, one-two-three, plain as day. Probably the call was a prank. Or somebody mistook a garden hose for a hot wire.

He instructed her to get out and have a poke around on foot. Could've fallen behind a bush or a fence. He didn't want to have to send her out twice.

Annoyed, Cindy Albright hopped down from the van and walked around to the sidewalk.

She stepped up onto the curb.

A bullet slammed into the side of the customer support unit van, puckering the ampersand in the utility company logo.

Cindy Albright jumped at the impact. She peered at the bullet hole. She had never been shot at and was slow to grasp how the hole had gotten there. Then a second bullet spliced the upright of the logo's *P* and she dropped screaming to her hands and knees.

Three more bullets followed in a tight grouping. An eyewitness at the bus stop on Walnut would describe the sound of them hitting the metal siding by rapidly smacking his lips: *mup-mup-mup.*

A bullet shattered the customer support unit van's passenger-side window.

Cindy Albright crawled to the driver's-side door. Hyperventilating, shaking, she hoisted herself behind the wheel. Pebbles of glass studded the seat fabric; there was glass on the dash and in the cushion crevices and glass embedded in her palms.

She tried to start the engine.

She dropped her keys.

A bullet pierced the van's right rear tire.

She retrieved the keys and started the engine and stamped the gas, and the van broke through the red light at Mission Boulevard, fishtailing northbound on the blown rear tire. Both lanes of traffic were dammed with cars going unacceptably, insanely slow. To get around them, Cindy Albright veered into the bike lane, running down twenty-five-year-old Fletcher Kohn.

Kohn's girlfriend, Jenn Volpe, was riding lead. She heard the growl of the oncoming van and turned to see Kohn disappear beneath the front bumper. Reflexively she jerked the handlebars. Her front wheel caught the curb and she pitched headfirst onto the sidewalk.

She was in the ambulance, being screened for concussion, when Lindsey Bagoyo and I arrived. The customer support unit van sat at an angle, haloed by flares. Up the block Cindy Albright was giving a statement to a uniform. The bulk of the police response was concentrated on sweeping the campus and surrounding neighborhoods. A shooter on the loose took priority.

Opinion was divided as to his intention. The first school of thought held that he'd waited for Cindy Albright to exit the van so he could take a potshot at her. But he had lousy aim and hit the van by mistake. Others believed that the van was the target. By letting Cindy get out, he'd tried to avoid hitting anyone inside.

One thing everyone could agree on: Cindy Albright was chosen at random. The *real* target was the utility company, the shooter enraged at having his power shut off for the third time in a calendar year. This theory would later be supported by the discovery, two hundred yards down Overacker, of a pile of rifle casings, alongside a Gatorade bottle containing a note.

Lights out bitches

Bagoyo and I erected privacy screens around Fletcher Kohn's body. She began the physical exam while I grabbed the camera and went to talk to Jenn Volpe.

She was young and tan, with pale stripes left by the stems of her missing sunglasses. She had scrapes on her face and forehead, large gauze pads on her scraped knees. A drop of clear liquid trembled at the end of a Roman nose. Her eyes were vacant. Three times while we spoke she said, "He was wearing a helmet," as if virtue trumped physics.

I got a phone number for Fletcher Kohn's parents and gave Jenn Volpe my card.

The ambulance took her away.

Bagoyo finished her exam and went to interview Cindy Albright.

I took photos and collected Fletcher Kohn's personal property. His bicycle, frame torqued, rear wheel like a shredded fingernail; a backpack containing his wallet, keys, and phone; his own sunglasses, miraculously unscathed and caught by a boxwood hedge. A crack ran up the left side of his helmet, nearly cleaving it into two unequal parts.

BACK AT THE BUREAU, Bagoyo braked to let the vehicle lot gate roll open.

"All good?" she said.

"Mm?"

"You keep checking your phone."

For a call from my father. From Andrea. From James Okafor.

A sick feeling came over me as I realized that I no longer expected to hear from Luke.

I put the phone away. "I was hoping they could tell me when my power's coming back on."

"And?"

"They don't know yet."

Bagoyo clucked her tongue in disapproval.

We weighed Fletcher Kohn and brought him inside to be photographed under bright clinical light, first clothed, then nude. I went to the van, hefting the bike on my shoulder and the backpack in the crook of my elbow.

When I reentered the intake bay, Lydia Januchak had joined us. She was folding Kohn's bloody jeans into an evidence bag. She saw the mangled bike and winced.

Hooking the bag on a free finger, I swiped into the property room.

Forty feet by thirty of cinder block and luggage lockers. The bus station that time forgot.

Stacks of clothing. Fewer shoes; an astonishing number of people die barefoot. Wallets and phones, handbags and watches. Eyeglasses. House keys. Jewelry. It smelled like Other People's Stuff; like a school gym after a long, contentious PTA meeting.

I wondered which lockers contained the valuables from Rory Vandervelde's home. The tiny fraction of a rich man's stash that Harkless and Bagoyo had deemed most worthy of protection.

I put away Fletcher Kohn's Stuff and took the elevator to the second floor.

EDMOND, THE PROPERTY CLERK, had his headphones on and didn't hear my knock.

I texted him: behind you

He glanced down, grabbed off the headphones, and

spun in his chair, gripping the armrests. "You're like a dang ninja," he said.

He handed me a chain-of-custody tag. I filled it out and he attached it to Fletcher Kohn's locker keys. A tinny voice issued from the headphones.

"What are you listening to?"

"Podcast." He hit PAUSE and rolled over to the master safe, a heavy-duty steel cube. A purple key carabiner hung on a lanyard around his neck. He unclipped it and selected a key.

"What about?" I asked.

He unlocked the safe, filed away Fletcher Kohn's locker keys, relocked the safe, twirled the carabiner on one finger. Grinned. "Ninjas."

SERGEANT CLARKSON'S OFFICE door was shut. I went to Bagoyo's cubicle.

"Hey," I said. "I may need to clock out a few minutes early. Are you set here?"

She faced up at me. Lindsey Bagoyo was a devout Catholic, active in her church choir, volunteering on the weekends. In the four years since she'd joined the bureau I had never heard her use profanity or raise her voice. The most she ever conceded was a mischievous smile.

"Go ahead," she said, her dark eyes crinkling. "I won't tell."

CHAPTER 15

————

I DROVE TO CONCORD.

I'd copied down Ivan Arias's address as well as addresses for the rest of Rosa's family. Maxwell and Stephanie both lived near their father. The younger son, Christian, was a student at UC Santa Cruz. Janet and Craig Vernon had divorced. She, too, lived in Concord.

None of them owned a truck of any color or had a criminal record.

I had no legal right to know that.

I hadn't been able to find a Craig Vernon in the vicinity, and there were too many men with that name to start chasing them all down.

I had to start somewhere, and Ivan felt like the best balance of risk versus reward.

Traffic through the Caldecott Tunnel was sparse. Over the 680 split, the message board declared:

HIGH WINDS—FIRE DANGER—AQI POOR—STAY INSIDE

I forked north. Big-box stores and housing developments bellied up to the roadside.

Roskelley Drive was a single block of ranch homes, a

quarter of a mile from Pixieland amusement park. The sidewalk smoldered white hot. Elms and oaks and palms cast weak pools of shadow. Lawns were trimmed to brown stubble or had been replaced by concrete or gravel. Ivan Arias might not own watercraft, but several of his neighbors did. They owned RVs and minivans. They owned trucks.

None white. None with tonneau covers.

Ivan Arias's ranch home was two cubes of peach stucco beneath an obtuse cap sheet roof. Silver Prius in the carport, curtains drawn against the heat. I stepped from the car into a parched stillness. No televisions or radios singing; no hair dryers or washing machines. A squirrel darted out along a power line and struck a pose as though electrocuted.

The man who came to the door was about five-eight, with wiry gray hair and a full gray beard, steel-rimmed aviator glasses resting on a broad nose. His T-shirt paunched softly. "Yes?"

"Ivan Arias?"

"Yes?"

I'd kept my uniform on. My surname was sewn onto the breast pocket. He didn't react to it or to my ID. He read it and gave it back and stood there, expressionless. It had to feel to him like déjà vu—a visit from the coroner. And what I was about to do was cruel.

But Luke . . .

"My name is Clay Edison," I said. "Luke Edison is my brother."

A tremor ran through him. "Excuse me?"

"Is anyone else home, Mr. Arias?"

"Is . . ." He clocked my face, my gun. "No."

"Can we talk?"

"What's there to talk about."

"Has my brother ever gotten in touch?"

"With me?"

"You, or any other members of your family."

"Why would he do that?"

"He spoke about wanting to ask your forgiveness."

Arias wound up to slam the door. Smiled, as if he'd thought of something absurd.

He said, "You're a cop."

"Yes, sir."

"And he's . . . who he is."

"Yes, sir."

"How come I don't remember you?"

"I wasn't at the trial," I said.

"Never?"

"No, sir."

"Why not?"

I said, "I don't know."

A few houses over, a leaf blower howled to life.

Ivan Arias stepped back. "Come in."

THE HOUSE HAD a typical midcentury layout, with kitchen, dining room, and living room forming an L around the carport. One dining chair was pulled out, manila folders stacked up on the table next to a laptop whose glow alone dented the gloom. I'd interrupted his work.

He pointed me to a sectional and went to a rear sliding glass door, tugging the chain to open the vertical blinds. The plastic slats swished and tapped as they parted, sallow light flashing on the carpet like a distress signal. In the backyard a flower bed enclosed by a brick border ran along one fence. There was a patio with a charcoal grill and a suite of sun-blasted outdoor furniture. It made for a forlorn tableau.

"I have water, orange juice, and Coke."

"No, thanks."

"Drink something," he said, making it sound like a command.

"Water would be great, thank you."

He put out coasters. "I have beer, too."

A test? *He's an alkie like his brother? Drinks on the job?*

"Water, please."

He went to the kitchen sink, shutting the laptop as he passed.

While his back was turned I slid over to look at the photo on the end table. It showed the whole family, the three children still children. Rosa wore a slender ruffled dress, her black hair pinned up and two glossy spirals hanging free. She carried the baby on her hip. His chin glistened with drool. The older boy smiled through large gapped teeth. The boys sported matching party outfits. The daughter, Stephanie, clung stubbornly to her father's leg, refusing to acknowledge the camera. Ivan's beard was dark. His face was red and happy.

My stomach churned. I had no right to be here, no right to his memories.

There were more photos in the dining area, staggered on the shelves of a wall unit. Too far to make out details, but I could see several male faces, a few of which had beards.

The faucet ran. Outside, the leaf blower ground like an auger.

Could I risk a quick look?

Ivan Arias was slumped over the sink.

I started to put my weight down. My boots sank into the pile.

The faucet shut off.

Ivan raised his head.

I sat back.

He brought two glasses of water and set them on the coasters.

"Thank you."

"You're welcome." He eased into a corduroy recliner.

"I can see it now. The similarity. He was a lot younger then. Now he must be, what. Forty?"

"Forty-one."

"Why"—with a soft exhalation he bent for his glass—"why does he want forgiveness now?"

"I guess he's had some time to think about what he did."

"He's had time. He had time in prison. What changed?"

"I'm not sure."

"So he sent you here to . . . set it up."

I skirted the lie. "For what it's worth, in my opinion, he's not the same person he was."

"I really hope not."

"I'm not defending him, Mr. Arias. No excuses."

"You should defend him. That's what family does." He sipped, ran his lips over each other. "If he does call and ask me to forgive him, I'll have nothing to say."

I nodded.

He wagged a finger at me. "You think I can't forgive him because what he did was unforgivable. That's not it. To forgive you need to feel. I feel nothing toward him. To me, he's not a person, he's a thing that happened. Like the weather. You don't forgive the weather."

He took another sip and nestled his glass carefully in the carpet. "Who else does he want forgiveness from? My kids? Janet?"

"I don't know."

"Have you talked to them yet?"

"No, sir. I came to you first."

"Good call."

"Why's that?"

"I loved my wife. I loved my niece. To lose them was more painful than I can describe. But the pain had a shape. It had borders. I could remember my wife and my niece. My children didn't have that. They were too young. Christian, he used to wake up at night and scream. I'd

have to hold him for hours till he calmed down. I knew
what he wanted, he wanted his mother. But he couldn't
express that, and I couldn't explain to him why it was me,
not her. My oldest son was six. Stephanie was barely four.
You don't know your mother at that age. She's not a person, she's a presence. Like God. So yes, they understand
something was taken from them. But they have nothing to
grab onto. It's an abstraction. I mourned for my Rosa.
They're mourning for themselves. That never goes away."

I said, "I'm sorry."

"Did he send you here to apologize?"

"No, sir. I'm on my own."

"You didn't come to the trial, though."

"No, sir."

He sat back, still wanting an explanation.

"I was angry at him," I said.

"*You* were."

"Yes, sir."

"Why?"

"He was an embarrassment."

"To you."

"To our family." I'd never spoken these words. "I hated
him."

"Do you, still?"

"Not anymore."

"You've forgiven him."

"I don't see that as up to me."

"Well, if it's not up to you, and it's not up to me, then
who's it up to?"

"I don't know, sir. Maybe he doesn't get forgiveness."

"Hard way to live."

"Not compared with you."

A cold smile. "It's not a competition. Everyone suf-
fers."

"Yes, sir."

"Your parents? How do they feel?"

"I think they were embarrassed, too."

"You think? You never talked about it?"

"No, sir."

"It must be strange for them," Ivan Arias said. "Him. And a cop."

The sound of the leaf blower died away.

"Your parents never said a single word to me," he said. "Not before the trial, not during, not after. It's okay. They were probably following their lawyer's instructions."

"What would you have liked to say to them?"

He thought a moment. "I would have told them about Rosa. Not to make them feel guilty. I gain nothing from that. But I do want the world to know what it lost. Afterward I had lawyers calling me left and right, wanting me to go after him in civil court. 'No, thank you. I don't need to watch the sequel.' Besides, what could we have gotten from him?"

Luke: unemployed, uninsured, sleeping under the freeway.

"Not much," I said.

"Correct. You start out fighting him but end up fighting yourself. Like my kids. Fighting who knows what. I'm pretty sure if he'd contacted them, they'd have told me. But let's find out."

He tapped a text, sent it off, and put the phone on the coffee table.

"I'm going to make a prediction," he said. "Stephanie will write back first. A minute or two. Max'll be five to ten. Christian," he said, chuckling, "we might get an answer next week."

I forced myself to smile. "Busy guy."

"Oh yes, yes. He's a double major, biology and physics."

"Wow."

"They're all like that. Smart, ambitious."

"What does your daughter do?"

"She's in law school. She wants to be a prosecutor. Who knows? Maybe you'll work with her one day. That would be ironic, don't you think?"

"Yes, sir. And your other son?"

"Max works for my brother-in-law, Raul. He's a contractor."

Contractors drove trucks.

"You must be very proud of them," I said.

"I am." Ivan scratched his elbow. "Do you have children?"

"One. One on the way."

"Does your brother?"

I shook my head.

"Is he married?"

"Yes, sir, he is."

"Good for him."

The phone chimed. He peered at it. "Stephanie says she's never heard from him."

He tapped a reply and put the phone in his lap. "What did I tell you? Right on time."

"Yes, sir."

"They don't change from when they're small. You'll see that."

"Yes, sir."

"You said your brother's a new person."

"In certain respects."

"Such as what."

"He's tried to stay out of trouble."

"Does he succeed?"

"I think so."

"And how is he?"

"Sir?"

"Is he well? Is he happy?"

"That's hard for me to say."

"What does he do to pay the bills?"

I hesitated. "He works at a cannabis company."

Ivan tilted his head. "Really?"

"Yes, sir."

"He's allowed to do that?"

"Apparently."

He burst into laughter. He took off his glasses and began cleaning them on the hem of his shirt. "Unbelievable . . . Is he allowed to drive?"

"Not for the first year. He can now."

"He hasn't killed anybody else, though."

A bright-green Camaro.

A garage door, stuck partway open.

A man with three holes in his back.

I said, "No, sir."

He replaced his glasses. "Well, that's progress."

"Yes, sir. May I ask about your sister?"

"I have five sisters."

"Your sister Janet. How do you think she'd react if Luke called her?"

"I don't know. I don't think she'd sit there with him like I'm sitting with you."

"I understand that she and her husband split up."

"Their marriage was never that great to begin with. Lucy was what they had, and once they didn't have her . . ." He fluttered his fingers like falling leaves.

"What about her husband?"

"He left town. I think he moved to Idaho."

"You're not in touch with him."

"Craig? No." Ivan Arias paused. "It made things tense between me and Janet, too. We don't talk as much as we used to. So in a way I lost her, too. Have you ever lost someone you loved?"

"No, sir, I have not." *Unless.*

"I don't wish that for you."

The phone chimed. He glanced at his lap. "Max hasn't heard from him either."

He tapped a reply. Seconds later the phone sounded

again. They made several more exchanges before Ivan laid the phone facedown on the table. "I'm getting a Coke. Want one?"

"No, thank you."

He started for the kitchen.

"One week till we hear from Christian," he called. "Start the clock."

I believed Ivan Arias was telling me the truth. He'd never seen my brother. As to his children's denials, there were too many unknowns.

How honest they were with their father; how he'd phrased the question. I began preparing a polite goodbye. Eyeing the wall unit, the photos of bearded faces. Could I pass close enough on my way out to get a look?

Ivan brought his can of Coke, sat down, and began to talk.

He told me about the first time he met Rosa, the summer she turned seventeen, when she worked at the mall. He told me about his big unruly family. He described Rosa's difficulty fitting in, Janet sticking up for her. He told me about Rosa teaching Lucy to sew and the quinceañera dress. He pointed to the photograph on the end table, taken at a wedding a month before Rosa's death. She'd made the boys' outfits. The last picture with the five of them together. He had others from that night, but— believe it or not—that was the best of the bunch. Without fail at least one child had their eyes shut, or was frowning or staring off into the distance.

"Law of nature," he said.

He smiled, remembering the gagging face Rosa made when Lucy described the chartreuse leopard print dress. After Rosa got off the phone, she said to Ivan it sounded like something a hooker would wear. The word she used, he told me, laughing, was *puta-licious.*

At the funeral it occurred to him that he would never hear his wife speak again. Her book had closed. A few days later he drove to the fabric store and the restaurant and asked them what they remembered. He learned that Rosa's last words on earth were when she checked to ensure that her children's chicken and noodles weren't spicy.

There had to be more words spoken, between her and Lucy in the car, prior to the crash. He would never know, though.

I sat in the prickly heat and listened, time slipping away, light ripening. Children ran by in the street, slap of sneakers and a basketball. How could they breathe in this air? Salt crusted my upper lip. I had stopped sweating. Ivan's voice had dropped to a near whisper; he was inhabiting the past. The leaf blower resumed its lament and I could scarcely hear what he was saying. Still I sat and I listened. I owed him that much.

The phone chimed, cutting him off in midsentence.

"Faster than a week," I said.

Ivan smiled faintly. He read the screen. His eyes narrowed. "It's Max."

"What did he say?"

"He's here."

CHAPTER 16

———

A SERIES OF CLICKS came from the front door, tumblers dropping, dead bolt shooting back, and I stood, wobbling on numb legs. I'd been sitting for forty minutes, listening to Ivan Arias's outpouring of grief, the forty minutes it took his son to get in the car or truck and drive over.

Max Arias stomped in and planted himself between the door and me. He wore scuffed work boots and loose denim shorts and an oversized T-shirt flecked with paint, standing with his thumbs and index fingers rigidly extended, like a child miming six-shooters.

"Who the fuck do you think you are," he said.

He was clean-shaven.

"Max," Ivan said. He had risen, too, blocking my path to the other point of exit, the sliding glass door.

The drowsiness had left me, driven out by a speedball of fight and flight.

Max Arias's T-shirt bore the logo of a lumber supply company. It bloused at the waist, wide enough to conceal a handgun. Cords stood out in his arms and neck. What

172 / JONATHAN KELLERMAN and JESSE KELLERMAN

had he and his father texted about? Why hadn't Ivan moved toward his son in greeting?

I said, "I'll go now."

"No no no," Max said. "You don't get to walk in, stir shit up, and walk out."

Ivan said, "Max."

"Your brother's too chickenshit to show his face?"

"I told your father, I'm here on my own."

"Why."

"I wanted to know if you'd spoken to Luke."

"Why the fuck would I do that?"

"Calm down, please," Ivan said.

"I'm calm, Pop. I'm asking questions. He asked his questions, now it's my turn. Why the fuck would I talk to your brother?"

"He said he might try to reach out to you," I said.

"He didn't."

"I understand."

"I don't," Max said. "I don't understand it at all. You want to know if he's talked to me, why don't you ask *him*?"

"I will when I speak to him."

"You didn't ask him."

"Not yet."

"Oh yeah? How come?"

"I haven't had a chance."

"You mean you didn't even try?"

"I haven't been able to reach him."

"He's a busy guy, huh."

"Sure."

"Yeah, sure," Max said. "Okay, well. Go ahead."

"Sorry?"

"Do it now. Give him a call him and ask."

"I don't know if he's available," I said.

"You haven't called him," Max said. "How do you know?"

A beat. I took out my phone.

"Put it on speaker," Max said.

I dialed Luke. It went straight to voicemail.

You've reached Luke Edison at Bay Area Therapeutics. Sorry I'm unavailable at the moment. Please leave your name, number, and a brief message, and I'll get back to you as soon as I can. Thanks and have a blessed day.

I hung up.

"You're not going to leave him a message? Your own brother?"

I said nothing.

"No," Max said. "I guess you're right, he's not available. Cause he's so busy. But it's too bad. I was hoping he could help me understand, you know? Cause, I dunno. *I* think it's kinda weird. I mean, you're a cop. It's your job to figure things out. You have a question about him, you don't ask him. You come here and ask my dad. You get him to ask me, and my brother, and my sister. Like, all the people in the world, it's our family who's the expert on him."

Ivan was watching me curiously.

"Is that it?" Max said. "You woke up this morning and said, *I have a question for my brother. Why don't I go talk to these people I've never met for no reason. That's what I'm in the mood to do.* Is that what you're telling me? Cause guess what? I don't fucking believe you."

"I asked you how he is," Ivan said. "You said it's hard for you to say."

I said, "Yes, sir."

"What does that mean?"

"I just . . . We're not close."

"You must speak to him," Ivan said. "You know that he wanted our forgiveness."

"Yes, sir."

"He told you he was coming here?"

"Not in so many words."

"What, then."

I said, "I talked to his wife."

"She said he came here."

"She wasn't sure if he had or hadn't."

Silence.

"Why are you here," Ivan asked. "Why today."

I glanced at Max. "Luke's gone."

"Gone where," Ivan said.

"He's missing."

"Your brother is."

I nodded.

"Missing how? What happened?"

"I don't know."

"You don't know if something happened to him?"

I said, "I'm not sure how to answer that."

"Answer it," Max said. "That's how."

In the silence I saw Ivan's face changing, falling like tumblers in a lock.

He said, "Are you accusing me of something?"

"No, sir."

"Are you accusing my son?"

"No."

Max snorted. "Okay, asshole."

Ivan said, "I let you into my home. I talked to you about her."

"I'm sorry."

"You let me do that. You looked me in the eye."

Max smiled sourly. "Why are you surprised by this, Pop? Same fucked-up family, same bullshit."

"Mr. Arias, I am very sorry."

Ivan felt for the arm of the recliner and lowered himself into the seat. He appeared both heavier and smaller; his belly staved in, he labored to breathe.

"I'd like you to leave, please," he said hoarsely.

"Yes, sir."

I faced the door.

Max didn't budge. A furious laugh exploded from him.

"What are you gonna do, man?" he said. "Shoot me? Choke me out?"

He flung his hands up over his head. "Go ahead. Unarmed."

"That's enough," Ivan said.

"What's wrong, Mr. Police Officer? You don't like how it feels when someone talks to you like that?"

"*Enough.*"

Max made a disgusted noise. He went behind the dining table.

Long shadows piled up on the lawn. A truck was parked in the driveway: a single-cab Toyota, navy blue. White lettering on the side of the bed read RAUL ARCELIA PERAL, LIC. CONTRACTOR. The bed didn't have a tonneau cover, though it did have a steel frame rack for securing lumber and tools.

Could a person confuse the two? Mistake that color for white?

Doubtful. Certainly not two separate people.

The front door opened. Max stepped from the house. He saw me looking at the truck.

I started for my car.

Max called, "I hope you never find him."

A FEW BLOCKS shy of the freeway, I veered to the curb, cut the engine, and sat, shaky and light-headed, strangling the steering wheel. Traffic hissed past, red streaks wiping the windshield. Each successive vehicle chunked against the same on-ramp pothole, like ax blows.

I climbed over the passenger seat, opened the door, leaned out, and tried to throw up, producing only dry heaves.

I slammed the door and fell back. My collar was damp

and curled. I rummaged in the center console for something solid to soak up the acid. I hadn't caught a proper meal in days. I wondered what my brother was eating. If he was eating.

All I could find was the ancient applesauce pouch. I uncapped it.

Amy Sandek would like FaceTime . . .

Taking three deep breaths, I connected. "Hey baby."

"Hi, hon." Her hair was flat and dark from the shower. Nursery rhymes tinkled in the background. "Are you in the car again? I can call you later."

I saw myself in the corner of the screen, a gray lump against gray. I punched on the dome light. "I'm just wiped out."

"I'm sorry. Hard day?"

"It was a day."

"Do you want to talk about it?"

Yes. Please. More than anything.

"Maybe later," I said. "Is she there?"

"She's almost ready for bed. Hang on."

The camera reversed. Charlotte sat on the bed, iPad in her lap, engrossed in YouTube.

"It's time to turn it off, honey pie."

"I don't want to."

"We said five minutes."

"I want *four* minutes."

"You got it, Priceline Negotiator."

"Hi, lovey."

No response.

"Say hi to Daddy."

"Hi, Daddy."

"How are you?"

"Good."

"I miss you."

Charlotte stared blankly. Moments like that brought home how young she was. She might possess the vocabulary of a child twice her age, but she had yet to absorb the social niceties.

"How was dinner?" I asked.

"Good."

"What did you get?"

"Mac and cheese."

Giddiness burbled up, my frayed nerves discharging. "Oh really. Not pizza?"

"Daddy, why are you laughing?"

"No reason, lovey. Was it yummy?"

"Uh-huh."

"Did you get dessert?"

"Uh-huh."

"What was it?"

"M&M's."

"Lucky girl. Did you say thank you to Mommy?"

"Thank you, Mommy."

"You're welcome, honey. Say good night to Daddy."

"Good night, Daddy."

"I love you, Charlotte."

"Mommy, I have to go poop."

"Can you get on the potty by yourself?" Amy said. "I'll come when it's time to wipe."

Charlotte dropped the phone. I saw the ceiling and heard her scamper out.

Amy came on the screen. "Mac and cheese is not the same as pizza."

"No."

"Totally different cuisines."

"Totally."

She smiled. "Hi."

"Hi."

"Good news. I booked our flights back."

Our conversation had carved out a small pocket of calm; instantly it was gone, like a mine collapse. "When?"

"Friday morning. We get into Oakland around ten."

Thirty-nine hours from now.

"Okay," I said.

"Don't get too excited."

"I am. I am. . . . I don't know if you saw. There's a new fire."

"Oh no. How bad?"

"They're saying it's going to get worse before it gets better."

"Ugh. I was really hoping to come home."

"I know. I so want you to."

True. I ached to have them near.

And not true, because I didn't know how I could manage the situation with them near.

I said, "We were concerned about the baby's health. It sucks, but nothing's changed on that count."

"Fine, but can we agree that that was an overreaction? It's not like hordes of pregnant women are fleeing the Bay Area."

"Why don't we see how things are in the morning?"

She scrutinized me. At times it can feel like being married to a mind reader. Only the fact that I was pixelated, on a five-inch screen, saved me.

"Okay," she said. "I love you."

"I love you, too. Have a good night."

Halfway home my mother called me. I let it go. She tried twice more and gave up.

EXCEPT SHE HADN'T. Coming up my block I saw her pinched shape pacing the front walk. I nearly made a U-turn. She spotted me and began bouncing on her toes, waving like a castaway. My father was there, too, on the porch, worrying the loose rail I hadn't gotten around to fixing.

I got out of the car and she rushed at me. "Why didn't you tell me Luke was missing?"

"Hang on a sec," I said. "Who told you that?"

"I saw it on Andrea's Facebook. I tried calling her but she won't tell me anything. I don't know what she expects me to do if she's not going to speak to me . . ."

She kept talking but I didn't listen, hurriedly swiping my phone.

Andrea Lamb • • •

One hour ago

****MISSING****LUKE EDISON****

Attention everybody, my husband Luke Edison has not been heard from in three days. He left the house on Sunday to take a drive and now he is not answering his phone. I am very concerned.

I am asking everyone to please spread this information so that we can find him as soon as possible and bring him home safely.

I am attaching a photo, please feel free to repost it. He is forty-one years old. He is six feet four inches tall with brown hair and . . . See More

The post had garnered a hundred and nine reactions, including likes, dislikes, crying emojis, shocked emojis, hearts. It had been shared eighty-one times.

"*Clay.*" My mother gripped my sleeve. "You're not listening."

I ushered them inside and into the living room. "Sit down, please."

"I don't want to sit down, I want you to tell me—Clay. Stop walking away from me."

I brought candles from the kitchen, lit them on the coffee table, took a chair. My father sat on the sofa. My mother stayed on her feet.

"When was the last time you heard from him?" I asked.

"You were aware this was going on and you didn't think to call us?" she said.

"Please stop yelling."

"Brunch," my father said.

"Not since then?"

He shook his head. He looked at my mother, who grunted in frustration and took the other end of the sofa.

"I don't remember," she said. "A few days."

"Check your phone."

She did. "Thursday."

"Do you remember what you talked about?"

"You should have called us."

Back and forth we went, like badminton, me asking about Luke, his marriage, finances, the loan, the Camaro, his behavior, the possibility of a relapse, while she pushed me on what I knew, what I'd done, why I hadn't called them, the police, *other* police.

"I've been busy."

"With what."

"Tracking him down."

"*How?*"

"I'm doing everything I can."

"You're one person, Clay. You can't—I just can't believe you've been letting this go by and not *once* did you think to pick up the phone."

"I didn't because I knew this was going to happen."

It was a dumb thing to say. I couldn't help myself. I was barreling along rusty old tracks, any semblance of restraint and professionalism kicked aside.

"What's *that* supposed to mean," she said.

"We cannot panic."

"Of *course* we should *panic*."

My father sat there as though catatonic. I knew what he was thinking about: The night he threw Luke out over the stolen necklace. Luke walking off with his middle fingers raised. My father's nose bleeding. My mother calling me up in tears, she and I driving the streets like deranged tourists.

This had happened before. Nobody called the police then, either.

Instead they called us, a week later, to tell us Luke was unconscious and what he'd done.

I said, "There's things you don't know—"

"So *tell me*!"

My father cut in quietly: "We're worried, Clay."

"Oh for God's sake," my mother said.

She shut her eyes and clasped her hands like a penitent. The bones of her forearm were prominent through crepey skin. She's always been lean. She was a collegiate long-jumper and excelled in several high school sports, including basketball. In childhood photos she wears her hair in a long braid, better to keep it out of her face while she runs and jumps. It had since thinned, as had the rest of her, stuffing pulled out by stress.

It struck me that both Luke and I had married our mother—deconstructed. Her form was Amy's. Her spirit was Andrea's. I doubted any of them would admit to any of it. But it helped explain something I'd never quite understood: why it was me living six blocks from my parents, while Luke had withdrawn to the hills.

An Amy could get along with a Mom. An Amy could get along with an Andrea.

But Mom and Andrea? They were both battling for the same ragged soul, each convinced they knew what was best for him.

My father said, "Tell us what we can do."

"What I need from you is to wait."

My mother opened her eyes. "You want us to sit on our hands."

"If you have a suggestion for where I should look, by all means tell me."

"I need an Advil," she said, rising.

I offered to bring it to her. She muttered that she was capable of getting it herself and went down the hall.

My father said, "I saw your email."

"I was hoping you and I could speak first."

"She feels a little deceived," he said. "Your coming to me separately reinforces that."

"You told her?"

"No. I didn't want to upset her even more than she is already. I trust you have your reasons for going about this the way you are and that you're doing the best you can. But—if I may offer a perspective?"

"Sure."

"It does look like you're dealing with a lot by yourself."

"I am. But that doesn't mean I'm not dealing with it. And you're right. I have my reasons."

"It might help if you shared them with her."

"It also might not."

He nodded. "That's true."

Unflappable. The veteran teacher's badge of honor.

He started right out of college, for four-plus decades working off the same lesson plans, performing the same in-class demonstrations. The bowling ball pendulum; the egg drop challenge. He's taught multiple generations, a constancy that's made him a beloved figure at his school. From him I received my analytical nature. The urge, when confronted with the unexpected, to move forward rather than away.

He slipped off his glasses and cleaned them on his shirt, reminding me uncomfortably of Ivan Arias. In another life they would get along just fine. "How are Amy and Charlotte?"

"They're having a good time in L.A."

"You're ready to have them back."

I nodded.

"You have a wonderful family," he said.

Pressure built behind my eyes. "Thank you."

He checked the lenses for clarity. The candle flames reflected and flickered. Perfect opportunity for a mini-lecture on refraction and the speed of light through a medium.

"We did this," he said.

"Did what."

He replaced his glasses and unfurled his arms, as if to suggest he had created the world from scratch. "Your mother and I. Together. It's our fault."

"Don't say that."

"Why shouldn't I? It's a fact."

"You're not responsible for him."

He gave me a pitying smile.

Of course we are.

MY MOTHER RETURNED from the bathroom. A truce had been composed in her own mind, no need to involve me.

I promised to call her with any news. She promised the same.

At the front door she threw herself against me. It had been many years since I felt her body next to mine. It was an unfamiliar feeling. I didn't know what to do with it. I don't think she did, either, though she kept pulling on me, hanging on my neck like a yoke, searching for a way to fit together.

CHAPTER 17

———

OPENED ANDREA'S FACEBOOK page and clicked SEE MORE.

> I am attaching a photo, please feel free to repost it. He is forty-one years old. He is six feet four inches tall with brown hair and light brown eyes, his beard is light reddish brown. He has a tattoo of a crown on the inside of his left arm (see photos). He was last seen wearing jeans and a blue T-shirt.
>
> Please get in touch with me if you know anything!!
>
> Please spread the word!!

A close-up of Luke's face, setting indeterminate. A wider shot, Luke shirtless, hoeing on their plot, his hard-earned musculature round and slick as river rocks, the tattoo visible.

Comments expressed concern, offered help and/or support, promised to pass along the news or put up flyers. Some wondered if she'd called the police. She hadn't answered them, and she'd had enough common sense not to mention Rory Vandervelde by name. But a user named G M Duggan asked another important question.

> Andrea I'm so sorry to hear this. What car was he driving

I opened her response.

> Its a bright green Camaro with black stripes thank u Gareth!!!

Facebook posts did not show up in ordinary searches. The effect of her going public was not yet apparent. Where the information might travel next, I had no idea.

The fuse was burning that much faster.

It was ten p.m. Official inquiries would have to wait for morning.

Unofficially, the night was young.

I CALLED EDMOND VALDEZ, the property clerk.

"Clay?" Sleep muddied his voice. "What time is it?"

"Sorry, man. Didn't mean to wake you up."

"S'okay. I was watching TV, musta passed out. What's going on?"

"We had a removal in Fremont today. The guy on the bike?"

". . . oh yeah."

"So I just got a call from his girlfriend. At the time of the accident he was carrying some of her stuff in his backpack. I didn't realize when I checked it in. Any way I can go grab it for her?"

"Now?"

"She's leaving the hospital and she's gonna be locked out of her apartment."

It was a plausible story. Similar things happened every so often. That they'd never happened to me added to the plausibility.

Edmond snuffled tiredly and gave me his locker combination. "Don't forget to update the tag."

"Right on. Appreciate it, man. Good night."

I showered and put on my last clean uniform. Tomorrow was my day off. The routine included taking Charlotte to the dry cleaner to collect whatever Amy had dropped off on Monday.

The dry cleaner was closed.

My family was in another world.

I filled a backpack with items I thought I might need and drove to the bureau.

A CCTV CAMERA goosenecked over the entrance. I didn't look at it. Nor did I look away. I kept my gaze level, like a person who belonged there.

I swiped my keycard, leaving a record of my entry, and walked deserted corridors under more cameras. The health lab was closed. The crime lab was closed. Only a skeleton crew of coroners was on site to cope with the victims of the night. The whole week had been slow. People sheltering. Less street crime. Fewer traffic accidents. Death never quits, but it had lifted its thumb off the scale, temporarily.

That night the deputy coroners on duty were Kat Davenport and Stevie Dixon. The sergeant was John Gruenhut. I knew all of them. I knew everyone, in every room, on every floor, day or night. They were my colleagues and my friends.

Outside the men's locker room I listened for running water. Heard nothing and went in and opened Edmond's locker.

Spare shirt. Spare towel. Deodorant. Bag of Sour Patch Kids.

The purple key carabiner.

I took it up to the second floor, let myself into his office, and unlocked the safe, using his computer to locate the keys to Rory Vandervelde's lockers. I stole them. I didn't bother with Fletcher Kohn's keys. I needed cover, not a ruined bike or a split helmet.

A camera hung over the property room door. I swiped my keycard.

Rory Vandervelde's belongings filled four lockers, a glittering assortment of small goods, individually bagged. Cuff links. Tie clips. Nancy Yap's pearls, her colossal diamond studs. Meds. The watches occupied two entire lockers.

Jed Harkless and Lindsey Bagoyo hadn't taken any of the other collections for safekeeping. A choice that might seem odd, but I understood. Once they started down that road, there was no end. If they took the antique knives, did they have to take the baseball cards? If they took the cards, did they have to take the footballs? Jerseys? Art? Car keys? They couldn't take everything.

The problem was that Vandervelde owned everything. Not a problem we often faced. Rich people tend not to get shot or shoot themselves or perish from exposure in alleyways. They die as they live: on their own terms.

In the bottom locker I found the house keys, five of them on an engraved silver fob. RWV.

I stole them and exited through the intake bay to the vehicle lot, passing beneath a red neon CORONER'S BUREAU sign, the sole surviving relic of the old morgue building, where for the better part of a century it hung over the sidewalk, burning luridly.

When we moved to the new building—ten years on, everyone still called it that—the decision was made to mount the sign out back, away from the gaze of anyone who might deem it in poor taste. It was supposed to evoke a sense of continuity, a romantic past.

Tonight, to save electricity, the sign had been switched off.

I still thought of myself as new, too. But that was fantasy. I'd spent most of my adult life here.

Seven vehicles lined the wall: three body vans, three Explorers, and the hulking mobile command center. A collection not quite worthy of Rory William Vandervelde.

I opened the middle van's rear doors, releasing a cloud of disinfectant fumes.

Gurneys. Sheets. Body bags. Shrink-wrapped disposable coveralls. Tool kit. Smaller miscellany: nitrile gloves, N95s, spare camera batteries, baby wipes.

Still Life, with Death.

I stole what I needed.

SEVEN MINUTES LATER I was easing over the speed bump on Kilmarnock Court, past the sign forbidding entrance to anyone other than members of the Chabot Park Summit Homeowners' Association or their guests. The paving smoothed out and I coasted between the trees.

Rory Vandervelde's driveway gates were shut. I parked around the bend, put on a mask, and doubled back on foot. Behind hedges and walls the estate homes brooded. With their hollow windows and high flat faces they resembled the lopped-off heads of giants.

I pulled on a crumpled pair of gloves and jumped the fence to Vandervelde's property, landing in a clump of sword ferns. I climbed from the planting bed and started up the driveway.

Even that much modest effort had my lungs on fire. I coughed and pounded as though I could jar loose the obstruction. But the obstruction was the air itself.

To my left, to my right, security cameras laid their blind stare on me.

I imagined the power surging on, exposing me—wouldn't that be opportune?

Streetlights, stoplights, neon, chandeliers, sconces, desk lamps, table lamps, floor lamps; microwaves chirping and printers booting up and idiotic oven clocks flashing twelve; an army of zombie devices resuming assigned tasks as though no time had passed.

Children jarred from their dreams, crying out.

And me, hiking up the hill to a dead man's house.

BENEATH FILTHY SCUDDING CLOUDS, the empty motor court looked immense. I hurried over it and took the front steps two at a time, preparing to commit my fourth crime of the evening. Or fifth, or sixth. Who could keep track?

A sticker joined the door to the jamb. Another covered the lock.

WARNING

ANY PERSON BREAKING OR MUTILATING THIS SEAL
OR ENTERING THESE PREMISES WILL BE PROSECUTED
TO THE FULLEST EXTENT OF THE LAW—AUTHORITY
27491.3 CA GOV'T CODE
ALAMEDA COUNTY SHERIFF'S OFFICE
CORONER'S BUREAU

Both seals were signed by Harkless, dated Tuesday, with a time of 1617.

Both were broken.

Jagged edges. Someone pushing through impatiently.

Neither lock nor frame showed sign of forced entry.

I drew my gun, clicked on my flashlight, and, pointing it down, let myself in.

The foyer was humid, overhung with a gamy odor. Absent the yellow evidence markers, the living room resembled the aftermath of a kegger.

I let my backpack down to the marble and paused to listen.

Feeble scratching, from deep in the house.

I crept after it, into the hallway, following the blood trail.

The sound got louder and more frenetic. The smell redoubled.

I reached the fork that led to the kill zone, paused again.

Close now.

I dared to extend my head.

A section of baseboard had been sawn away to allow retrieval of the slug. The pool of blood had shrunk down to black enamel, shot through with cracks, like the inside of a saucepan accidentally left on the fire. Constellation of spatter. Drag marks into the office.

The scratching noise was coming from there.

Frantic, staticky, animal.

I edged up and pivoted into the doorway, sweeping the beam, trigger at the ready.

The desk had been ransacked. Papers littered the floor. The Rolodex was in place but the silver-framed snapshots were knocked over. The desk window was thrown open to the night.

Wind gusted in, flapping a plastic shopping bag on the blotter.

I lowered the sash. The air went limp, the bag drooped, the scratching sound died.

I played the flashlight over the display cases. The bathroom door was shut.

In the bag were a pair of baseballs, the '89 World Series commemorative autographed by Eck and another with what looked like Ken Griffey, Jr.'s signature. There was a Nolan Ryan rookie card in a hard protective case. The makings of a nice little shopping spree.

I started forward to check the bathroom.

A faint cough wheeled me around.

I moved back into the hall, toward the next door, the next, drawn by a living presence. We know when others are near. We crave them and fear them and sometimes we destroy them.

I came to a door. The parlor. Where the knives were kept.

The emanation changed. It listened back. It felt me, too.

CHAPTER 18

——

SEAN VANDERVELDE WAS leaning over a display table, its lid raised forty-five degrees, using his phone's flashlight to browse. He was wearing the same jeans and polo and had a black bandanna pressed to his nose and mouth, and when I charged in yelling *police hands hands hands* he tripped over his own feet, dropping the phone with a soft thud and sending up the cloth like a penalty flag.

"Get down. Let me see your hands. *Hands*."

He didn't put up a fight. I rolled him onto his stomach. He reeked of booze.

"Get the *fuck* off me."

I frisked him, released him, stood back as he crawled toward his phone.

"I'm going to sue your dick off," he slurred.

He pulled himself up on a club chair. His eyes went wide. "The fuck are you doing here."

"Let's start by asking you that."

"It's my house."

"It's sealed. Maybe you noticed that on the way in, when you violated the order."

A bottle of Japanese scotch sat uncorked on the mantel. He grabbed it down and took a belt.

"I saw the stuff in the office," I said. "What else have you taken?"

He took another swallow. Flexed his elbow. "You fucked up my arm."

"Mr. Vandervelde, what else have you taken?"

"*Nothing*. I haven't taken anything. Nothing's left the premises."

"What else have you touched?"

His gaze strayed to the open display table. I inspected it. Knives in an intact grid, five by five. He hadn't finished making his selection before I tackled him.

I shut the lid. "What else?"

"Nothing that isn't mine."

"You can work that out on your own time."

"I'm not talking about all of it," he said petulantly. "There's things that belong to me, that he gave *to me*. The baseball . . . There's a knife, he bought it for me when I was twelve. It's sentimental value, *she* won't miss it."

"So you decided to help yourself."

"Like she isn't going to do the same thing."

"She's not the one breaking and entering. How'd you get in?"

"Hopped the fence." He tipped the bottle toward me with a small smile. Proud of his agility.

"How'd you get into the house."

"I have a key."

"I'll take it, please."

"I don't have to do that."

"I don't have to arrest you, either."

Defiance puffed up his chest. But it was a chemical bravery, swiftly dissipated. He fished the key out and tossed it to me. Flimsy wire ring; plastic tab with a paper insert. DAD.

"Have you been into any of the other rooms?"

"Just the office."

"What about the desk? What'd you take?"

"God's sake, *nothing*."

"What were you looking for?"

"His will."

"It's not here," I said. "We have it."

A long silence.

"What does it say?" he asked.

"Ask the lawyer for a copy."

"I don't trust a thing that cocksucker says."

"Come on. Time to go."

He bent to grab the bandanna and almost keeled over. Scotch splashed the rug. With exaggerated, drunken care, he folded the bandanna into quarters, covered his nose and mouth, and walked ahead of me into the hall.

A few steps along he halted, staring at the giant bloodstain.

He must have seen it on his way in. Maybe he'd been too intoxicated to care; too hell-bent on collecting his birthright.

He wheezed through the cloth, causing it to pouch in and bulge out. The bottle tilted, about to spill. I put a hand on his shoulder and he allowed himself to be led to the foyer.

"Last chance," I said. "This is a crime scene. Did you take or touch anything else?"

"No."

"That?"

Sean peered at the scotch. "You can't be serious."

"I'm serious."

He feinted as if he were going to shotgun the booze, then gave an arrogant snicker. I realized then that my backpack was directly behind him, in the shadow of the entry table. He hadn't seen it. If he did, he might wonder what was inside. Why I had a backpack with me in the first place.

He set the bottle delicately on the tiles. Curtsied. "As you wish."

I steered him outside and over the motor court. He moved with a shambling gait, loafers scraping.

"How'd you get here?" I asked.

"Uber."

"Call it."

Down by the gates, I picked my way through the planting bed to the shrub that concealed the motor unit. I lifted off the housing, grasped the crank, and began winding. The gates parted with excruciating slowness. I opened them eighteen inches and we shimmied through.

I walked him to the curb. I needed to make sure he was good and gone.

"All I wanted was the Ken Griffey, Jr.," he said. "That's all. There was a baseball card show and we went. He *took* me. Stood in line for two hours to get it autographed. All right? I didn't . . . I could've taken anything, there's things worth more. Way more."

I didn't point out that the shopping bag held several other collectibles.

Headlights drew near. A black Escalade pulled up.

"Have a good night, Mr. Vandervelde."

I started for the gates.

"Hang on," Sean said.

I pretended not to hear him.

"Hey. I said wait."

I turned. I could see him blundering toward sobriety, his native intelligence piqued. "I need to close the gates," I said.

The driver peeked out at us. "For Sean?"

"One minute," Sean said.

The driver withdrew.

Sean said to me, "How did you know I was here?"

"We received a call from one of the neighbors. They must've seen you climbing the fence."

I didn't stick around for the follow-up questions.

Why would a coroner respond to a break-in?

Where was my vehicle?

Why was I wearing gloves?

"Safe travels," I said and slipped through the gates.

IN RORY VANDERVELDE's office I spun the Rolodex to *L*.

Three from the end.

Luke Camaro guy

My brother's phone number.

I pulled out the card.

It was my first proof of a prior relationship between the two men.

Exasperated as I was with Andrea, I didn't think she'd lied about not recognizing Vandervelde's name. Which meant Luke had chosen to withhold that relationship from her.

She wouldn't approve. Or he knew better than to try to interest her. She had more important things on her mind.

I pocketed the card and spun the Rolodex to a random entry.

The last time I was here—two days and a hundred years ago—I'd gone through the desk.

Maybe I'd missed something.

A quick search of the drawers failed to turn up a Camaro key or a car key of any kind.

But I'd planned for this contingency.

I restored the baseballs and cards to their cases, sheaved the loose papers in a file folder, stood the snapshots up on the desktop.

I retrieved the bottle of scotch from the foyer and replaced it behind the living room bar.

I shouldered my backpack, left the house, and walked to the garage.

Frail moonlight filtered through the redwoods. Grit blew steadily into my face. The hangar door was cranked shut. Harkless and Bagoyo had gone to town: three seals on each side, four at the bottom, and four more along the top.

The pedestrian door had one over the jamb and one over the lock.

Intellectually, I'd accepted the necessity of what I was about to do. It was no worse than anything else I had done in the last two days: destroying and removing evidence, misrepresenting myself, intruding on a private citizen, lying to my colleagues and my wife.

Nevertheless my hands shook as I used a plastic knife to scrape the seals from the pedestrian door. The paper was designed to show signs of tampering. No matter how slowly I went, it shredded into wisps. One at a time I peeled them off, cleaning the surfaces with adhesive remover.

Letting myself in with the stolen house keys, I crossed the display floor to the Camaro.

I took out another set of items lifted from the body van: a vehicle lockout kit, consisting of a plastic wedge, a second inflatable wedge, and a rod with a curved tip.

With the flashlight in my teeth I worked the plastic wedge between the driver's-side door and the frame to create a thin gap, which I widened incrementally with the inflatable wedge. The Camaro's door locks were flared like golf tees. I inserted the rod and snagged the top of the lock.

Hesitated. I didn't want to set off an alarm.

Late-sixties Camaros didn't have alarms.

Unless Luke had added one.

He liked to rhapsodize about the art and science of vintage car restoration. What to preserve. What to modernize. Which changes raised value and which lowered it. I tended to zone out. Now I wished I'd listened.

In for a penny.

I popped the lock.

The door opened silently.

I got behind the wheel.

The seat, upgraded from vinyl to leather, was soft and cool through my clothes, its stitching neat as Braille. Woodwork like velvet. Mirror-bright chrome. I curled my fingers around the gearshift and it felt alive. Everything from knobs to vents was solid and crisp and perfect, as if the Camaro had rolled off the showroom that morning, ready to eat up the road.

It was a beautiful car, a stunning achievement; the culmination of a process begun when my brother walked out of prison half a man. Hours and hours alone under the hood, fixing, polishing; keeping company with the trees, with the deer and the sparrows; with his thoughts, and memories, and guilt. Man and machine, evolving, improving, together.

A sad, breathless admiration filled me.

This might be all that was left of him.

The glove box held the registration, a box of tissues, and a chocolate protein shake.

I reached beneath the seats to unearth a paperback. *Achieving—and Sustaining!—a Growth Mindset.*

I popped the trunk.

Jumper cables, bundled car cover, tire patch kit. I lifted the cover on a black pouch, a larger version of the one Andrea used to protect herself from the dangerous tumor-causing radiation emitted by her phone.

Inside the pouch was a space-gray MacBook.

I touched the power button. Dead.

I tucked the laptop in my backpack, cleaned up, and exited the garage.

———

I'D BROUGHT ALONG several blank coroner's seals. Copying the date and time from the original seals, doing my best to forge Harkless's atrocious signature, I applied the new seals to the garage door.

I repeated the process at the main house. Erasing proof of my trespassing, but also Sean's. Now neither of us had been there.

Eleven minutes later I was pulling up to the bureau.

I returned the lockout kit to the body van.

I returned Rory Vandervelde's house keys to the property room, sealing them in a new evidence bag that I filled out with Harkless's name and the old time and date.

In Edmond's office I put the locker keys in the master safe. I updated the tag on Fletcher Kohn's locker keys to make it appear as though I had used them.

Down in the men's room I replaced the purple carabiner in Edmond's locker.

I kept Sean Vandervelde's house key.

It was one thirty in the morning. My keycard had been active innumerable times. Cameras had caught me coming and going. But no one would review the log. No one would watch the tape. On the off chance that they did, I had a compelling excuse: I was going beyond the call of duty to help a grieving woman in need.

A few inconsistencies marred that story. It did not, for instance, account for why I'd left the bureau, only to return several hours later. I wasn't worried. The people in this building were my colleagues and friends. We had a culture, a culture I had helped to foster, grounded in trust. Ten years is a long time.

I emerged into the hall.

"Clay?"

Kat Davenport was walking toward me. She smiled and drew me in for a shoulder bump. "What's up, dude?"

Davenport was a relative newcomer. She'd never worked in the old building. I'd spent a year with her on night shift, our bond cemented by the trauma of digging up an infant buried in a public park. For months nobody came forward to claim the remains. The family turned out to be a bunch of homicidal neo-Nazis.

She said, "What brings you here at this godforsaken hour?"

I told Kat Davenport the Fabulous Tale of Fletcher Kohn's Girlfriend.

She shook her head. "Get outta here, bro. You look like shit."

THE DRIVE HOME was too short for the laptop to charge. I hung my uniform in the bathroom for reuse and went to the Great Wall of Cardboard.

Column three, second from the top: BREAD MACHINE.

I took down a different box, labeled BOOKS (CLAY).

Stack of noir, biography of Jerry West, nine-hundred-page history of Europe that I'd never read, and an equally weighty tome called *A Practical Guide to Death Investigation* that I had.

I pried out the history book and riffled its pages. Tucked into the chapter about the Ottoman wars was a personal check, made out to my daughter in the amount of a quarter of a million dollars and signed by a man whose missing sister I had found. The case was an outgrowth of the investigation into the dead infant in the park. I'd solved it off the clock. I'd never submitted the requisite paperwork for permission to moonlight and thus was not entitled to any compensation.

I rubbed the check between my fingers. It felt strangely insubstantial, as though the amount of money it represented ought to give it more weight. What I should have done was tear it up a long time ago. It was a temptation and a comfort; half insurance policy, half grenade. Cashing it would cause problems. Could, conceivably, kill my career.

If that wasn't dead already.

CHAPTER 19

——

Thursday. Eighty-six hours in the dark.

ON A BICYCLE I zigzagged the bombed-out avenues of a dreary industrial town, Rust Belt or Eastern Europe, miles of sterile apartment blocks and belching smokestacks. My legs jerked like ungreased pistons, the frame bucked wildly, an unbroken horse fighting to throw me; pedals scraped, metal shrieked, sparks flew, a shovel trenched the inside of my skull.

I swatted the phone chirping on the nightstand.

My pillow was soaked. The bedroom was icy and viscous, dark as the inside of a barrel.

Too dark for six thirty.

I lifted the phone. Six thirty.

Stumbling over to the window, I drew back the curtain on a world gone wrong.

The sky was molten orange. There was no horizon. No skyline. No clouds. No depth whatsoever: Haze grouted the empty space, flattening everything into a single, imminent sheet, the vaults of heaven pressing down on my rain gutters.

I touched the glass. It was freezing.

Every instinct screamed not to go outside. That to do so was to invite death.

I put on my unclean uniform.

Smoke and mist made a frigid slurry that stuck to my skin as I walked to my car. I knew it was there but I couldn't smell anything at all.

UNION CITY MARKED the southernmost limit of the shut-off zone. I lurched through traffic toward the Dumbarton Bridge, driving like an amateur. I wasn't the only one. The sun had never risen. Nobody had woken up. Vehicles appeared from nowhere, surging up out of the murk and vanishing just as suddenly. In twelve miles I'd passed three accidents.

I told the phone to call Amy.

"Good morning," she said. "How was your night?"

"I've had better."

"I'm so sorry. Is it smoky in the house? It sounds like you're in the car again."

"Charging," I said, which was true: I had Luke's laptop on the passenger seat. "What's on the agenda for today?"

"I think we're just going to hang out here and swim. I feel like we've filled our virtuous educational activity quota for the week. Should we talk about tomorrow?"

"Tomorrow?"

"We were supposed to discuss coming home."

"Have you seen what's happening up here?"

"No."

"Check the news."

"Hang on."

She was gone for a minute.

"Oh my God," she said. "What *is* that?"

"I have no idea."

I'd meant to coax her into staying put. But of course she reacted as I knew she would.

"Get out of there, Clay. Please."

"I don't know if I can."

"What do you mean? Go to the airport. Take the first flight."

A FedEx truck stopped short. I stomped the brake.

"Can we see how the day goes?" I said. "I need to get a few things done around here."

"Honey. Whatever it is, it can wait."

"I'm concerned they might call me in."

"To work? Did they say that?"

"They might." I hated myself. "It's not as bad as it looks. The air smells better, actually."

"Clay. The actual sky is falling."

"Please don't get mad at me."

"I'm not mad, I'm confused."

"Believe me, I would like nothing more than to see you right now."

"So?"

My body hurt, my soul hurt, lies piling up like bad debt. "I'm asking, please, if we can talk about it later."

A beat.

"Whatever you want," she said.

"Thank you. Is she around?"

"One sec . . . Say hi to Daddy."

"Hi, Daddy," Charlotte said.

The sound of her voice was unbearable. My voice broke in reply. "Hi, lovey. How are you?"

"Good."

"Are you being a good girl for Mommy?"

No answer.

"She really is," Amy said.

"That's great. I'm so proud of you. I hope you both have a wonderful day."

"Say thank you."

"Thank you, Daddy."

A honk prodded at my back.

"You're welcome. I love you, Charlotte."

"I love you, too," Charlotte said.

"Thank you for saying that, lovey."

"You're welcome, too."

PAST THE TOLL PLAZA, the highway sank flush with the surrounding marshlands. The waters of the Bay were the same uniform, saturated orange as the sky and their surface oddly featureless and still, a lack of natural motion that was not tranquil but desolate. Commuters to either side of me jabbered in their steel cages. Overcome by claustrophobia, I cracked the window. Stiff brackish air flooded in. I quickly shut the window and told the phone to call Andrea.

No answer. I called Billy Watts, the Berkeley detective I'd been playing phone tag with, and left him a voicemail. I switched on the radio and let it babble while I crept over the bridge into Menlo Park, low and dry as a griddle.

Stanford Hospital was a concrete abscess amid the stucco and red tile of the university. The receptionist at the cancer center told me that Dr. Yap was in clinic.

"Can I leave her a note? It's an urgent matter."

The receptionist frowned. What could be more urgent than cancer? "I can't guarantee she'll get back to you."

I gave her my card and headed to the lobby. Wan residents lined up for the coffee cart. My order of six espresso shots did not impress the barista. I dumped in dairy and sugar and occupied a bench near a power outlet.

Luke's laptop prompted me for a password. Using the list Andrea had given me, I got in on the second try.

Feeling deliriously lucky, I opened the browser. Google defaulted to his work account. I clicked over to his personal account. The password autofilled. Angels sang.

Everything that had come into his Gmail since Saturday was spam. I put *Vandervelde* and *Rory* into the search bar and got nothing.

Camaro, on the other hand, summoned hundreds of hits. Luke ordering parts. Guys offering to buy the car from him. Guys sending proud pictures of their own Camaros, like birth announcements. *One hundred eighty-eight inches! Thirty-seven hundred pounds! Everyone is doing great.*

I came to an email, two years old, subject line blank, sender RWV.

Luke

Good meeting you. Happy to show you the collection whenever it suits you. Phone is best.

Take care

R

PS You ever change your mind on the Camaro I have dibs

Contact information followed. I dialed the number.

This is Rory. I'm unavailable at the moment.

I'd never heard his voice. Thinner than I'd expected. I disconnected.

The email was the one and only communication from RWV, no hint of how they'd met or if Luke had taken him up on the invitation. Scrolling back I discovered a promotional email for a swap meet held the weekend prior. Luke regularly drove three or more hours for such events, mostly to spectate, sometimes to deal.

Good bet Vandervelde frequented the same events. No matter that he could buy any car he wanted. The thrill was in the chase. In the tribal sense of belonging. Sizing up the competition. Comparing rides.

A place where guys like Rory and guys like Luke, men from vastly different universes, could become friends.

What a beauty. How much you want for her?

She's so sweet. Think I might hold on to her a little while.

The last website Luke had visited, at four twenty-four Sunday afternoon, was the Wikipedia page for Bentley Azures.

Before that, he'd read up on Ferrari Testarossas.

Before that: Davis Divan. A quirky miniature with three wheels.

Koenigsegg One:1.

In the hours before his disappearance, Luke had made fourteen similar searches, all for vehicles in Rory Vandervelde's car barn. As though cramming for an exam.

My phone rang with a 650 number. A brisk voice said, "This is Nancy Yap. I only have a few minutes."

"I'll be right up."

"Come to the cafeteria."

SHE WAS AT the register when I got there, shepherding a tray with a salad and a bottle of green juice. Spotting me, she flung a hand toward the tables, *any table, pick one.*

Her white coat billowed as she approached and sat. "You don't mind if I eat."

She was even more luminously beautiful in person than in the vacation photo, notwithstanding the effects of acute stress: lopsided hair and one lapel folded over.

"Please. I appreciate your taking the time, Doctor. First off, my condolences."

"I assume this is about the body. I spoke to someone from your office yesterday. Harden?"

"Harkless."

She gulped juice, wiped her mouth. "He said the autopsy was complete and you'd be ready to release it today. He assured me he'd inform the funeral home."

"Deputy Harkless is out of the office, but someone will handle it."

"As long as we get it done today. Rory's son is throwing a tantrum. He told my lawyer he's filing for a restraining order."

"From what I read the will provides instructions for burial."

"It does, but I'd prefer not to have to go to court to get it enforced, and I don't want Rory lying in a mortuary basement for weeks and months. Just so you know," she said, prying open the plastic clamshell, "I didn't ask for any of this. I begged him not to do it. He wouldn't budge."

"As soon as we're done I'll call my office and make sure they're aware of the situation."

"I'd appreciate it." She raised a forkful of leaves, paused. "Is that not why you're here? They told me you said it was urgent."

"I have a few questions about Mr. Vandervelde's activities prior to his passing."

"I've been over this several times."

"I realize that, and I'm sorry to make you repeat yourself."

She put down the fork and sighed. Solemn, as if delivering bad news to a patient.

"I last saw him on Saturday night. My daughter's boyfriend came in from out of town and the four of us went out to dinner. We met at seven, at a restaurant in San Mateo. Wursthall. Rory was in a good mood and I noticed nothing unusual about his behavior. He didn't drink more than usual. He didn't seem preoccupied or concerned for his safety. I suggested he spend the night at my house, rather than have to drive home. He declined and left the restaurant around nine."

"Did he give a reason for not staying?"

"No. But I'm used to it."

A wisp of irritation. She caught herself and softened. "It's not his fault. He's a light sleeper. He wakes up when I turn over, or he gets up to go to the bathroom and can't fall back asleep. It's more comfortable for him in his own bed. The majority of the nights I'm in Oakland I end up in a guest room. So I always ask, but I don't expect him to say yes."

"Did you talk to him on Sunday?"

"He called in the afternoon to let me know his power had gone out. I wanted him to move in with me for a few days, so he wouldn't have to go without air-conditioning. I told him I'd take the guest room and give him the master. He said he'd think about it. That was the last time we spoke."

Her posture caved under the weight of finality. Only for a second: She snatched up the fork and tore into her salad, eating against the clock. "That's it."

"Are you aware of anyone else he might've been in contact with on Sunday?"

"No."

"Is it possible he went home on Saturday intending to meet someone the next day?"

"Who would he be meeting?"

I'd touched a nerve. If Sean was to be believed, his mother was still alive when Nancy Yap and Rory Vandervelde took up together. Like any relationship begun in infidelity, theirs contained the anxious seeds of its own undoing. Rory had strayed once. Why wouldn't he do it again?

"A repair person, for example," I said. "Or a friend."

"He didn't say so, but that doesn't mean there wasn't. We respected each other's space. That's one of the things that made it work. We knew what to expect from each other. At this stage of life, you can't start recalibrating who you are. Service people, his housekeeper doesn't come on the weekends. It's a big house, though. Something's always breaking."

She shoveled in another mouthful of leaves. "I told the detective all of this."

"Our departments work in parallel."

"That seems less than efficient."

It was, as was my entire line of questioning. I was circling toward the crux of the matter, trying not to stoke suspicion. "Mr. Vandervelde was something of a collector."

That got a laugh. Bits of green showed in her teeth. It took the austere edge off her good looks, made her human and fallible. "One way to describe it."

"Say he was going to buy or sell something of significant value. Would he discuss it with you?"

"I guess it depends on what. Not that he needed my permission."

"A car."

"You seem to have an idea of what you're after."

I took a chance. "The garage door was left open."

"When?"

"It was like that when we responded to the call. I wondered if he had a meeting set up with a potential buyer or seller. Or he was showing the collection to someone. Do you recall him talking about anything like that?"

"No, I—no."

She frowned, lost in troubled thoughts.

"He had a man who worked on the cars," she said finally. "He used to come to the house."

I remembered the bespoke mechanic's station. "Used to."

"Rory fired him. Months ago."

"What's this person's name?"

"Sammy."

"Last name?"

"I don't know. I don't think I ever knew it."

"Why did Mr. Vandervelde fire him?"

"He scratched one of the cars. Rory drives some of them more than others, so it's part of the duties to take them out in rotation and keep the batteries charged. Rory noticed a scratch on the bumper—the Porsche, I think it was. Sammy panicked and denied it. He accused Rory of doing it and trying to blame him. He said Rory needed to get his eyes checked. Due to his age. You can imagine how well that went over."

"Did it get acrimonious?"

"Well, I don't think anyone came away happy."

"Was there any physical violence?"

The question jolted her. "Of course not. You don't think I would've told the detective that?"

"What did you tell him?"

"Nothing. I didn't think of it at the time." To avoid being labeled a person who didn't think of things, she added, "Like I said, it happened months ago, and anyway, Rory's fired hundreds of people over the years. He had two thousand employees at one point. Sometimes you have to let people go. It's inevitable. He hired his current housekeeper because the old one loved Martha and was rude to me. She refused to make my bed."

Her watch dinged. She tapped the screen. "I have to go."

"One more question, please, Doctor. Had Mr. Vandervelde found a replacement?"

"For Sammy?"

I nodded.

"Not that I know of. I'm sure he meant to get around to it at some point. The cars are a lot of work. Rory wasn't going to do it himself."

I was reevaluating Luke's browser history in light of what she'd told me.

Not just a casual visit. A job interview.

Would Luke leave a cushy start-up to become a glorified mechanic?

He might. No need to broach the subject with Andrea, though, not before he'd sat with Rory, talked it over, figured out for himself what he wanted. Same went for telling me or my parents or Scott. We'd criticize the move as a step down, the latest in a series of questionable choices.

Nancy Yap dabbed at her lips, getting ready to leave.

I said, "Did he ever mention the name Tom?"

"I don't think so. Who is that? Is this connected to Sammy?"

"Not necessarily. What about Scott?" I said, grabbing more names out of the air, insulation to hide the real question. "Or James or Luke? Any of those ring a bell?"

"No."

"What about these last names: Starks, Lamb, Edison."

Her watch dinged again. She stood, tapping. ". . . no. Sorry, excuse me . . ."

She hurried out, taking the juice and leaving me to clear her tray.

CHAPTER 20

――――

PLEASANT VALLEY STATE PRISON lies off Interstate 5 in the Central Valley. The drive from the East Bay takes two and a half to three hours. My mother made it often, pressuring me to accompany her and occasionally succeeding.

Luke was always grateful to see me, but our conversations went nowhere. He had no life to speak of and I shared little of mine. Soon I stopped going altogether. Only as his sentence began drawing to a close did remorse rear up. On my final visit I brought Amy along. Our second date.

I thought about that as I left the hospital and set out for my meeting with Assistant Warden Gluck. How clumsy of me to ask her. How generous of her to accept.

I joined a caravan of big rigs shuttling along the spine of the state, through limitless tracts of dark fertile soil birthing avocados, almonds, citrus, garlic, grapes; crook-backed farmworkers in caps and facecloths, one hundred seventy miles of mounting dread.

I never made it.

———

I GOT AS far as Gilroy. The sky had eased to a matte brown and the temperature had rebounded forty degrees. At the 152 cloverleaf my fuel light came on. I exited for the first gas station. While I dipped my credit card, Evelyn Girgis called. She and James Okafor had pulled the security footage from outside Bay Area Therapetutics HQ.

"I need to warn you, the quality's not great."

"I'll take whatever I can get. Thank you so much."

I started the pump and headed into the convenience store to escape the heat, holing up by the refrigerator case.

The clip was about three and a half minutes long, time- and date-stamped the morning of May 11. There was no sound, and her caveat had led me to expect something grainy and stilted, but the image was vivid and in full color, bowed at the edges by a fish-eye lens. I saw the sidewalk in front of the building, the street, the storefronts opposite.

At 07:42:21 my brother arrived and swiped in.

At 07:42:58 a white single-cab truck nosed into the upper right corner of the frame and parked across the street. Glare bleached the interior. The angle rendered the tag illegible and made it impossible to tell if the bed had a tonneau cover.

At 07:43:40, Luke reemerged, having forgotten his lunch. He stopped short and stared briefly at the truck before walking offscreen to the left. The driver's-side window went down and then a shape leaned into the open window frame, aiming a small object. A cameraphone.

I hit PAUSE.

Shadow split the man's face. He was wearing dark glasses. Zooming in scrubbed away his features. But I could tell that he was white.

With a beard.

I studied the screen for a few minutes but could not identify him. I pressed PLAY.

At 7:44:51, the man in the truck retracted his arm.

Fifteen seconds later Luke returned carrying an insulated bag, his expression tense. He went inside.

I waited for the truck to drive away.

It didn't.

The truck's passenger door opened.

A second man got out.

He let a car go past, then stepped haltingly off the curb. The fish-eye caused him to distend monstrously, so that he seemed to be forcing his way through the tissue of time and space.

He took a step toward the building.

White. Clean-shaven. And young; there was an ungainliness in his carriage, a body gotten too big, too fast; a ship with no one at the helm. His thighs were like grain sacks. If he had more growing to do, his full size would be terrifying.

He took another step.

I hunched closer to the screen, as if I could meet him halfway.

The driver's arm shot out and began waving to get his attention. The clean-shaven man stopped and turned to look at the driver. The driver pointed to the building, and then they both stared toward the security camera.

They'd spotted it.

The clean-shaven man backed away. He stepped onto the curb and got into the truck.

The driver put his window up.

At 07:46:08, they drove off. The clip ended.

I watched it twice, three times, six. Slowing the playback, pausing, rewinding, trying frame by frame to squeeze out a good look at the tag, at either man, a tickle forming at the back of my brain.

The second man. The one without a beard.

I'd seen him. Some version of him.

My teeth ground.

The memory was there, I couldn't retrieve it.

"Mister? You okay?"

The convenience store clerk eyed me from behind Plexi. I'd been standing in the same spot, by the energy drinks, for half an hour. I was going to be late for Assistant Warden Gluck.

I texted my gratitude to Evelyn Girgis and James Okafor and jogged to my car.

My phone rang as I was merging onto the freeway. The caller was a Berkeley cop named Nate Schickman, another former collaborator.

"Hey," I said. "I'm on the road. Can I call you a little later?"

"Where are you?"

"Gilroy."

"Shit. How soon can you get back here?"

He sounded nothing like his regular, equable self.

"Where's here?"

"Highland Hospital," he said. "Somebody shot Billy Watts."

NINETY MINUTES LATER I pulled into the hospital lot.

I knew as much as Schickman had told me over the phone. That morning, around seven thirty, Billy Watts left the house to go to work. His wife, Rashida, was in the kitchen, cutting fruit for the boys' lunches. Through the window she saw Billy pause by his car to fiddle with his cell.

He looked up abruptly.

A series of loud claps and he crumpled on the sidewalk.

I ran for the ER. The automatic doors parted on babel, children pawing at infected ears and groaning men massaging their hairy breasts while on the television Judge Judy dispensed tough love.

I received multiple sets of wrong instructions before finding my way to a swampy third-floor conference room crowded with people, all but one of them cops. The table had been scooted against the wall and loaded with cheap sustenance: oily pink bakery boxes and boxed coffee. The chief of Berkeley police was on hand, attended by several Berkeley uniforms and Nate Schickman in a black BPD polo shirt. Oakland PD occupied a circle of their own. The crime had occurred on their territory, outside Billy Watts's house, a meticulously restored Craftsman east of Dimond Park.

Billy and I weren't close friends, but we liked each other, and our families occasionally socialized. Rashida was a dietitian. Their younger son was around Charlotte's age. They'd bought their house in a state of disrepair and done much of the work themselves. The first time they had us over for dinner, Billy showed me built-ins he and Rashida had refinished by hand, rooms they'd repainted together, tomatoes run riot in their garden.

I saw her now, in the corner of the conference room. Willowy, with high cheekbones and beaded cornrows. Bloody sweatpants and bloody sneakers. She was folded over in a faded gray chair, her face a silvery map of grief, one of three people forming a bubble of privacy. The other two were a white male detective I didn't know and a Black female detective I did.

Delilah Nwodo was an ace I'd worked with, friend to both Billy and me. She was talking in hushed tones, holding Rashida's hands while Rashida rocked silently.

Schickman detached from the Berkeley group to greet me.

"You look like shit," he murmured.

I asked for an update.

He skated a hand over his crew cut. "Still in surgery."

Rashida let out a low keen.

Nwodo rubbed her back, acknowledging me with a shallow nod.

I thanked Schickman and went to get coffee. Another thing he'd told me over the phone was that Delilah Nwodo had examined Billy Watts's cellphone and noted our failed attempts to communicate since Monday morning. At the moment of the shooting, Watts had been keying my name into his contacts. She wanted to ask me about it.

I wanted to talk to her, too. I'd spent the ninety minutes from Gilroy assembling my own theory about Billy Watts and the case that had brought us together.

A buried infant, a blanket full of bones.

"THANKS FOR GETTING here so quickly," Nwodo said.

"Thanks for calling me."

We'd stepped into the hall to talk. The other detective introduced himself as Ryan Hanlon and offered a grinding handshake.

"Who's taking care of the boys?" I asked.

"Grandma," Hanlon said.

"Rashida ran outside when she heard the shots," Nwodo said. "They followed her out and saw him bleeding on the lawn."

"Fuck," I said. "Anyone get a look at the shooter?"

"Not a good one."

"There was a driver, too, but she didn't see him at all," Hanlon said.

"Wild guess," I said. "White pickup truck, single cab. Tonneau cover over the bed."

Hanlon stared. He was a young guy, pug-nosed, with pale cheeks lit up by rosacea.

Nwodo folded her arms. "Go ahead."

I LEFT A LOT OUT. Told them about Luke going missing and showed the footage from his work, but said nothing about Rory Vandervelde's murder, the Camaro, the gun in a gas station restroom.

Hanlon frowned. "I don't see what it's got to do with Watts."

"A while back, Delilah, you remember we dug up a body in People's Park."

"The baby," Nwodo said.

"That's the one. The DNA came back a paternal match to this neo-Nazi, Fritz Dormer, doing a life bid up in San Quentin. He refused to cover burial costs, so I found his sons. There's three of them, also white power types, living on a compound way out in the middle of nowhere. Wives, kids, dogs, everyone piled into trailers. I go to them, 'This individual is your biological brother, no one else is gonna give him a proper burial.' They showed me out at gunpoint. Next thing I know, a brick with a swastika on it comes through my window."

She nodded. "Billy told me he was looking into it for you."

"He did. He paid them a visit and put them on notice."

"That doesn't seem like a reason to shoot him," Hanlon said.

"Maybe not to you, but these people aren't normal. Daddy's in for a hate crime. He beat a Black man to death for smoking on the sidewalk. A Black cop comes onto their turf and dresses them down? I think that's plenty of reason."

Hanlon chewed his cheek. "When was this?"

"Two years, give or take."

"They're acting up now?"

"Hang on, there's more. I had several run-ins with them after that. Fast-forward a few months. A couple of the brothers get into an argument, and one of them, Dale, ends up shooting the other, Gunnar. Our office gets the call about the body. I know the location, so I volunteer to take it. Gunnar was a big guy, two fifty, two sixty. Dale used a shotgun on him at close range. It's a horror show. My partner and I had to squeegee him into the bag. I look over, and one of the kids is standing in the doorway to the trailer, watching us with a look on his face."

I moved the video slider to show the clean-shaven man's face. "That's him. The kid."

"Hold up," Hanlon said. "I'm not following you. Who are we talking about?"

"One of the Dormer brothers' sons. Gunnar's, probably, from the size of him. He was sixteen or seventeen back then. So we're talking eighteen, nineteen, twenty now."

"You're positive," Nwodo said.

"I couldn't place him at first, because he's grown up, a lot. It clicked when Schickman told me about Billy."

"Who's the second guy?" Nwodo said. "The driver."

"The kid has an identical twin."

A smile played around Hanlon's mouth. "Like *The Shining*."

Nwodo stayed poker-faced. "You believe they blame you and Billy for what happened to their father."

"It's how they've been raised," I said. "Rage and blame, making some other group of people responsible for all the shit in your life. On top of that, they're young males, angry, isolated. Their dad's dead, their uncle killed him."

"Two brothers," Nwodo said.

"Right. Exactly. Me and Luke. Eye for an eye. It's how you think at that age, everything's symbolic. Look, even at the time, something about this kid felt wrong. He's watching me mop up his father's guts and he's got on this crazy, fucked-up grin. I thought he might try to kill me right then and there."

"He didn't," Hanlon said.

"He will. *They* will. They're orchestrating something."

"*Or*chestrating," he said, as if learning a new word.

"Luke's been gone since Sunday," Nwodo said. "That's four days they've had to move on you. Why wait? Why wait to shoot Billy?"

"Maybe they got held up, or they haven't had the opportunity. Whatever it is, I think Billy knew something was up. You saw yourself how many times he's called me."

"Is there another reason he might've been trying to get in touch with you?"

"I can't think of one."

Nwodo nodded thoughtfully. "I want to show Rashida the video."

She took my phone into the conference room.

Hanlon arched his back. "Cool story, bro."

"It's more than that, it's true."

"Mm."

"The truck's the same."

"It's a white truck."

I did not respond.

Monitors beeped, high-pressure toilets bellowed.

Nwodo returned. "It might be the guy she saw. She's not sure. She's upset, I'm not going to make her keep watching it."

She gave back my phone. "If Billy knew he was being followed, he didn't tell her. I asked Schickman, the rest of the Berkeley guys, too. Nobody heard a word about it."

No surprise. Luke hadn't told Andrea. I hadn't told Amy.

All three of us practicing the same soothing self-deception.

It'd turn out to be nothing.

No call for panic.

"You haven't noticed anyone following you, either," Nwodo said.

"No. I haven't been looking, though."

Hanlon smirked and took out his cell.

"Okay," Nwodo said. "Let's start by gathering some intel on the Dormers."

"Lieutenant." Hanlon's hand dropped to his side. The screen showed Instagram. "Really?"

"Call the uniforms," she said to him. "Find out what they picked up on canvass."

With a glance at me, he walked off.

"Thank you," I said to Nwodo.

"Don't thank me yet. Nothing's happening till I have more information. That pans out, I'll drive out there and see what's up."

"Fine. Great. I need to go home first and get my gear. I can meet you—"

"Uh-uh," she said. "If I go—that's *if*—you're not coming."

"Delilah—"

"You've done your part. I'll take it from here."

"I've been there, I know the layout."

"Clay. Forget it. It's out of the question."

"These fuckers are dangerous. You can't just roll up on them. You need a tac team."

"More reason for you to stay away. They really are that dangerous, I don't want you going home, either. Find someplace to camp out."

"And do what?"

"Get yourself safe and stay that way."

She was right. I was an interested party, running on fumes, a liability to myself and others.

I said, "At least let me draw you a map."

She handed me her notebook.

"The entrance is hard to see," I said, sketching. "There's a barbed-wire fence. Look for a double post.

That's the gate. Six trailers, half a mile back from the road."

She looked it over. "This is good. Thank you. Now go find a place to crash."

"Can I talk to Rashida?"

"Depends on what you're going to say."

"I just want to give her some support."

"Fine, but no questions. She's been through enough."

I started into the conference room. Nwodo touched me on the arm. Her gaze, usually sharp, was warm, searching, sisterly. "When was the last time you got some sleep?"

"I'll get some now."

"Will you?"

"I got nothing else to do."

"I want to believe you," she said. "But I've known you too long."

I heard myself making a weird sound, felt my lips crack. I realized I was laughing.

RASHIDA WATTS FELL against me. Her shirt was stiff with dried blood. I could feel her heart through her ribs. "It's nice of you to come."

"I'm so sorry, Rashida."

"Thank you." She released me. "How's Amy?"

"Fine, thanks."

"Send her my love, will you? And Charlotte? How's she doing? She's so smart."

"Great."

"We need to get everyone together." She wiped her eyes on her sleeves. "We need to do that soon."

CHAPTER 21

———

FALSE NIGHT CLOAKED THE CITY, a rim of sour orange light curdling at the horizon like fat on soup. The renewed odor of smoke exerted itself on my limbs and in my chest. I hurried to my car, scanning for white trucks and seeing them everywhere.

The Dormer twins had spent two years nursing a grudge and doing research. They knew about my brother. Why wouldn't they know about my parents? Or Amy's?

I did a drive-by of both houses. Nothing looked out of order. I was tempted to stop and knock. But Paul and Theresa would have no clue what I was talking about.

My parents would go to pieces.

I went home. I didn't plan on staying any longer than necessary. I put on jeans and a sweatshirt, tossed spare socks and underwear into a duffel bag. I wasn't sure how long I was packing for. What I was packing for. Where I was going next.

Ride around all night, maybe, searching uselessly for Luke.

Just like old times.

Nwodo's advice was wise. Find a motel and sleep.

I added my bulletproof vest to the duffel. I took the SIG Sauer and a box of ammunition from the gun safe and started for the bathroom. Nwodo called.

"Uniforms talked to Billy's neighbor up the block. He has a security camera that runs on a mini solar panel. They checked back to last week. A white truck goes past on Saturday and Monday, both around seven thirty a.m. Same time Billy got shot."

"That's them. It's gotta be them. They're doing recon."

"Or they got scared off. Either way, I'd like to ask them in person."

"Good. Great. How soon can you get out there?"

"You know how this works. You're telling me I need a team, that takes time."

"All right." I paused. "Whatever happens with Luke—"

"You'll be the first to know," she said.

"Thank you."

"Head on a swivel," she said.

The bathroom mirror confirmed what everyone was telling me: I looked like shit. My hair lay smashed atop my crown. Scorched pits ringed my eyes, the lids fluttered like a broken doll's.

Every explanation I'd come up with for Luke's disappearance centered on him and his character.

Crimes he could have committed.

People he had hurt and who might hurt him.

Never had it occurred to me that I was the explanation.

I opened the medicine cabinet, shook out four Advil, swallowed them.

I hefted the duffel.

At the front door I checked the peephole.

The porch, with its wobbly railing. Clear.

I parted the ugly scarlet tartan curtains and peeked

through the leaky front window at the traffic sailing by. Our house was three blocks from the freeway, along a main entry route. It got noisy. It was what we could afford. The lawn needed attention. The front-walk pavers were chipped and cracked.

So many projects, so little time, even less skill. We weren't Billy and Rashida Watts.

The sidewalk was clear.

I stepped onto the porch and turned to set the dead bolt.

Brakes whined, tires crunched, too close.

I spun, yanking at the duffel zipper. Why hadn't I taken the extra minute to put on the vest? Thrusting elbow deep I rooted through socks and underwear, knuckles grazing the box of ammo, its sharp corners. I touched the knurled butt of the gun. My finger found the trigger.

Car at the curb. Dark-blue sedan.

The driver got out, swaggering.

Cesar Rigo.

"Good evening, Deputy."

I pulled my arm from the duffel and returned the greeting.

He came tapping up the pavers. Smiled his smile and chinned. "Going somewhere?"

The duffel hung on my stomach. The undone zipper gaped. I shifted the bag to my hip and pinned it shut with my elbow. "Just till the power comes back on."

"How fortuitous that I caught you. Can you spare a moment to talk?"

I glanced at the street.

"Why don't we go inside?" he said. "Rather than stand out here in public."

I opened the door for him.

"After you," he said.

———

Rigo strolled around the living room while I lit candles.

"Where will you go until power is restored?"

I shook out the match. "Someplace with airconditioning, I hope."

He'd planted himself by the Great Wall of Cardboard and was reading the labels, hips shoved out like an Elvis impersonator. Today's suit was green with matching necktie in an abstract pattern. Where the hell did he shop? Not off the rack, surely; nothing would fit him, his compact gymnast's body. Maybe he shelled out for custom. Or haunted the boys' section.

"Did you move in recently?"

"I'm embarrassed to say how long it's been."

He smiled. Rapped the box marked BREAD MACHINE. "We have one of these."

My heart began to pound. No way he could know what it concealed. But I fought not to fall on the box like a loose ball. "No kidding."

"We received it for a wedding present but have never used it."

"Same."

"Interesting. And yet neither of us has ever thought to dispose of it. Why is that?"

"Everybody needs something to aspire to."

"I take it from the clothing that you have a daughter, or daughters."

"One."

"She's with your wife?"

"They left town for a few days."

"Do you enjoy having peace and quiet?"

How many times had I done this with a suspect, worked to build rapport? But Rigo was lousy at it. He knew it. And he knew that I knew it.

"Whatever it is you'd like to know," I said, "come out and ask it."

"I appreciate your candor, Deputy. I will strive to reciprocate." He pressed his palms together. "Shall we?"

We sat.

"I received a phone call today from Mr. Vandervelde's son. He was quite irate."

"About what?"

"According to him, he was at the victim's house last night and encountered you."

Sean, you prick.

"Did he happen to mention why he was there?" I said.

"He claims he wanted to ensure that the property was secure. He was concerned Dr. Yap might misappropriate items of value. He is convinced—you will forgive me—but he insists that you returned to the scene with the same intention. Under most circumstances I would dismiss any such accusations as the ramblings of a man in a state of distress."

"You should."

"Yes, but—and again, forgive me—I recalled that the victim possesses a photograph of you in his collection of sports memorabilia. As you are aware, I, too, was an athlete. I can appreciate that one experiences nostalgia for that period of one's life. Perhaps one wishes to acquire a memento."

"You're insinuating that I stole from a decedent."

"I'm providing you an opportunity to clarify the matter."

I'd conducted interrogations. This wasn't about an autographed photo. Rigo was dangling an easy out, enticing me to commit to a story he could then proceed to blow up.

I said, "I went to the house because I thought Sean might try to break in. And I was right."

Admiration in his smile, one chess player to another. "Why would you think that?"

"He made clear his dislike of Dr. Yap and was adamant that she didn't deserve to inherit his father's estate. I figured it couldn't hurt to check the seals."

"Is that something you typically do?"

"This isn't a typical situation, in terms of the amount of money or the personalities involved."

"Did you inform any of your colleagues of your decision?"

"I only thought of it after I'd left work."

"I see. You had a—what is the expression . . . a *brainwave*. I believe there was a comic book character by that name. My father was an engineer. He often traveled to the United States for conferences, and he would bring me American comic books and other materials to improve my English. In those days we did not have ready access to American television shows."

All hail the King of Casual Rapport.

"Bummer," I said.

"It was for the best. It made me a reader. You worked yesterday, did you not?"

He knew the answer. He'd seen me at the autopsy. "Yes."

"And today?"

"I was off."

"May I ask what time your shift ends?"

"Five. Although sometimes it can take a while to get out of there."

"Yesterday evening, did you go straight from your office to the victim's house?"

I'd gone straight to Ivan Arias's house. A different victim. "No."

"Where did you go?"

"Home."

"How long does it take you to get home from work?"

"About ten minutes."

"On average, I imagine, you are walking in the door between five thirty and six, yes?"

"Something like that."

"Do you remember what time you got home yesterday evening?"

"Not exactly."

"But not much later or earlier than usual."

"I don't think so, no."

"Very good. How long after you arrived home did you have your brainwave?"

"I couldn't really say."

"Did you eat dinner first?"

I'd eaten nothing.

I nodded.

"May I ask what you had?"

"For dinner?"

"Everything in your refrigerator must have spoiled by now."

"Beef jerky."

"Very nutritious. After you ate, what did you do?"

"Took a shower."

"And then?"

"I went to the victim's house."

"Having had your brainwave."

"Yes."

"In the shower, perhaps," he said. "I find showers a conducive atmosphere for thinking. Tell me: You didn't call one of your colleagues on duty to suggest they perform this task?"

"I didn't want to interrupt them. I figured it would turn out to be a fool's errand."

Rigo beamed. "Such dedication. If only everyone was so devoted to their work."

"I had nothing to do and it's ten minutes away."

"You're selling yourself short, Deputy. You had to climb the fence to get in, no?"

"I needed the exercise."

"Describe, please, what happened when you arrived."

"The seal on the front door was broken."

"That must have been vindicating for you. Did you enter the house?"

"I had to. There was evidence of tampering."

"Naturally. And when you did?"

"I ran into Sean."

I expected Rigo to ask about my tackling him, but evidently that part had been cropped from Sean's rendition—minor editing to assuage his bruised ego.

"What was he doing?"

"Going through the knife collection. He'd also set aside some baseballs and baseball cards."

"Our department retained a set of keys from Ms. Santos, the victim's housekeeper," Rigo said. "I was thus able to inspect the office. And several other rooms."

Say it. *Garage*.

"To my eye," he said, "no items were missing."

"That's because I put everything back."

"Ah. Of course."

"So you know very well I didn't take anything."

"It was not my intention to mischaracterize you, Deputy Edison."

Not a question; I didn't answer. I listened to the sounds from the street, keyed to the heavy tread of a truck.

He said, "After you encountered Sean Vandervelde, what did you do?"

"Escorted him off the property."

"I noticed that you resealed the front door. I could be wrong, but it appeared to me that you removed the old seal, rather than apply the new one over it. Is that correct?"

"Yes."

"Can you help me understand why you did that?"

"I thought it would help the new seal adhere better."

"First you restored the baseballs and baseball cards to their rightful places."

"Yes."

"When did you peform these tasks? Before or after you escorted Sean Vandervelde off the property?"

I could see where he was going. Sean must've said that I'd walked him down, then headed back through the gates—something Rigo could corroborate by talking to the Uber driver.

Had he gone to that length?

"After," I said.

"Why did you choose to do things in that order? That is to say, it would appear to me simpler to clean up the baseballs and baseball cards first, exit the house, apply the seal, and escort Sean out, rather than have to walk up the hill a second time."

"I needed the exercise."

Rigo beamed. "Really, though. What was the reason for that sequence of events?"

"He was drunk and belligerent, and I wanted him out of my hair so I could deal with putting away everything he'd tried to steal."

"Sensible. Now then, to avoid any possible ambiguity: After Sean departed, you reentered the house, unaccompanied."

"Yes."

"Do you recall which specific rooms you went into?"

"The foyer. The office and the one with the knives. He'd also drunk half a bottle of scotch. I put it behind the living room bar."

"No other rooms?"

Come on, Cesar. Say it. *Garage.*

I'd worn gloves. I'd been careful.

Time for defense or for offense?

Offense.

"No," I said.

My voice had taken on an edge.

"Very good. Let us review, please, what you have told

me thus far. You depart your place of work at five p.m., or perhaps a trifle later, and go home. Ordinarily you would dine with your family, but on this night you are alone, with only beef jerky to nourish you. You take a shower. Reflecting upon the events of the day, you are seized by the thought that in view of Sean Vandervelde's prior expression of anger, he may attempt to burgle his father's residence. This thought concerns you to the extent that you elect to take matters into your own hands. Once again you dress and drive to the victim's residence. What time do you arrive?"

Like all guilty people, I said, "I don't know."

Rigo crossed a green trouser leg. "Perhaps we can work backward. Sean Vandervelde was able to furnish a record of his Uber receipt, indicating that he was picked up from the residence at eleven thirty-seven p.m. Once you encountered him inside the house, how long was it before you saw him off?"

"I don't know."

"Let us suppose it was an hour. Does that sound reasonable?"

It didn't sound reasonable to claim any longer than that. I nodded.

"Therefore your arrival at the victim's house would have taken place around ten thirty."

"Thus it would appear."

He smiled at my mockery. "Does it appear otherwise to you?"

"Nope."

"Therefore you left your house to drive to Mr. Vandervelde's house shortly before that. By your description it is ten minutes away. Let us call your time of departure ten fifteen p.m. This, in turn, implies an interval of four and one quarter hours between your arrival at your own home, at six the latest, and your visit to Mr. Vandervelde's residence. Some of that is spent eating din-

ner and what have you. But, of course, beef jerky requires
no cooking time, and as you stated, you had nothing to
do. So there would seem to be several hours unaccounted
for. I presume you did not take a four-and-one-quarter-
hour shower. To that end, it would be helpful to know,
more precisely, at what time you had your brainwave. Perhaps it occurred later than you initially suggested. Not in
the shower, but while you were brushing your teeth, for
example. Or while you were getting into bed. If so, you
had to change out of your pajamas. One can only aspire,
Deputy Edison, to have such dedication. Another possibility is that you departed your house earlier than ten fifteen and went to another destination in the interim. That,
too, could explain the lost hours. Incidentally, I forgot to
ask: How did you obtain a key to enter into the victim's
house?"

Who had he spoken to? What had they said? Edmond,
the property clerk? Kat Davenport? Did they know they
were selling me out?

Had he checked the keycard records? The CCTV?

How much credit should I give him?

The better question was how much longer I felt like
keeping this up, doing what guilty people did, improvis-
ing, freaking out and scrambling and committing one
dumb messy error after another. The reckoning had to
come sooner or later.

What I wanted was to lay my head on my arms and
rest, like guilty people do.

"One other point of clarification," he said, "and,
again, I apologize for not mentioning this earlier. I noticed that the signatures on the newly applied seals re-
semble that of your colleague, Deputy Harkless, rather
than yours. I grant you, the seals are a little hard to read.
But comparing them to your signature on the autographed
photo in the victim's office, the disparity strikes me as
greater than expected, even taking into consideration the

degradation of penmanship that can occur over time. Since, as you say, you came to the victim's house for a legitimate purpose, signing your colleague's name in place of your own would appear—let us call it *nonstandard*. I can't conceive of why you would do it, unless for some reason you wished to conceal your actions. I wonder: What might that reason be?"

As a suspect, I detested Rigo. As a cop, I applauded him.

"While you decide on your answers," Rigo said, taking out his phone, "there is some additional information you may find of interest. During their investigation of the crime scene, forensics recovered fragments of two glass tumblers that bore fingerprints. One set of prints belonged to the victim. The other was submitted to the state crime lab for expedited analysis, and the results issued earlier today. You are familiar with an individual by the name of Luke Alan Edison."

He showed me my brother's mugshot. "Would you like to have a closer look?"

"I can see it, thanks."

"Very well." He put the phone away. "It is peculiar. The last twenty-four hours have witnessed significant social media activity regarding Mr. Edison. The other Mr. Edison. As of Sunday, he looks to have disappeared, though there is no active missing persons report. From the tenor of the discussion, however, one can infer that his wife and friends are extremely concerned for his safety. I expect you must share their concerns."

I said nothing.

"Please take the foregoing in the spirit of professional courtesy," Rigo said.

I couldn't help but laugh.

"I'm glad you can appreciate the humor in these circumstances," he said. "Though at this juncture I think it might be beneficial to relocate to a more neutral setting."

"The PD."

"We have air-conditioning."

Busting a fellow cop embarrasses both parties and creates headaches. What was the worst Rigo could produce? Destroying evidence? I'd plead out. Slap on the wrist.

It wasn't me he wanted to nail. He wanted a solve on his murder.

I could give that to him. I'd found his killers.

Or I was wrong and I hadn't.

Ryan Hanlon thought I was full of shit.

Delilah Nwodo and I had history. She trusted my instincts. But she was smart, with every reason to proceed with caution, and having Rigo call her created its own set of problems. Once she learned about the murder, she'd know I'd lied to her by omission. Good chance she'd feel—justifiably—that I'd taken advantage of our friendship.

That happened, she might hold on visiting the Dormers till she'd sorted out the facts.

How long before she assembled a team? Two hours? Three? Twelve?

What was my play?

Open the virgin bread machine and hand Rigo the gun?

"Deputy?" he said. "May we proceed to the station?"

A request? Or a command?

How much did he have, really?

My pocket buzzed.

In a perfect world, Nwodo calling. She was en route to the Dormer compound.

"I have to take this," I said, fishing out my phone.

Not Nwodo.

A text message. An image.

The sender was Luke Edison.

I touched the thumbnail.

My brother's face filled the screen. The picture had been taken in poor light. Flash wiped out the background.

His face, and what had been done to it.

One eye a purple egg. Lips split; red and brown crust in his beard, at his temple. The line of his nose deviated grotesquely. His head was averted. I couldn't see the other eye, whether it still had the wet sheen that fades with death.

A second text arrived. A map and a pin, red dot floating in a gridded beige field.

Rigo tilted forward eagerly. "Deputy."

A third text.

30 minutes alone or he dies

CHAPTER 22

———

RIGO ROSE, ANGLING to see the screen.

"You look unwell, Deputy. Are you all right?"

Concern in the words. Suspicion in the tone.

I slid down the sofa, away from him, and snatched the duffel off the floor. "Something's come up. I need to go."

"How unfortunate. I had hoped we could continue with our conversation."

"We will. Later." I stood up and walked toward the door. "Stay as long as you'd like."

He came along, first blowing out the candles.

STRIDING OVER THE LAWN I tapped the red pinhead to explode out the map, a set of coordinates hovering in the heart of the Altamont wind farm. The shortest route, thirty-one point eight miles, had a projected drive time of fifty-eight minutes.

I slung the duffel into the passenger seat and got into the car and waited with my hand on the ignition while Rigo got into his. I didn't want him following me.

The sedan didn't move. He was making notes, maybe. Waiting for *me* to leave.

I sat another twenty seconds, twenty seconds I did not have.

The sedan's headlights came on. It drove away.

I let him reach the end of the block, then reversed squealing into the street.

I thought he might circle back after me, but the sedan's brake lights shrank in the rearview. He was a homicide detective, like most of his ilk considered himself an intellectual, not some high-speed-pursuit hotshot. He'd come for me in due time.

I blew through the intersection and whipped onto 580, pressed centrifugally to the door. At the top of the ramp I came to a dead stop. It was 6:27, the peak of rush hour. Fires and outages had taken a few cars off the road, but any slack was offset by closures, short tempers, and wretched driving conditions.

My brother was scheduled to die at 6:53. GPS estimated a 7:24 arrival.

I forced in front of a semi and began bullying toward the interior shoulder.

"Call Luke," I barked.

Voicemail.

"Text Luke."

A robotic lady inquired sweetly what I'd like to say.

"I'm coming as fast as I can. There's traffic. Please wait."

She parroted my words. Was I ready to send? Yes, I yelled, ready, send, *send*. I was pushing from one lane to the next, perpendicular to traffic, raising honks and soundless screams of indignation, the Most Hated Man in the East Bay.

"Call Delilah Nwodo."

". . . Clay?"

"They texted me."

"Who did?"

"Whoever has Luke. They're going to kill him if I'm not there in twenty-five minutes. They sent a location for the meet. I'm forwarding it to you. When can you have a team?"

"Whoa, whoa, hang on. Where are you?"

"In the car. Be quiet on approach, they're expecting me alone."

"Clay. Wait a second."

"I need to make some calls. Get back to me as soon as you have an ETA."

"Wait wait wait wait wait. How do you know it's them?"

"They have his phone. They sent a picture of him. He's messed up, Delilah."

"Clay. Listen to me. I hear you're in a bad way, but you need to think. I'm sorry to have to say it but Luke could be gone."

"I know that."

"They're playing you. Think about it like it's someone else."

"It's not someone else."

"Pull over and we'll figure this out together."

I'd reached the shoulder. "Send the team."

I disconnected and pressed my foot to the floor.

Immediately she was calling me back. I ignored it, accelerating to forty miles per hour, fifty, sixty. I called Gabe Zaragoza, a former coroner now at the ACSO Special Response Unit, and left a rushed voicemail. Nwodo called again. Too soon for her to have done anything. She meant to talk me down. I sent her the picture of Luke's ruined face and ran the needle up to eighty-five. Every pebble or crevice rammed a fist through the chassis. The engine sobbed. My car had a hundred thirty-four thousand miles on it. I maintained it, but this was a lot to ask.

"Half a mile ahead," the nice robot said, "stop-and-go traffic."

A Day-Glo orange work zone ran at me.

I braked and was thrown forward. The steering wheel bit into my rib cage. The orange resolved to a cautionary sign and cones. Beyond them, the shoulder was open, no break in the road and no work crew. I edged around and sped up.

"Call work."

Deputy Lisa Shupfer answered: "What's up, buttercup?"

I'd known her for ten years. Like Lindsey Bagoyo and Kat Davenport and Brad Moffett and everyone in an Alameda County Coroner's uniform, she was my colleague and my friend.

I told her to contact Dublin station; coordinate with Delilah Nwodo at OPD. "She'll fill you in."

Shupfer said, "Okay."

I covered the next eleven miles in eight minutes. Gridlock streaked past. The GPS kept doing double takes, unable to comprehend how I was making such superb time in the face of bumper-to-bumper traffic. It warned me of snarls and slowdowns then hastened to revise my ETA as I rocketed by. The shoulder contracted dramatically, forcing me to ride the yellow line till I got too close and scraped the center divider. My side mirror ripped off and I shot the gap toward encroaching darkness, night and false night fusing to bring forth a horrifying sight: a seam of flame limning the far eastern horizon, as though the new day had dawned early and full of wrath; as though the points of the compass had been reversed.

I accelerated.

The seam widened, smearing its halo against a cyclorama of turgid gray-brown smoke, yawning like the mouth of a forge to feast on the line of cars offering themselves in sacrifice, exurbanites plodding toward planned communities on evacuation standby. Tonight they would toss in their beds, coughing, hearts clenched, giving up on sleep and getting up to check their go-bags for medications, photo albums, jewelry.

Was it worth it—their tiny slice of the promised land?

California was an abuser. Every year it strangled you, every year you forgave.

Nwodo called. This time I answered. "Tell me you've got a team in place."

"Nobody can get there in under an hour. Your people are saying the same."

"I'll stall as long as I can."

"Absolutely not. You do not engage. Under no circumstances."

"I'm sorry, Delilah."

"Clay. Pull over, stop the car, and *wait*."

"I can keep apologizing, if it'll help."

She said, "Can I ask what it is you think you're going to do when you get there?"

"Figure it out."

My tires whistled.

"Hold shit down," Nwodo said. "I'll do my best."

"Thank you. For everything."

"Don't talk like that," she said.

Then she said, "Good luck."

It was 6:42. "Luke Edison" had not replied to my text begging for a grace period. I sent another: On my way.

The nice robot bade me take the exit for South Vasco Road. I wedged into the stalled fast lane and began bushwhacking toward the off-ramp.

"Call my wife."

". . . hey there," Amy said brightly. "How are you?"

My mouth felt gummy.

"Clay? Did I lose you?"

"I'm here."

A red-faced man in a Subaru brandished his middle finger at me and leaned on the horn.

"On the road again," Amy said. She sang: "I can't wait to get on the road again."

She was singing because she was still a little annoyed at me. Working not to be. I'd never met a better person.

I wanted to tell her that: *You are the best person I know.*

I said, "How was your day?"

"We're about to sit down to dinner. Can I call you when we're done?"

No, let's talk now, let's not wait.

"What's for dinner?" I said.

"One guess."

"Mac and cheese."

"Pizza," she said.

I laughed. She did, too. "I'm pretty sure Charlotte has scurvy," she said.

We laughed more together.

"Did you get your errands done?" she asked.

"I did. I'm sorry we fought this morning."

"That wasn't a fight. That was a discussion."

"Right, that's what I thought, too."

I felt her smile from hundreds of miles away.

"Talk soon," she said.

"Amy? I love you."

Silence.

She had to know something was wrong.

One of my moods, maybe, kicked up by being alone.

She said, "I love you, too."

I barreled down the ramp, south and then east, through a hodgepodge of industrial parks and housing developments. Across Greenville Road blocky corporate campuses yielded to sad ranches where rawboned cattle gnawed stubble. Pumpjacks prayed. The boulevard devolved to a twisting country lane, and I pitched up into shorn hills, dwarfed by a tsunami of smoke that bore down like a murderous leer.

I thought about what would happen if I died. That I was putting myself in harm's way not for a stranger but for Luke was no consolation. In a certain sense it was worse: Amy and I had a framework for death in the line of duty.

I'd voided the contract. Set it ablaze.

I swerved on the turnouts, rising toward the saddleback over asphalt that rippled like burnt skin, each crest the last, each layer of smoke peeling back to reveal another. A sawhorse got in my way, ROAD CLOSED NO ENTRY CAL FIRE—I obliterated it. Tried Nwodo. Tried Shupfer. Both calls fizzled. Luke would die in three minutes. I was fifteen minutes away.

"Call Cesar Rigo."

Scratchy ringing.

". . . Deputy. I did not expect to hear from you again so soon."

"My brother didn't kill Rory Vandervelde," I said. "He was kidnapped by the men who did. They're using him as bait for me. I'm going to meet them now. I need backup."

"Surely you must agree that additional evidence is called for."

He was breaking up, words crackling like crushed bone.

"Call Delilah Nwodo. She'll vouch. She's getting a team but I don't know how long it'll take. The end point is east of Livermore. I'm sending a map. Freeway's fucked. I rode the shoulder. Just get here. Please."

The map started to transmit.

The progress bar stopped halfway.

"Rigo," I yelled. "Can you hear me?"

Electronic hash.

High along the ridgeline a row of wind turbines cycled their giant arms through torrents of smoke. My phone gave up trying to send the map and displayed a red exclamation mark. Sharp turn ahead, twenty miles per hour, I took it at fifty, gravel sprayed the guardrail, I righted the wheel just in time to avoid flying off the edge of the world and spit through a cleft in the bedrock, the road pared back to nothing, I hugged the cliffside while below me a gash opened in the earth, a steep terraced ravine, miles long, boiling with smoke. Wind savaged the slopes, harrying thousands more turbines stitched to the dirt like the souls of the damned, flailing in desperation, trapped between here and nowhere by a moat of fire.

The clock ticked to 6:53. My brother was dead.

The land sealed up behind, the grade plummeted, and I ran a gauntlet of electrical stanchions and high-voltage lines that delivered me out of the hills and to the verge of a vast, smoke-shrouded plain.

I was still descending, but gradually. Some accident of topography had stifled the wind and caused the accumulation of smoke, a woolen malignancy that bellied low, smothering the moon and the stars and muting the fires' distant glow. I touched down in the depression. Smoke mobbed the car. I slapped shut the vents but could smell it streaming in. It wormed relentlessly into my sinuses, my eyes ran. Visibility halved and halved again. I wove over the rumble strips, navigating as much by the phone as by sight. The map had me passing through ranchland, but I saw no sign of life, nothing but curtains of smoke and barbed wire and the margins of dry grass. Stanchions came marching from every direction. A skeleton army with only its feet visible, converging on a single point: a mammoth power substation, four miles out.

The pinhead lay just past it, at the corner of Millar Ranch Road.

It was 6:59. My brother had been dead for six minutes.

I tore past a deserted employee lot. The substation loomed. Behind concrete walls towers and transformers bristled in smoke. I rounded onto the final stretch, chasing the smoke which whirled teasingly up and away. The intersection assumed shape. I braced for a bullet. For Luke's broken body in the road.

I skidded to a stop.

The pinhead was right here.

I saw nothing. Nobody.

Smoke licked the blacktop.

I checked my phone: 7:02.

No reception.

Before losing contact with the network, the map application had loaded the destination and portions of the surrounding area. I brought up the satellite image and matched its features as best I could to the shadows on the other side of the glass: naked hills to the north, country road snaking eastward toward the county line, substation at my back.

Millar Ranch Road stuck out like a thorn, lancing southeast for half a mile to end at a group of structures with holes in their roofs. The Millar Ranch. A ranch no longer. More profitable to lease the land to the power company. Stanchions sprouted like freakish outliers in fields of chest-high weeds.

I put on my vest and loaded the SIG Sauer.

Took my knife and my flashlight and my mask and got out with the engine running.

The stench was instant and acrid and intense. It pooled like oil in my lungs. I began to cough uncontrollably. The sound died inches from my face, as though I were shouting underwater. Dozens of incoming power lines ran overhead. I couldn't see them through the haze but I could hear sizzling. All the hair on my body was standing on end.

I blinked out tears, coughed out gunk, squinted. The greenish pall of the substation floodlights seeped over the fields and gasped out to nothingness. Along Millar Ranch

Road, trash was strewn on the roadside. Particles swirled in the flashlight beam. A plywood sign read DEAD END. A shopping bag with knotted handles hung from an orphaned fence post.

Smoke crowded in like a silent enemy.

I aimed the flashlight at the bag. It was from Target, its red logo a puncture wound.

Something inside was pulling it taut.

I inched up.

My name was written on the ash-flecked plastic.

It could contain an explosive. It could go off if I opened the bag. If I got close enough.

Just because I couldn't see them didn't mean they couldn't see me.

I didn't think they'd settle for killing me remotely. They wanted the pleasure of direct violence.

I lifted the bag off the post and untied the handles. Inside was a green-and-black five-channel walkie-talkie, set to channel one.

I looked back the way I'd come, wishing for a battalion of emergency vehicles.

It was 7:05. My brother had been dead for twelve minutes.

I switched on the walkie-talkie and held the CALL button. "I'm here."

CHAPTER 23

————

THE RECEIVER BLIPPED.

"You're late."

I turned, trying to place him.

Fields. Stanchions. Weeds. Smoke.

"I'm here now," I said.

No answer.

"Hello?" I said.

"Start walking."

Flat voice, fighting to avoid the upper register.

A boy, masquerading as a man.

Each time I forced him to think or speak or adjust it tipped the balance of power in my favor. Every second I stretched was one more I gave to Nwodo or Shupfer or Rigo.

I ran to the car, got in, and shut the door. Turned on the radio and detuned it to white noise.

"Hello?" I said. "Are you there? I can't hear you."

"I said start walking."

I raised the volume. "Sorry. I'm having a lot of trouble hearing you. Say that again?"

"*Walk,* fuckhead."

Not *Get out of the car and walk.*

He couldn't see me.

The smoke.

It was giving him problems, too.

The enemy of my enemy.

"*Hello,*" he demanded.

"I'm sorry," I said. "It's really hard to hear you. Maybe we can try another channel."

Ten precious seconds ticked by. I studied the map on my phone.

The receiver blipped. "Channel two."

I cranked the static up higher and switched to channel two.

"That's worse," I shouted.

"Just *walk.*"

"I'm switching to three," I said. "Can you hear me? Channel three."

"*Four.*"

"What?"

"*Channel f—*" He dissolved into coughs. "*Channel four.*"

"I think you're saying four. Is that what you said?"

"*Ye—*" More coughing. "*Yeah,*" he croaked.

He was feeling it.

He was outside.

I dialed the noise down to a murmur and switched to channel four. "Are you there? Can you hear me now?"

"Yeah." He cleared his throat noisily. "Can you hear me?"

"It's a little better," I said. "You said walk?"

"Yeah."

"Do you want to tell me where I'm going? Give me some instructions?"

"Follow the road."

"Follow the road."

"That's what I said."

Other than the substation, the ranch was the only human structure for miles. They had to be back there somewhere.

They were putting me in a funnel. Monitoring my approach from a safe remove.

They had a vision of how this was supposed to go.

I grabbed a Post-it and pen from the center console. "Which road? The one I'm on? Or the other one?"

"What other one?"

"Right now I'm on the highway," I said, scribbling *ATTN first responder*. "Is that the one you mean?"

"No—you got the bag, just keep going that way."

"Okay." *Proceeding on foot Millar Ranch Road SE.* "So Millar Ranch Road."

"Yeah."

I climbed out of the car, trapped the Post-it beneath a wiper blade, and ran toward the field at the southwest corner of the intersection. "Southeast."

Twelve glorious seconds elapsed while he figured it out.

". . . yeah," he said uncertainly.

"Okay. Southeast. How far do you want me to go?"

"Just get going, asshole. I'll tell you when to stop."

Switching off the flashlight I ducked into the weeds and began crabbing due south, using the substation and the nearest stanchions as reference points. "Let me talk to Luke first."

"Bitch, you don't make the rules."

"For all I know you killed him," I said, parting stalks. "I need to know he's alive."

There was no answer. I maintained south, diverging from the road, moving as quickly as I could while staying low. Which was not very quick, because the terrain was pitted and uneven, and the weeds were high but not that high, and I'm tall, and the smoke while thick was unpredictable. Light erratic wind brushed it this way and that, slicing short-lived windows of transparency. One badly timed movement and I'd be exposed.

Within fifty paces my legs and back were cramping. I sucked at the inside of my mask, struggling to draw enough oxygen, my heart beating triple time. I covered another fifty paces and paused to poke my head up.

I was in the middle of a dark, trembling sea.

Smoke eddied, languid as ink in water.

I could no longer see the road.

I adjusted southeast and crouched down and began moving again, parallel to the invisible road. The boy hadn't spoken since I'd asked for proof of life.

Either Luke was dead and they couldn't produce him.

Or they'd kept him alive for a reason.

The receiver blipped.

". . . Clay . . ."

My brother's voice, altered horribly, shivved with pain.

"Luke," I said. "It's hard to hear you. Are you there?"

The boy said, "Move it, bitch."

He hadn't seen me enter the field.

He thought I was still at the intersection.

"Put Luke back on."

"Fucking *move*."

"He said one word. How do I know that wasn't a recording? Put him on and let me talk to him."

Another silence.

". . . it's me," Luke said.

"You're alive."

". . . yes."

"Are you okay?"

". . . yeah."

The boy came on: "That's it."

"One second."

"*Start walking* or he's *dead*."

"I need to ask him something only he knows. Otherwise you haven't proved anything."

Head down I advanced through the smoke, parting stalks, counting paces. Sweat stung my raw eyes. The mask stuck to my face. I inhaled with my mouth wide stretched painfully wide, suppressing an urge to cough that bulged against my soft palate like vomit.

Luke spoke again: ". . . it's me."

"It's really you."

". . . yeah."

"Mics," I said.

Reference to a Fugees song. A code from our playing days.

Back to the basket: How many defenders in my way?

I crept forward, holding the walkie-talkie close, squeezing the casing. There was nothing and then more nothing and fear gripped me.

I'd overstepped. They'd kill him now.

Or Luke hadn't heard me, hadn't understood, his head cloudy, his body weak, starved, faint from blood loss.

Or he'd simply forgotten, our private language fossilized by adulthood. How could I expect him to remember? It was so long ago. We were different then. We moved like one body. But that hadn't been true for a long time. I should have asked something innocuous. What poster did he have on our bedroom wall? Our mother's maiden name.

"Left," he blurted.

Two hostiles.

"Hang in there," I said. "I'm coming for you. I—"

"Shut the fuck up and walk," the boy said.

"Okay," I said. "I'm walking. I'm setting out now. I'm going."

Best guess I'd covered about a third the distance to the farm—a five-minute head start.

But my pace was much slower than it would be on an open road.

They would be expecting me soon.

Distract them. Keep them talking.

"You're Gunnar's son, right?" I said. "You and your brother."

Silence.

"I remember you."

No response.

"Let's talk about this."

"That's the plan, motherfucker."

"What should I call you?"

"You"—a chesty grunt—"don't call me shit."

"It's me you want," I said. "Let him go."

No response.

"Whatever you think has happened," I said, sidling past a stanchion, "you can change your mind. It's not as bad as you think it is. Billy Watts? He's alive. You didn't kill him."

No response.

"I was just at the hospital. I spoke to his wife. Spoke to his doctors. He's going to survive and recover. So however bad you think it is, you still have options. But you need to talk to me. To figure this out so it's best for you."

No response.

"Are you there?"

No response.

"I know you're angry," I said.

The receiver blipped and a new voice spoke. Harsher, slightly deeper.

"You don't know a fucking thing."

The receiver blipped and the first boy said, "Shut up."

New picture: They weren't together. One twin was out front, as a first line of defense. The other was in a separate location, keeping watch over Luke, listening in on a third receiver. To communicate without my overhearing, they'd need a private channel.

Channel three. The one he'd had me skip.

I switched to three. It was silent. I changed back to four.

"—your ass over here *now*," the first boy was saying. "You don't think I will?"

"I'm coming as fast as I can," I said. "Can you give me something to look for? Like a landmark?"

"How hard is it to walk?"

"I'm just saying, it's hard to see out here." *For you, too.*

I wiped my eyes on the hem of my shirt and sneaked a glimpse. No buildings yet, but to the east, where the road ought to be, I discerned a line of tall scratches that flickered like gray flames. Trees.

I crouched and pressed on. "What happened to your father—he didn't deserve it."

"What happened," the second boy said, "*you* happened."

"Shut up," the first boy said.

"I've met your grandfather," I said. "I've met your whole family. Your uncle Kelly? I tried to help him. Ask him."

"I don't care what that piece of shit thinks," the second boy said, starting to cough.

"Shut up, Jace."

A name.

"I met you, too, Jace," I said quietly. "I remember you. I remember both of you."

No response.

"What happened to you was a nightmare. You shouldn't've had to see it. Nobody should. I am truly sorry you did. You were kids and you didn't deserve any of it. We can talk about it."

"Nothing to talk about."

"Jace *shut the f*—"

He erupted into coughs.

I froze.

I could hear him, in stereo to sound on the receiver.

The signal cut out and I heard him still, coughing and talking.

Faint, but unmistakable.

Coming from the tree line.

I switched to channel three.

"—can't concentrate if you can't stop fucking talking."

"It's fucked up," Jace said. "Something's fucked up."

"Just shut up and lemme think."

"Ask him where he is. Ask him what he sees."

"No."

"Move up and see if you can see him."

"*Fu*—" A violent cough. "*No.* St—"

I switched off the walkie-talkie and oriented east, toward his voice. Weeds tickled the skin around my eyes, smoke feathered in my chest, the power lines crackled and zapped, they emitted a constant damp hum like the drone of carrion flies. The boy went quiet. I thought I knew where he was but the dense vegetation and the heavy air played tricks with sound, I could hear my boots in the dry earth like dirt being shoveled, my breath roared inside the mask, and I slowed further to avoid drawing his attention, moving between the stalks, feeling the weight of each step as though performing a walking meditation. The treetops came into view, leaning forth through the smoke, trunks growing outward from their centers as they surfaced. They were planted at regular intervals to form a corridor. Smoke crowned the canopy, dripped from the branches like Spanish moss.

"Hurry the *fuck up.*"

Talking to me. Annoyed by my dawdling.

I closed another few yards.

Switched on my walkie-talkie and toggled the CALL button.

His receiver blipped.

Ahead. To the left.

I was behind him.

CHAPTER 24

——

I SAW HIS DARK shape through a drifting white tide, fifteen feet away, stationed in the road facing north with his back to me. He'd parked the truck diagonally to serve as a barricade. A rifle with a scope was propped on the tonneau cover. The butt of the rifle was pulled into his shoulder. His left hand, the hand he used to aim, cradled the walkie-talkie receiver. He was staring at it, wondering why it had blipped and fallen silent.

I had a shot.

Firing and alerting the other twin was too risky.

I unsheathed my knife and rushed from the weeds.

He turned. He was wearing a baseball cap with a camouflage pattern and a dark shirt and camouflage pants. A camouflage neck gaiter covered his nose and mouth. Over its top his eyes flew open. I saw them change, from surprise to shame and then to fury. For two years he and his brother had been cultivating their hatred, sharing it between them, anticipating this moment. He'd pictured the outcome often enough that it had calcified into inevitabil-

ity. In a thousand simulations it had never happened this
way. It couldn't. His cause was righteous.

His left hand still held the walkie-talkie. He lacked the
presence of mind to drop it, and when he tried to take
hold of the rifle to shoot me the barrel knocked against
plastic and bobbled up. His eyes, now full of fear, left me
to follow the barrel's errant path. He let go of the receiver,
almost reluctantly, as if it were glued to his palm.

By then I had reached him. Knife out I crushed into
him, pinning him against the truck with the rifle between
us. The blade went in, slick warmth flooded out of him,
he made a guttural sound. I clamped my hand over his
mouth and hammered the base of his skull against the
tonneau cover. His hat flew off and he thrashed, straining
to head-butt me, to bite my fingers, to knee me in the
groin, to work the rifle loose. His gaiter had slipped
down. He was the one with a beard. His cheeks were distended with effort. His fallen walkie-talkie blipped on the
ground.

"D'you see him yet?" it said.

The boy's bulging eyes rolled toward the receiver, as if
to communicate without speaking. A scar bisected his left
eyebrow. I wondered how he'd gotten it. Wrestling with
his brother. Whupped with a belt. He was not far from
childhood. He was strong. I thought about Billy Watts
and his two sons. I thought about my brother, about my
wife and my daughter.

I dragged the knife through the boy's abdomen till it
hit bone.

The rifle clattered down.

I stepped back. My shirt adhered to his for a moment
before peeling away and slapping against my skin, heavy
and cold and wet.

The receiver blipped again. "Ty?"

The boy, Ty Dormer, looked down at his opened body.
He fell to his knees and onto his face.

I searched him. I did it efficiently, I had ten years of experience turning out the pockets of dead men, to preserve and protect their property. His legs twitched senselessly.

Ty Dormer's property consisted of a wallet, an iPhone with a Bay Area Therapeutics logo on the case, a set of keys, four zip-ties, and an unopened teriyaki-flavored Slim Jim.

I took the rifle. I took everything except the Slim Jim. I never wanted to eat jerky again.

I got into the truck and turned hard toward the ranch, speeding along the tree corridor. The blaze of the headlights was worse than nothing, reflecting in the smoke and whiting everything out; I killed them. Two splintery posts rose like the pillars of a destroyed palace. I passed beneath a large rusty *M*. Shapes solidified: wormholed sheds, a barn more air than wood, ravaged machinery, a paddock.

I steered between them on dirt paths, SIG Sauer pressed against the wheel.

Atop a shallow rise sat the dilapidated farmhouse. A long low structure stuck out its snout behind.

I rolled up at a crawl. The structure was a cattle shed with open sides and a wavy roof and stalls of tubular metal.

A figure came strutting out of the shadows.

Jace Dormer thought I was his brother. He was carrying his walkie-talkie, coming to help. Looking forward to dealing with me. He jogged toward me and then he stopped. He knew his brother's form; it was his own, and mine was different.

I threw on the brights, blinding him.

He scrambled backward.

I stamped the pedal and drove at him.

He hurled himself clear. I crashed into an exterior stall

railing. The front end of the truck kicked up. The airbag exploded in my face.

I clawed it away and shoved open the door.

Jace had run into the shed and was stumbling up the center aisle striped in the headlights' icy glare. I squeezed off a shot that went wide and ran after him. My shirt, drenched with his brother's blood, swung like some obscene piece of meat. He turned into a rear stall and fell on a heap of rags with my brother's face. His arm pumped, driving a short knife repeatedly into Luke's body. I couldn't fire again without fear of hitting Luke. I burst into the stall and grabbed Jace around the throat and hauled him off, and we staggered around, bashing into railings. He was taller than me and stronger than his brother. I could smell his unwashed neck. He had to realize that if I was here, his brother was dead. The point of the knife had broken off, leaving a sawtooth. He swung it wildly over his shoulder, I blocked his arm with my gun hand. He swung again and I jerked my head to avoid getting gouged in the eye and the jagged end of the knife incised a six-inch line through my scalp. Hot blood streamed over my ear and down the side of my face and down my neck. I held on to him. He brought the knife down and back in an arc and the blade punched deep into the meat of my thigh.

I let go.

Jace pulled out the knife and rounded on me.

Lunged.

The sawtooth hit the vest and bounced off.

He tottered back, bewildered. Then he lunged for my throat.

His front foot slipped. He tumbled past me, limbs flying. I saw the thing he had slipped on, a paperback novel with a creased spine. My brother was on the ground, not moving. Jace Dormer rose on one knee, knife in hand. His body rotated through a quarter turn. I buried the SIG

Sauer in the soft tissue of his flank below his ribs and fired four times. The other side of him blew out in a red cone. He went to the dirt.

I put an insurance shot in his head and crawled to Luke.

He was bleeding freshly from numerous stab wounds to his gut and chest. One hand was cuffed to the stall railing. I took off my bloody shirt and stuffed it against his torso.

"Hold this here. Put pressure."

He clutched at me, *don't go*.

"I need to find the cuff keys. I'll be right back."

There was nothing in Jace Dormer's pockets but a coil of wire.

I sprinted, limping, to the truck. My right leg was numb from the waist down. My right shoe was full of blood.

When I returned with the keys Luke's eyes had closed. I uncuffed him and eased him up against the stall railing. He blinked lethargically.

"Stand up. Can you stand up? Luke."

I got my shoulder into his armpit. He let out a wet sough. His breath stank of blood, his body of waste. I stood up with him and started out of the stall and into the aisle. He wasn't walking right, his feet dragged. His ankles were bound with zip-ties. I picked him up under the knees. He was hideously light. I carried him to the truck.

I lifted him into the passenger seat and buckled him in and limped around to the wheel.

His eyes had closed again. His chest cycled shallowly. Strands of red saliva stretched between his lips.

"Hey," I said. "Luke. Open your eyes, bud."

I started the motor and tried to back out.

The truck strained, caught on a railing.

I swore and shifted into drive and floored it. The tires spun. I threw it into reverse. Luke drooped forward and I pinned him against the seat with a forearm, not thinking about what damage I might be doing to his insides as I plunged the truck forward and back and wrenched the wheel from side to side till the bumper sheared halfway off and we shot free over the lumpy dirt.

Luke's head bounced and rolled.

"Luke."

I reached the ranch entrance and hurtled up the tree corridor through smoke, bumper scraping, narrowly avoiding Ty Dormer's body splayed in the road.

My unattended car was at the intersection. The truck's gas gauge was a third full. The nearest hospital was in Tracy, ten miles to the east. Ash snowed down softly. Luke slumped against me, I eased him straight again and started to make the turn. Vehicles were approaching from the west. They had their sirens off but their flashers on, red and blue diffusing in the smoke. I put the truck in park and got out, waving my arms.

CHAPTER 25

————

H E CAME OUT of surgery in pain but out of danger. They had brought him to Highland, and for the next several days Andrea and my parents pulled shifts by his bedside.

On Wednesday my dad called. Luke was awake, he was alert, and he was ready to talk.

I met Cesar Rigo in the hospital lobby. We rode the elevator to the fourth floor. I knocked on the door and my father emerged. He told us he'd take a walk for the duration of the interview.

To give us privacy, he said.

His eyes were wet. Whatever Luke had told him, he didn't need to hear it twice.

"Great thing you did," he said to me.

My brother lay sunken in the bedsheets. Light slanted across his chest. Rigo started his recorder. Luke beckoned me close and began to speak.

————

MOST DAYS HE got up before Andrea, but the previous night he'd had trouble sleeping, and in the late morning he woke alone.

He brewed coffee and sat on the longhouse steps facing the forest. Her car was gone. The sun had come up muddy, and a bitter note complicated the familiar morning smells of dirt and dew and grass.

So far as he could tell, their fight—yet another—had begun as a normal conversation, him proposing that they escape for a few days. Just hop in the Camaro and go. They were both stressed. Had been for so long. A change of scenery might help.

She'd looked at him, astonished.

Didn't he *get* it? For months, *years,* she had been working *so hard* to fine-tune their environment; to reduce variables and keep everything as *stable and consistent as possible.* A change of scenery was *literally the opposite* of what she needed.

He'd tried to redirect but she was in a groove, not shouting but using her patient voice that plowed forward like an earthmover in low gear. Easy for him to say things like quote-unquote *just hop in the car.* It showed, clearly, that he still wasn't treating this as a shared responsibility. Did he actually think racing around for hours on end in the Camaro would help her relax? She got nauseous *sitting up* too fast. Her medications had to be kept cold; how was that supposed to work?

He knew she was suffering. He'd grown accustomed to a heightened level of drama. But for whatever stupid reason, he opened his mouth: There was this amazing invention called ice packs.

Well, then.

He blew on his coffee. If he was honest with himself, he'd known what he was doing, pushing back. She accused him of not stopping to consider what taking a trip might mean for her. Had she considered what *not* taking the trip might mean for him?

His needs had ceased to exist, chased out by the all-consuming goal of having a child.

But you couldn't live forever in crisis mode. Eventually it stopped feeling like a crisis.

You had to listen to what the universe was telling you.

He wished he had someone to talk to. Apart from James, the people at work were kids. And he and James didn't have that kind of relationship; they were men past the age when forming new strong bonds was possible. Whatever you'd acquired for yourself by forty—that was what you got, and you counted yourself lucky to have it. To ask for more felt inappropriate, almost childish.

Still.

A week ago, it had gotten to the point where he'd texted his brother.

R u around. Can we talk

No reply. No surprise. Clay had a lot going on in his own life. His busy, busy brother.

The forest stirred. A deer, a young male, high-stepped through a thicket.

Luke smiled. "How about you."

The buck raised its head.

"You want to hear my problems?"

The buck galloped off.

Soon Andrea returned with a trunkful of farmers' market produce in canvas bags. Luke got up to help her. He told her he was sorry and reached to take the bags.

She shied away. "Sorry for what."

Before he could answer, she went into the longhouse.

One of those days. He watched the trees for a bit, hoping the buck would reappear.

Time to get some work done. He carried his mug to the car shelter.

———

THERE WAS A tiny pebble mark on the underside of the Camaro's front bumper. It happened. Lots of guys would treat the car like a museum piece, only trotting it out on big occasions. Luke disagreed. Cars needed to move.

He got out the masking tape and the touch-up paint and the clear coat. While waiting for the first coat to dry his mind wandered to a conversation with Rory Vandervelde. They'd met at the Lodi swap meet a while back and hit it off. Luke had toured the collection once or twice. It was mind-blowing, and Vandervelde himself was so enthusiastic, like a little kid on his birthday, that you couldn't even be jealous.

In the end, of course, how much did they have in common? Same as with James: easy come, easy go. Didn't bother Luke, he accepted it. They'd been out of touch for probably a year when, over the spring, Vandervelde phoned out of the blue. They exchanged pleasantries and then Vandervelde mentioned that his maintenance guy had upped and quit. He never offered Luke the job, just talked around it, testing the waters. Know anyone good?

Luke promised he'd keep his ear to the ground.

Six months had passed without a second call. Obviously Vandervelde would've found someone by now, and it shamed Luke to feel a pang of regret. He had a job, a good one, reliable, respectable. Scott took care of him.

Still.

He worked on the Camaro for several hours. At lunchtime Andrea came outside and began puttering around the chicken coop. She was making noise, shutting the door harder than necessary and sighing and shooting glances at him, expecting him to take the first step.

He wiped his hands on a rag.

He did his best. Before long, though, they were at it again. He decided to get some space. Her high sharp voice pursued him across the clearing. Where did he think he was going? Did he think he could leave her like that? It felt mean—but good—to rev the motor and drown her out. He drove through the trees, over the culvert bridge, and onto the main road. A truck was parked up the roadside. But his mind was elsewhere.

HE STOPPED AT a vegan taqueria in Oakland for a late lunch, bringing in his laptop so he could work while he ate. He couldn't concentrate and closed it when his food came.

The server warned him the power could go out at any minute. Luke thanked her.

He gnawed at the burrito, nursed his lemonade. Andrea wasn't answering her phone, which didn't mean anything in itself. She left it switched off and in her car. He kept trying her anyway, every twenty or thirty minutes. That way, when she did think to check the phone, she'd see the missed calls and know that she was important to him, at the forefront of his mind. He regretted the way he'd left, and he felt ready not to be alone. But he couldn't bring himself to go home just yet. At the very least he wanted to hear her voice and get a feel for what he was walking into.

Rory Vandervelde popped into his head again.

Why not?

Vandervelde sounded pleased to hear from him. Without being asked, he invited Luke to drop by. They arranged for six p.m. They didn't discuss if this was to be a social call or a job interview. Even if the job was open, Luke wasn't sure he wanted it. After they hung up, he did some googling on cars he knew Vandervelde owned. Couldn't hurt to be prepared.

———

268 / JONATHAN KELLERMAN and JESSE KELLERMAN

AT FOUR THIRTYISH the restaurant lights went off. To kill time Luke drove to Mosswood and watched the pickup players. They looked to be running in slow motion. The afternoon had turned brutally hot and the air smelled like lighter fluid.

The game broke up, and he tooled around some more, arriving at Vandervelde's driveway a few minutes early. The gates were open.

Foot on the brake, he sent Andrea a text. Baby I'm sorry

He couldn't leave it at that. She expected him to be specific with his apologies. Sorry for what? As he sat there, weighing what to write next, he heard a car coming and glanced up.

A white truck cruised past and went around the bend.

Two memories hit him, like a gut-punch combination.

That morning, the truck on the roadside.

A white truck, following him to his work. The guy with a camera.

Upsetting, at the time. But nothing happened. Nothing ever did.

Prison had carved a paranoid streak into him. He worked not to cater to it. *The world is not a threat* Andrea liked to say. Sound advice, even if he didn't think she totally believed it herself.

He tried to recall if the truck he'd seen that morning was white, too. He wasn't sure.

Not that that would have proved anything. Millions of white trucks. They were the boneless skinless chicken breast of commercial vehicles.

He stayed for a few more minutes, watching the road. The truck didn't come back.

Six oh four. Somehow he'd managed to make himself late.

———

RORY VANDERVELDE MET him at the door with drink in hand, a big smile on his rough red face.

"*There* he is." He clapped Luke on the shoulder and tilted the tumbler toward the Camaro. "And there *she* is. The Green Goddess."

He bounded down the steps to the motor court, ran a caressing hand over the hood. "I got a space all picked out and ready for her. Say the word, I'll get my checkbook."

Luke smiled weakly. "Anything's possible."

"Don't be a tease, amigo. Well. To the Batcave." Vandervelde started for the garage but stopped and slapped his thighs. "Ah, dammit. You know what, come on in for a sec."

Luke trailed him into the darkened house. The living room picture windows framed the setting sun.

"Friend of mine sent me this whisky," Vandervelde said. "Japanese. Fantastic stuff."

"Water's fine, thanks."

"You sure? You're missing out."

Luke was sure.

Vandervelde brought a second tumbler from the wet bar, and, leaving his own drink on an end table, disappeared down the hall.

Luke wasn't thirsty. He'd only accepted to be polite. He put his tumbler next to Vandervelde's and went to the window. The coppered waters of the Bay rose in sudden peaks and melted away like unfinished thoughts.

"I never get tired of it."

Vandervelde was crossing the foyer, carrying a pair of foot-long Maglites.

He joined Luke at the window and together they took in the view.

"I wouldn't, either," Luke said, knowing this to be untrue. He got tired of everything, that was his problem. One of many.

"For you," Vandervelde said, handing him a flashlight.

Luke grasped it. Its heft stoked a strong scary urge to smash out the window and leap through the frame; flee westward through the hot doused city streets till he collided with the shore. Where he went from there was anybody's guess.

He said, "Did you get your checkbook?"

He heard these words from outside himself, like an unauthorized third party had spoken.

Vandervelde's smile got a little wider, a little flatter. No longer your and everybody's best friend, but the shrewd businessman that he was. "Did you want me to?"

Luke's pulse was racing, as if he had committed an intractable sin. "Let's bring her in and see how she looks."

THEY HAD TO crank the hangar door by hand. The mechanism was hidden behind a portrait of Frank Sinatra. The spot Vandervelde had picked out was close to the entrance, next to a Ferrari giving six inches of clearance. Luke eased in while Vandervelde called out instructions and waved the flashlights like an aircraft marshaller guiding a 747 to the gate.

They stood before the Camaro in reverential silence.

"I think she looks pretty good," Vandervelde said.

Luke nodded morosely. The effort involved in moving the car made a sale feel like a done deal, when really he'd only meant to try the idea on. But he couldn't back out now, he was trapped. He'd acted impulsively. Nothing good ever came of that.

"What's on your mind, son?"

Vandervelde was looking at him with curiosity. Compassion.

What was on his mind.

The warm, drowsy darkness acted as an intoxicant. The fact that Vandervelde was a virtual stranger helped, too, opening up a confessional space and giving Luke permission to unburden himself, like he'd sat down next to someone friendly on a long train ride. Once he started talking, he couldn't stop. Their miscarriages, the arguments, the monotony of his job, money—everything coalescing into a single yearning, a fire hotter and more painful than the sum of its parts.

He wanted something else. Something different. Even if *different* was not *better*.

He said, "It feels wrong to complain."

"Oh, I don't know about that. Complaining is a human right. If I can do it, you sure can."

Luke laughed.

"What it sounds like to me," Rory said, "is you don't think you're allowed to be happy."

Luke said nothing.

"I'll let you in on a secret. That's what I used to think. And—okay. I know what it looks like," Rory said, waving to encompass the cars, the outsized garage, his outsized life. "But you're seeing me now. For the longest time I thought that by denying myself I was setting myself up for a reward down the line. It doesn't work that way. You have to live while you're alive."

Outside the wind had picked up, howling past the open hangar door. The gaps in the trees were blue-black.

"Offer rescinded," Rory said. "You still want to sell her to me, six months from now, that's another thing. Tonight I'm not buying."

Luke nodded, relieved.

"But." Rory grinned. The businessman was back. He pointed at the Camaro. "First dibs."

"All yours."

"Atta boy. We'll drink to it."

Luke didn't have the heart to turn him down. He'd pretend to take a sip.

There was a bar in the garage, but Rory was dead set

on him tasting this killer whisky. Meantime Luke should feel free to look around.

Alone, Luke strolled the display floor, running the flashlight over one treasure after another. He ought to be heading home. It was getting late and he felt pretty talked out. He didn't want to be rude, though, especially not after the kindness Rory had shown him.

He realized he'd forgotten to ask about the mechanic job.

Five minutes went by, then fifteen. Rory didn't return. Maybe Luke had misunderstood, and he was supposed to find his way back to the house on his own time. He locked the Camaro—force of habit—and left the garage to head up the path. The wind hissed, showering him with pine-cones and needles.

He stepped out of the redwoods.

A white truck sat on the motor court.

Luke got a head rush, his fingers tingled.

He stared at it, then came forward, mesmerized, following the flashlight's bobbing spot.

The truck was parked by the front steps. Enervated moonlight dyed it a pale blue. Tonneau cover on the bed.

He got closer.

The truck's cab was unoccupied.

He looked at the house.

The front door was ajar.

He reached for his phone.

The door banged open.

"Don't fuckin move."

The man in the doorway was broad as a coffin. He wore a mask and was aiming a rifle at Luke's chest. Luke couldn't see past him, into the house, to know what he had done.

"Rory," Luke called.

"Shut up," the man said.

He ordered Luke inside, keeping a bead as Luke climbed the steps and entered the foyer.

Rory was sitting on a living room sofa. A second masked man stood over him with a pistol. On the end table glinted the two tumblers, whisky and water, as though Rory and the man had been sharing a drink.

The rifleman told Luke to put the flashlight on the ground. Luke set it on the tiles.

"Lie down," the rifleman said. "Hands on your head."

"Take anything you want," Rory said.

The second man pistol-whipped Rory, felling him to the marble.

The rifleman said, "Lie down."

Luke lay on his stomach. He could hear Rory moaning in pain.

"Get over here'n help me," the rifleman said.

The man with the pistol came over and held it to Luke's cheek while the rifleman zip-tied Luke's wrists behind his back and cleaned out his pockets.

The man with the pistol said, "Fuck we do with *him*."

"Your problem, you deal with it."

"How's it my problem?"

"You're the one so wet you can't wait till he comes down the driveway."

"He wasn't coming."

"He would, you could learn to sit still for five fuckin minutes."

Behind them Luke saw Rory struggling to pull himself up on the end table.

"How d'you know?" the man with the pistol said. "You don't know that."

"Tell you what I know, I know you're a fuckin moron."

The table tipped, dumping the tumblers to the floor with a crash.

Both men spun around.

Rory lurched up and across the foyer and down the hall.

The man with the pistol swore and took off after him.

Seizing on the distraction, Luke rolled onto his side and began kicking at the rifleman's legs. He heaved up at the waist and had almost managed to stand when something hard caught him square in the temple.

Several loud bangs; a long buzzing silence.

". . . 'spect me to do? He was getting away."

"Yeah cause you *let* him get away."

Luke stirred. His head throbbed. He was on his stomach again. His ankles were bound, too.

"*You asked me* to help you."

"Yeah, okay. Problem solved. Nice job, idiot."

"Fuck you."

"Stay here."

"Where you going."

"Just stay here." A snicker. "Hey, Jace: Try not to let him get away."

"Eat a dick."

Footsteps went and came back.

"Whad you do?"

"Put him in the bathroom."

"Fucks'at spose to do?"

"You want me to leave him out where they're gonna see him?"

"They're *gonna* see him. There's blood everywhere."

"Hey. Hey. Shut up. I don't take lessons from you. It's your fuckin mess I'm cleaning up here. Fuckin idiot. Whatever, let's get the fuck out of here already."

Luke readied himself to die. They had come for Rory but run into him; now he must be eliminated. He took a deep breath and felt himself leave the ground. The thought crossed his mind that his spirit was leaving his body. He found it encouraging that he was going up instead of in the other direction.

The men carried him to the truck. They raised the tonneau cover and locked him in.

HE COULD HEAR them arguing in the cab, their words unintelligible over the churn of the engine. They drove a short distance and braked hard, throwing him headfirst into the front panel.

A door opened, a door slammed, they resumed driving.

Luke tried to keep track of the turns but he was dizzy and had bagpipes whining in his skull. He wriggled around in search of a weapon or a means to free himself. Found nothing and lay still, conserving his energy.

They got onto the freeway. He felt the rhythm of the seams in the concrete.

Then came a road that curved and rose and fell.

The truck slowed and shuddered. He guessed they'd been traveling for an hour but he had no idea in which direction.

The tonneau cover lifted. He kicked at them with his bound feet. He'd gotten disoriented in the lightless chamber of the truck bed, and he was facing the wrong way, battling air. They dragged him over the tailgate and onto the stony dirt, pummeling him with the rifle stock, the pistol butt, fists, boots. He considered himself a strong guy, but so were they, and he was trussed like a pig.

Hoisting him by the elbows they hauled him drooling and bleeding into shadows. He still expected to die at any moment. He thought they were stringing it out, for fun.

They held him down, cut the zip-ties from his wrists, and handcuffed him to something cold.

They were bickering again. They'd ripped off their masks and were slashing at each other with the beams of their flashlights. To Luke's dismay there were now four of them.

No. Just two, he was seeing double.

He forced the images into alignment, piecing their faces together from brief illuminated fragments, like a mosaic displaced in time. The similarity of their voices and builds and their combative shorthand led him to conclude that they were brothers. One had a beard and the other did not. The beard made its possessor seem older and larger and lent him an air of authority.

By shooting the "old guy" No Beard had gone off book. Beard berated him for his stupidity. Now the pistol tied them to the crime scene. They had to ditch it.

No Beard opposed this suggestion. If they did that, they'd only have the rifle left.

Beard retorted: Whose fault was that. But he had an idea. He'd head out to some random spot, turn on the phone, and toss the pistol there. Then turn off the phone. That way if the cops traced the phone, or the gun got found, they'd be looking way over in the wrong place. Lemons to fucking lemonade.

"Give it," Beard said.

No Beard glared but surrendered the pistol. Beard tucked it in his waistband, like a movie gangster. He crouched and stuck Luke's phone in Luke's face. "Code, bitch."

Luke didn't answer fast enough. Beard raised the pistol over Luke's head like a tomahawk.

"Okay," Luke said. His mouth was full of mashed tissue and blood. "Okay."

He recited the passcode.

"You tell me right," Beard said. "Cause I get there and that's *not* right, you know what I'm going to do?"

Luke nodded.

Beard smiled. "Okay. Stay the fuck here," he said to No Beard, and left.

The truck drove away.

No Beard paced, as if he could walk off his humiliation.

Luke's eyes had begun to adjust to the dim. He was in some sort of pen. The surrounding structure was unwalled, similar to his car shelter but much larger. Through the open sides he could see the smudged charcoal outlines of other buildings. No lights were on.

Blood and snot dripped down his throat.

He said, "Can I have some water, please."

No Beard startled. He stared at Luke, then took a two-step run-up and kicked him in the stomach. Pain radiated out from Luke's belly to his fingertips.

IN THE MORNING he turned over and surveyed his new home.

His stall was one of eight, each measuring about thirty feet wide and fifteen feet deep, four on either side of a center aisle. The floor was dirt, tamped by hooves and flecked with old hay. His right wrist was cuffed to a rear railing, his ankles still zip-tied. His nostrils felt blocked solid but he could taste ammonia and smoke. Fading tang of manure.

Sunrise backlit a welter of tumbledown buildings. Nearest was a farmhouse. The truck was parked outside it. Overgrown fields stretched to the hills. A scrim of haze made it difficult to tell if the hills were high and far away or low and close. Electrical towers threw spiky shadows. The lines met at a place with long walls like a prison yard. Antennas stuck up. A power station.

He felt his face. The skin was taut and warm and his nose had taken a sharp left turn. It flared with pain at the slightest touch. With his tongue he probed the pits of missing teeth. Dried vomit scaled his shirt and pants. Bruises spread like an oil spill around the bulge of a snapped rib.

He grabbed the railing, shook it as hard as he could. It didn't move. It was made of steel, formed in large sections, free of bolts, and anchored in concrete.

He got slowly to his feet and hopped along. The cuff allowed him six feet of lateral movement before he hit a cross-weld. Cupping his mouth with one hand he called toward the power station for help. He tried for a couple of minutes before deciding it was pointless. The station was farther off than he'd realized, and the fact that they'd brought him here, shackled him in the wide open, demonstrated that they weren't worried about him attracting attention.

The exertion and the shouting had made his body ache. A cramp doubled him over. He couldn't believe he'd chosen a burrito for his last proper meal. He breathed through it, then hopped to the corner and started to unfasten his pants.

Footsteps approached.

No Beard.

Stolid and dull. An overgrown kid.

He carried a canteen and a sandwich. "Down, fuck-head."

Luke complied.

No Beard came into the stall and set the food and water just within Luke's reach. Then he retreated to the aisle, like Luke was the dangerous one.

The sandwich was peanut butter on white. Luke choked down two or three bites. His throat was inflamed, chewing was agony. He drank the whole canteen.

No Beard said, "Throw it back."

Luke resisted the urge to wing the canteen at the guy's head. He lobbed it pathetically.

No Beard made to leave.

"Hang on, please," Luke said. "I need to use the bathroom."

"Go on the ground."

"Can I have some paper or something?"

No Beard bit his lip.

He humped away to the farmhouse, coming back with a paperback book, which he tossed at Luke's feet.

"Thank you," Luke said.

No Beard left.

Squatting with bound ankles proved a challenge. Luke wondered if the blows to his head had done something to affect his balance. He steadied himself on the railing. After using several pages to wipe, he leafed through the paperback. It was a legal thriller.

BREAKFAST WAS THE ONLY meal he received, both that day and the next two. There were periodic checks to make sure he hadn't escaped. His attempts at conversation went ignored.

They hadn't killed him. So they needed him for something. It followed that he was the one they had come looking for, Rory the innocent victim.

Luke felt like weeping. Another life he had destroyed.

He wondered which part of his past this was, come to collect.

He meditated. He hopped his six feet of railing, watched the white truck come and go. The book's courtroom scenes were more exciting than what he remembered from his own trial.

ON DAY FOUR he woke shivering. The truck had left in the predawn, and the darkness had a speckled quality to it, like a damaged negative. His face burned with fever, the rest of him was cold. The cuff rattled on his scabby wrist. In the last seventy-two hours he'd eaten less than one full sandwich. His body couldn't hang on to water, he was peeing like crazy, drying out like a wrestler trying to make weight. Hopefully he could get skinny enough to slip the cuff.

He tested it. Not yet.

A few more days.

Did he truly think he would be here in a few more days?

More concerning to him were his feet. They had ballooned, his toes were hard as rocks, they were purple and severely tender, except at the tips, where they were beginning to blacken and lose sensation. Around his ankles the zip-ties bit into angry red flesh. He'd tried every method he could think of for getting them off: filing them against the railing or against the chain of the cuff, torquing his shins to stretch the plastic until the pain became too much to bear. He couldn't get proper leverage. He lacked the strength. The will.

He was weak. Always had been.

He lay on his side, shivering, waiting for the sun to top the hills. Instead a viscid orange oozed out, coating the sky and everything beneath like a broken yolk.

The truck came back.

No one brought breakfast. No one checked on him.

He tried to read but he was shaking so hard the words wouldn't stay in focus.

The sky began to lighten, to lower, floating downward like a bedsheet and breaking against the earth in a white froth that spread across the land.

A singed reek filled the air. Smoke wound through the stall posts. It collected around him. Inside him. He opened his mouth to call toward the farmhouse and coughs tore through him. It felt like his bones were separating.

It was evening again when they appeared. For hours he had been holding still, passing in and out of consciousness, trying not to provoke another coughing fit. Meanwhile the smoke continued to gather, forming a cataract over reality.

They climbed the rise, symmetrical figures relieved against the darkness.

The instant they entered the shed Luke sensed the change in them. Masked, dressed in camouflage, they walked up the aisle, brimming with fraught, nervous energy.

This was the time they had been waiting for.

Beard used Luke's phone to take a picture of him. He tapped the screen. Frowned.

"It's not sending."

"Lemme see," No Beard said.

Beard ignored him.

"Ty. Give it."

Luke remembered, during the home invasion, hearing one of them call the other Jace. Therefore Jace was No Beard, and Beard was Ty.

"There's no fucking bars," Ty said. "I'll drive around till it sends."

"You need to get back fore he shows up."

"Just shut up, okay?"

They left, still jawing at each other.

A few minutes later, the truck drove off.

A LITTLE WHILE after that, Jace returned. A walkie-talkie was clipped to his grubby jeans. He stood in the aisle, took a coil of wire from his pocket, unspooled it.

"Who's coming?" Luke asked.

Jace used a small folding knife to trim off a few inches of wire, then wrapped the ends around his hands to form a garrote.

"Is someone coming?" Luke asked.

"He's your brother." Jace yanked the wire, testing it for strength. "You tell me."

His walkie-talkie blipped.

Clay said, "I'm here."

CHAPTER 26

——

LUKE HAD BEEN TALKING, on and off, for three hours. A nurse came to take his vitals.

"That's enough visiting," she said.

Rigo and I stepped from the room.

My mother was at the nurses' station. Andrea was with her, elbows on the counter, features slack as if she'd fallen asleep standing up.

My mother saw me and murmured something.

Andrea opened her eyes.

She pushed upright and came straight at me.

I got ready for a tongue-lashing: Everything that had happened to Luke was my fault.

My mother seemed to expect the same thing. She hurried behind Andrea, hand outstretched to restrain her, not quite making contact.

I squared toward Andrea. She walked right into me. Her arms wrapped my waist and she clung to me tightly. I peered down at the top of her head. Gray lined the part in her hair.

My mother looked on with a puzzled smile.

Cesar Rigo was writing in his notebook, like a scientist charting animal behavior.

Andrea gave a squeeze, released me, and went into Luke's room.

My mother pecked me on the cheek and followed her.

I LIMPED TO the elevator, Rigo at my side.

"I neglected to thank you," he said. "The firearm you furnished is a match for my murder weapon. Though I confess I would have preferred that you furnish it sooner."

The elevator arrived. We got in. Rigo pressed the button for the lobby. I pressed two.

My mind kept returning to the coil of wire in Jace Dormer's pocket.

They'd kept my brother alive for four days.

They were never going to kill him.

They were going to force me to do it. Like their uncle had done to their father.

"I understand you have taken a leave of absence from the Coroner's Bureau," Rigo said.

"It wasn't a choice."

"Please know that it was not my desire to cause problems for you."

"You didn't cause them, I did."

The doors opened on the second floor.

Rigo gave a shallow bow. "I wish you a speedy recovery."

I LIMPED TO Billy Watts's room and knocked.

Rashida said, "Come in."

They'd taken out his breathing tube. He was reclined on pillows, looking ashen and flayed. Rashida perched on the pulled-out sleeper chair. I said, "Don't get up," but she did.

Nwodo was there, too, notebook in her lap. "We were wrapping up."

I smiled at Billy. "How are you?"

Watts flashed a thumbs-up. He tried to say "Not bad" but it became a hacking fit. Rashida fed him water.

"How's your brother?" she asked.

"Better, thanks. They're going to keep him here a little bit longer."

"And you?"

I touched the bandage on my head. "Couple of stitches."

Thirty-eight, plus thirteen for the quad.

Billy Watts pushed the straw out of his mouth. In a voice barely there, he said, "Pussy."

Rashida clucked her tongue at him but smiled.

Nwodo turned off her recorder. "I'll walk you out."

BILLY WATTS HAD spotted the white truck outside his house twice, first on Saturday afternoon and again early Monday morning. He didn't like how it was idling in the street or the look of the driver; nor did he like how it took off in a hurry when he walked toward it. The second time he caught most of the tag. He ran it and the registration came back expired. The name of the owner gave him a jolt: Sherri Dormer, Gunnar Dormer's widow.

"He figured they were trying to put a scare into him," Nwodo said. "Like the brick in your window. He thought maybe you'd heard from them, too."

The elevator bumped to a stop. We crossed the lobby.

She said, "I brought Sherri in. She swears up and down the boys moved out last year and took the truck, she hasn't seen them since, has nothing to do with it."

"You believe her?"

"Doesn't matter what I believe. They're both dead, it's her word."

Outside the air was better than it had been for weeks. Far from perfect, though.

I said, "You do realize there's a whole tribe of them."

"Four boys, eight girls, including the cousins. The next oldest is sixteen. I spoke to her, too."

"Should I be worried?"

"Who knows? You dealt them some pretty heavy casualties. They'd be smart to cut bait."

"They're not smart."

Nwodo turned up her face. "Feel that?"

"What?" I said.

Then I did: a prick of rain.

We stood there, staring with our necks cricked. Whatever was coming, it was taking its time.

I PICKED UP Charlotte and drove to the supermarket. The lights along Washington Avenue burned gaudily, as though it were the Las Vegas Strip, and Safeway held the promise of riches.

With Charlotte in the cart seat, I limped the aisles, piling in eggs, milk, cheese, greens. I asked again what she'd done at preschool. She gave the same answer.

"Nothing."

"Who'd you play with?"

"Lila."

"Lila F. or Lila N.?"

"Both."

"What did you play?"

"*Frozen Two.*"

"Were you Anna or Elsa?"

"I was the water horse."

"Nice. Should we pick you up some oats?"

"*No.*"

"What about water oats?"

"What's water oats?"

"It's what water horses eat."

"They don't need to eat," Charlotte said. "They're magic."

BOOTS KICKED OFF; a squealing stampede. *Mommy.*

"I smell frittata."

"Mommy I cracked the eggs."

"Great job."

Amy lifted Charlotte to her hip. Trunk and branch, fine and sturdy. For a moment I thought about the twins. Someone's kids.

I set the hot pan on the range and kissed Amy. "How was your day?"

"Fine. Tiring."

"Mommy, I had *so* much fun today."

"That's wonderful. Let's set the table and you can tell me about it."

"I played with Lila F. . . ."

AMY AND I began disassembling the Great Wall of Cardboard late one night. She gave the bread machine to her mother, who needed a replacement for her old one. When we were done there was a long rectangle of compressed carpet. We vacuumed but it wouldn't go away.

"We should rip it out," Amy said.

"The carpet?"

"It's so ugly."

"Okay. Sure. Do you want me to look into that?"

"Eventually." She sat down and patted the sofa.

I sat beside her.

"I've been waiting to have this conversation, Clay. But we need to have it."

I nodded.

"I know you think you were protecting us. I get that it

came from a good place. But you almost died. And—please, please don't say you didn't, because that is completely beside the point. It's unacceptable and I'm furious with you."

"I'm sorry."

"I believe you mean that."

"I do. I—"

"I believe you mean it right now," she said. "I'm not talking about right now. I'm talking about the next time."

"Honey. Nothing like this is ever going to happen again."

"That's not an answer."

"You're right. I'm sorry. I didn't know what else to do."

"Start by not putting yourself in danger."

"I won't."

"Don't lie to me. Ever again."

"I won't."

She let out a short, sad laugh.

She walked to the bookcase and took down the nine-hundred-page history of Europe I'd never gotten around to reading. From the chapter on the Ottoman wars she removed the personal check made out to our daughter for a quarter of a million dollars. She dropped the book on the ugly carpet, slapped the check on the coffee table, and looked at me expectantly.

I said, "Peter Franchette gave it to me. He's the guy I—"

"I remember who he is. *Why* did he give it to you?"

"As a thank-you for finding his sister."

"Why is it in a book?"

"I can't cash it. I could be fired if I did."

"So you hid it from me."

"No. No. I didn't want to be tempted. Amy—"

"Someone gave you this money, money for our daughter, and you didn't tell me about it."

"I meant to. I forgot."

She left the room.

I let a few minutes go by.

She was plucking her eyebrows in the bathroom.

I said, "I'm sorry."

She put down the tweezers. "This is a terrible pattern, Clay."

"You're right."

"We need to deal with it."

"We will."

"I want us to go into couples therapy."

"I think that's a good idea."

She said to me in the mirror, "You are so lucky I love you."

She turned. Her hand came up sharply, as if she was going to slap me.

She brushed my cheek. "Let's change your dressings."

LATER, NAKED, IN BED, entwined, we saw the walls flash white, heard a far-off rumble, followed by tapping on the roof, tentative and sporadic, then picking up speed.

Amy sat up. She wrapped the blanket around her long, lean body; around the gentle swell of new life. She took my hand and led me to the window, and we watched the sky release its mercy.

ACKNOWLEDGMENTS

———

Rafi Rosen, Rafi Silberblatt, Ariel Resnikoff, Ezra Malmuth, Jo-Ellen Posner Zeitlin, Boris Shcharansky, Patricia Wilson, Jesse Grant, Ben Mantell, Alisa Givental, Michel Banda.

Read on for a thrilling excerpt from

The Lost Coast

By Jonathan Kellerman and Jesse Kellerman
Coming soon from Ballantine Books

ONE

T HE WOMAN BEHIND the glass stared at Clay Edison like he'd asked her to do something illegal.

For all he knew, he had.

He had no experience handling a check this large. He hadn't handled any check, of any amount, in years. Nobody used checks anymore. You had direct deposit, PayPal, Venmo. You had mobile deposit. Clay couldn't remember the last time he'd set foot inside an actual branch bank. He wasn't sure why branch banks still existed; why they hadn't gone the way of the video store. People still wanted a personal relationship with their banker, he guessed. Wanted to believe there was someone you could count on in a pinch. A human being, with a name, instead of a chatbot. Face-to-face interaction was important for one's mental health.

The face-to-face interaction he was having with the teller consisted of her looking at the check, looking at him, squinting at the check, squinting at him.

She held the check up to the light.

If it had been possible for her reach through the Plexi

barrier and hold him up to the light, she would have done that, too.

She said, "One moment, sir," and disappeared through a door at the back.

Two tills over, a second teller dealt out a fan of twenties for an elderly man with a bamboo cane and heavy-soled black sneakers. A sleepy-eyed security guard leaned near the main entrance. Otherwise the place was empty.

The elderly man shuffled out with his money.

The security guard coughed into his elbow.

To the right of the teller windows, a concealed door opened in the wall. Out stepped a middle-aged white man in a slouchy gray suit, a Post-it pinched between his fingers.

"Mr. Edison. Darren Prince. I'm the manager here. Nice to meet you. Please."

Clay followed him to a desk with an ancient-looking computer terminal. They sat, and Prince stuck the Post-it to the edge of the monitor where Clay couldn't see it.

"You've been a client," Prince said, palming the mouse, "for fourteen years."

"Sounds about right."

"We appreciate your loyalty. Now, I understand you'd like to make a deposit."

Clay nodded.

"I'm sure you understand, situation such as this, we have certain boxes we have to tick."

"A situation such as what?"

"Well, there's the amount, for one. Anything over ten thousand dollars, we're required to place an automatic hold. This is . . . more than that. Obviously. There's also the issue of the payee. I'm seeing a joint account," Prince said, clicking, "in your name and the name of Amy Sandek."

"That's my wife."

"Gotcha. And Charlotte Edison—"

"Is our daughter."

"The money's for her?"

Clay nodded.

"Wow. Lucky kid. Must have a big fan in . . ." Prince checked the Post-it. "Peter Franchette."

Clay smiled politely.

"Charlotte doesn't appear to have an account of her own."

"She's five. So, no. I asked the teller about opening up a custodial for her."

"Oh sure. Never too young to start learning fiscal responsibility. Mr. Franchette—he's grandpa, or an uncle?"

"A friend."

"Must be a very good friend, he's giving her a quarter of a million dollars."

Clay said nothing.

"The date on the check," Prince said, clicking, "that's also a little bit of an issue."

His gaze stayed glued to the monitor. Not a flat-screen, but a boxy CRT from the late eighties, housed in yellowing plastic. The rest of the bank was similarly old-fashioned, with terra-cotta floor tiles, exposed wood, white plaster. Yellow-brick exterior. Red tile roof. Much of San Leandro shared the same modest Spanish aesthetic, low and compact, contributing to a small-town vibe. Clay liked it. It felt comfortable. The house he'd grown up in was a few blocks away, the house he and his family lived in, a few blocks from that. Since he and Amy had moved back he'd been getting reacquainted with the city. It fascinated him to see how things had changed and not changed. Prices kept climbing. More and better restaurants. But the meters still accepted quarters only.

Prince let go of the mouse and swiveled to face Clay. "Is there a reason you've been holding on to it for almost four years?"

Because I'm not supposed to have this money.

Because I could be fired for accepting it.

Clay said, "The timing wasn't right."

"I see. But it is now."

"Yes."

"May I ask what changed?"

Captain Bakke's top-floor office at the Coroner's Bureau.

Her flat voice mouthing words of concern.

We need to be realistic, Clay.

That was the theme of the conversation: realism, and his need for it.

We need to have appropriate expectations.

It's not that I don't appreciate everything you've done.

But we need, you and I, to be honest about your service record, and think realistically about your future.

Clay said, "Is there a problem?"

"No no no no no no no," Prince said. "No problem."

Clay had a theory: The number of noes in a denial equaled its degree of bullshit.

"We just like to understand our clients' needs and get a sense for their overall financial picture. And you know," Prince said, "because of the issues I mentioned, it's important to take certain steps, for everyone's safety, privacy, and security."

"Great. Let's take them."

Prince eyed him. "Well, first off, I'm going to need a copy of your driver's license. I'm also going to have to contact Mr. Franchette for written authorization."

"That's what the check is. Written authorization."

"I understand, but it's more than six months old, so we're not legally required—"

Clay's phone buzzed.

"Look," he said, tugging it out, "I can tell this is going to take longer than I have right now. Why don't I speak to Peter, and we can set up a time to get this done."

The caller ID read NUMBER NOT AVAILABLE, which meant work.

Never mind that it was his day off. Allegedly.

He plugged his ear and answered the call. "This is Edison."

"Clay, it's Brad."

Brad Moffett was a fellow coroner, the on-duty lieutenant.

"Hey," Clay said. "I'm right in the middle of something, let me call you in ten."

"Wait wait wait, listen to me. Safe Harbor—that's the clinic Amy works at?"

"One of them, yeah. Why."

"I heard on the radio," Moffett said. "There's been a shooting."